The God Factor

A Novel

Karen Spickerman

Trilogy Christian Publishers
A Wholly Owned Subsidiary of Trinity Broadcasting Network
2442 Michelle Drive
Tustin, CA 92780

For information, address Trilogy Christian Publishing
Rights Department, 2442 Michelle Drive, Tustin, Ca 92780.
Trilogy Christian Publishing/ TBN and colophon are trademarks of Trinity Broadcasting Network.

For information about special discounts for bulk purchases, please contact Trilogy Christian Publishing.

Manufactured in the United States of America

10 9 8 7 6 5 4 3 2 1

Library of Congress Cataloging-in-Publication Data is available.

ISBN 978-1-64773-861-7 (Print Book)
ISBN 978-1-64773-862-4 (ebook)

To my sons, daughters-in-law, and grandchildren, who have for years now, put up with the *crazy lady*. They have continued to love me, to claim me as mom/grandma, and have even occasionally conceded that I might be onto something. I love you all and assert that you guys are my best *product*.

Contents

Acknowledgments

I would like to thank Jerry Spickerman for providing insight into the world of investing and gaining wealth through that means. Any error in the book on that topic is mine.

I would also like to thank Gene Notestine for providing information on what might go wrong with a small plane that has not been properly maintained. Again, any error in the book on that topic is mine.

I greatly appreciate your help and insight, guys!

Prologue

On September 11, 2001, thousands of people died in a terrorist attack on America. A large number of the almost three-thousand victims died in the initial impact and subsequent collapse of the twin towers of the World Trade Center in New York City. Of those who died in those buildings, most of the bodies were not recovered. Families mourned without having the closure of burying any remains of their loved ones.

On that day, with no idea the attack was imminent, people were living their daily lives, going about their normal routines. So…what if someone had planned his own disappearance, unintentionally coinciding with the impending event, and was inadvertently helped along in his deception, by the event?

The following is that story.

C H A  P T E R

September 10, 2001. On his office computer, he had scrolled back to the top of the document, a letter to his wife, and added today's date.

The light streaming from the lamp at his desk adequately covered his work area; it was the only full source of light in the large room. Night-lights, emitting much dimmer illumination around the vast work area, had automatically come on hours earlier. The ever-present lights of Manhattan twinkled from the surrounding large windows. He could hear a distant vacuum cleaner running in one of the other rooms on this vast ninety-sixth floor of the North Tower of New York's World Trade Center. This prestigious, high-rent space was occupied by the home office of Devlin, Burke, and Associates—Jason Brigholtz's employer. Jason was the only representative of the company who was currently physically present in the building.

He looked at the clock: 10:27 pm. He would need to leave soon. The computer system would begin its nightly back-up at eleven, shutting out any users prior to doing so, which was fine. He was sure he'd accomplished all the necessities. Jason had been working late at the office almost every evening for weeks now. He wanted to be sure he had all his bases covered. If his wife, Serene, were to be sorry to have him absent from her life, it wouldn't be because of any financial hardship; he intended to make sure of that. No one would be able to accuse him of leaving her and his thirteen-year-old daughter without financial means. The one thing he'd done well in his adult life was the accumulation and management of wealth.

Married during their last year of college, when Serene had informed him she was pregnant with their first child, the young couple had lived very frugally those first several years. Serene had engaged every trick she could find to stretch her meager household allowance just as far as she could, while Jason had poured every cent they could spare into investments until he'd finally amassed enough to begin buying stocks of well-established companies that had a time-tested stability and would pay him back in dividends, dividends he most often used to purchase more stock. It had gradually paid off, built up, and continued to become more profitable every year. There had also been several risky investments over the years, but Jason stayed on top of the market, studying it like a pirate studied a treasure map. With few exceptions, he was able to pull his funds at just the right time to prevent any serious loss that hit the market. With his company-matched 401(k), Roth IRA, stocks, and other investments, his wife and daughter would be well able to continue their affluent lifestyle. He had even set up a trust for Keisha, stipulating that she must come of age before she would receive it. That was just in case Serene fell under the influence of a money-grabbing charlatan, his daughter's future would still be protected.

Tonight he'd completed the last of the paperwork that turned over the management of these very lucrative investments to his fellow banker and colleague, John Barbour, a man he'd found to be honest to a fault. After making that change online for each account, he wrote a letter to John on his computer and printed it out, not fully trusting that company e-mail was confidential. He signed the letter and placed it in the out basket on his desk. It would be picked up by that gangly kid from the mail room and delivered to John's desk tomorrow—along about midmorning was the usual routine. In the letter, he had explained to John, whom he'd always suspected was a dedicated Christian, that he would be away for an extended period and wanted someone trustworthy to manage the accounts for Serene. Of his colleagues, Jason believed John to be the most astute and also the most likely to be completely honest. In the letter, he asked John to check in with Serene in about a week to assure her that he would have her finances under control and well protected.

Then there was the second letter, to Serene. Proofreading it one last time, he hit Print and listened to the printer several feet away come to life, once again complying with the print command. He then deleted the document from his computer. Retrieving the single page from the printer, Jason sat holding it in shaky hands. He remembered the first time he'd ever seen the beautiful redhead that night he'd walked into the library at Michigan State University, out of Michigan's cold winter chill. She had taken his breath away for a moment, not that he'd let on. You never let a female believe that she has the upper hand. If the big-man-on-campus types hadn't taught him that, it wouldn't have mattered; he'd learned it by example from his father.

He stared, unblinking and unseeing, at the paper in his hand for so long that his eyes began watering. *Get ahold of yourself, Jason. It's the only way.* He grabbed a pen and signed his first name with his usual confident flourish, folded the sheet in half, then the half into thirds so that it fit nicely into a personal-size mailing envelope. He sealed the envelope and addressed it to their residence, a Manhattan high-rise several blocks from the WTC. Rummaging through the desk ordinarily manned by Zoe, the secretary for the four investors in this partitioned zone, he located her stamps. Snagging two of them, he applied the postage to his envelope. If one stamp was sufficient, then two should assure that she'd receive the letter. Back at his own desk, he dropped it in his out basket, where, along with the letter to John, it would be picked up midmorning and sorted into the mail that was leaving the building, to begin its journey via the US Postal Service. He could take it home tonight and leave it where she'd be sure to find it, but this way, he'd have at least a one-day head start. He didn't want to be pursued.

The letter to Serene had been a little more difficult to write than the all-business note to John. He'd pushed through the emotions and labored over the wording until he'd finally managed to transmit his thoughts into the words on the page, frequently assuring himself that he was doing the right thing. Misery was eating him alive, and had been for a long time. The best thing he could do for Keisha and Serene, since he couldn't remove the misery from himself, was to remove himself from them, as far away as he could manage. And that was exactly what he told her.

September 10, 2001

My dearest Serene:

> *I am so sorry for my poor excuse for parenting, which has resulted in our son's death. I am sorry that I've been unable to show my love for you, something you deserve to experience lavishly. I guess, never expe-*

riencing affection from my own parents, I have never learned how to appropriately give it. You and the children have suffered for my deficiencies, and I seek, now, to free you to experience a better life.

This is not a suicide note. I do not have the courage to remove myself in that way, but I will be leaving my rat race of a career that I've pursued for all our married years, subjecting you and the children to it as well. Don't try to find me. Just file for divorce on the grounds of desertion, which will be easy enough to do, and move on with your life.

My colleague John Barbour should be contacting you soon to discuss your financial situation, which I assure you will be stable and abundant. I have transferred the management of our various investments to him, investments that are now yours. John will be able to answer any questions you have regarding the funds.

Please don't let anyone suggest that you have any fault in this. You don't. You have been the most loving, kind, selfless, and wonderful wife any man could ever ask for, not to mention the most beautiful. You just picked the wrong man to share those things with.

I am haunted by my failure as a husband and as a father. For all my success as a material provider, I have found no satisfaction in that. There is an emptiness in me I cannot explain and that I have been unable to fill. And so, being unable to remove this misery from my existence, I will do what I can; I will remove my existence from you and Keisha.

Please start over and be happy, and in that knowledge, I will find some measure of contentment.

Your loving husband,
Jason

He let himself into the apartment, locking the door behind him, and headed for the kitchen. Switching on the light, he laid his briefcase on the counter, opened the fridge, and looked at his options. Grabbing the carton of orange juice, he took a long pull from it, put it back, and grabbed a bottle of water, having found nothing else that enticed him. Closing the fridge door, he grabbed his briefcase, turned off the kitchen light, and by the subtle radiance from an inconspicuously placed night-light, he made his way down the hall to the small bedroom that he used as his home office. Avoidance of conversation was his usual routine. Keisha would already be in bed and asleep since it was a school night, and when he was reasonably sure Serene would be asleep, he'd go get ready for bed himself.

She had heard him come in. Following the familiar sounds, Serene knew when he was in the kitchen and when he went on into his office. She also knew, from experience, it would do her no good to follow him in there and try to talk. So she turned her attention back to the book she had been reading.

After a while, realizing that she'd read that last paragraph three times and still didn't know what it said, she replaced the bookmark in the novel and allowed it to slip gently to the floor beside the bed. She reached over and switched off the light on her nightstand, fluffed her pillow, and pulled the cover up over her shoulder. She was thinking, *I really should pray before I go to sleep*, but she'd not even fully completed the thought before slumber overtook her. However, not more than five minutes after surrendering to sleep, she came partially awake with a sensation that made her think she'd been bitten by some insect on her back. Drifting off once more, she felt another bite, this time on her shoulder, and this one was accompanied by a caress over the curve of her hip.

"Do you have carpool tomorrow?" His warm breath tickled her ear.

"No. What's tomorrow, Tuesday?" Her voice was groggy. She was half-awake now.

"Mmm, the eleventh."

Goose bumps rose on her stimulated skin. "It's Jack Mason's day, you know, Sondra's dad."

"Mmm." Featherlight kisses and nibbles covered her ear, jawline, and neck. She wanted to be angry. She so craved connection with him, but it needed to start with meaningful conversation.

She was fully awake now. "Jason…"

"No talking, Serene." He quickly interrupted her. "I just need to cuddle right now."

Right. *I just need to cuddle!* She was familiar with the phrase. In better days, they'd used it playfully, knowing it would lead to intimacy. Normally, hearing him say it would leave her with a warm feeling of being loved, but she was not fooled. Tonight it was just his way of ignoring the deep emotional chasm between them, while fulfilling his physical desires. She should kick this biting insect out of her bed, but her affection-starved body didn't seem to agree. She rolled toward him, once again trying for conversation, but her mouth was quickly covered by a crushing kiss filled with passion and what almost felt like desperation. That was the last conversation Serene attempted that night. She would later cry herself to sleep in his arms, his silence persisting, other than a few murmured platitudes.

C H A  T E R

That beeping alarm clock sound, was that in the distance somewhere? No, he realized, it was right next to his head on the nightstand. It was 6:00 a.m. on September 11, 2001. In his Manhattan bedroom suite, Jason awoke after sleeping only a few short hours. He was immediately awake, surprisingly alert and energetic, and was instantly filled with enthusiasm about his upcoming day. The anticipation of his pre-planned adventure was only slightly frightening. Mostly, he was experiencing an adrenaline rush that had been absent in his life for so long he couldn't even recall the last time he felt this alive. He was surprised that he'd fallen asleep at all, but it was definitely the sound of the alarm that had shaken him from slumber and triggered the first thought of the day: *My God, this is the day. It's really the day!*

Most days, Jason had to drag his miserable frame out of bed and force it through the morning rituals of readying for the day, weighed down heavily by guilt, depression, and dissatisfaction that were so deeply embedded in his being they could not be washed off in the morning shower. Nor could the beautiful woman lying on the other side of the king-size bed lift his spirits. There had been a huge gulf between Jason and Serene for years now. Although he would no longer allow himself to think about it, Jason knew the wedge began with the death of their son, Michael, three years ago. No matter. Today, he had his answer, and today he'd pursue it, with each carefully planned step to be just as carefully executed.

Although the alarm had also awakened Serene, she faked sleep. No point in beginning another day with the same futile argument. Bringing to her husband's attention the observation that their marriage had declined into an empty shell hadn't produced any progress toward resolving that issue. In fact, directing his attention to that topic had stopped working altogether and just led to arguing. Perhaps she'd just have to take up his habit of ignoring it, or rather stuffing it down inside, as he seemed content to do.

Serene lay still, feeling the shift of the mattress as Jason rolled out of bed and headed for the bathroom to begin the routine of getting ready for work. Her thoughts gravitated to last night, her mind reliving it in detail, though she knew she shouldn't be dwelling on it. When her thoughts threatened to bring on a fresh crying jag, she made the effort to pull her mind back to the needs of the day, even though doing so felt like she was dragging something very heavy. She knew this was a sign of depression. She concentrated on the one bright spot in her day, the prearranged phone call from her friend Miranda in Hawaii.

Maybe it was because Miranda was so far away that Serene felt safe talking with her about the deeper things in life, or maybe it was just that her friend had a way of making her feel completely at ease. Whatever the reason, Serene had talked to Miranda about everything in her life that had deep meaning, her loneliness in her marriage, the grief over Michael's death, which she'd never successfully been able to share with Jason, and the concerns of being the mother of a discontented teenage daughter who was also hurting from the loss of her brother.

Miranda's encouragement was always refreshing to her, and Serene knew that Miranda's Christian faith was a big factor in the value of her counsel. They always ended their phone conversations with prayer as well, and Serene welcomed the feeling of well-being which that always brought her. Her friendship with Miranda had been the one discernable good thing to come out of the trip to Hawaii, Serene thought to herself, a trip that was supposed to help the Brigholtz family to reconnect and find a deep place of communication that could bring about the soul healing that they all desperately needed. How, then, had Jason and Serene virtually gone their separate ways in tropical paradise? Actually, they had slipped quite easily into it. Jason surely wasn't about to go shopping and sightseeing, and Serene was just as surely not into trekking the rugged terrain of the more rustic islands, so splitting up seemed the natural thing to do.

Curiously, each had found something special, not with each other, as Serene had hoped they would, but by each pursuing interests that excluded the other. Serene had found Miranda, and with that friendship had come a thirst for the peace that so obviously covered Miranda's life like an invisible umbrella of protection. What she didn't know was that Jason had found Del Mayhew. Though Jason was aware of and acquainted with Serene's newfound friend, Serene had no idea Jason had made an acquaintance that would prove to be life-changing for him.

While Jason was showering, Serene splashed water on her face, brushed her thick auburn hair, and pulled it back into a scrunchie, then brushed her teeth. Performing these morning rituals while he showered made it easy for her to move on to the kitchen and start the coffee without interacting with him. Lately, it was almost as if she had to rehearse in her head how she would approach him. She didn't want to start a fight and had to consciously focus on not being passive-aggressive in her demeanor. It was a sad way to live, but she didn't want Keisha to overhear any more fights than she already had.

It was the smell of freshly brewing coffee that awakened Keisha. She breathed deeply. She loved that smell, even though she hated the taste of the stuff. It was that aroma, not any particular sound, that usually awakened her. It was one of the few dependable things in her life these days. The familiar routine of waking up in her own bed, in her own room, knowing that her mom would be in the kitchen, her dad would usually be out of the apartment already, on his way to work, and she would get ready for school. The familiar. The routine. No surprises. No tragedy. The routine. She clung to it, the only definition of normal she could find.

For Keisha, the anticipation of seeing a couple of close friends was Drake High School's only draw, not the academics, not the sports, not the extracurricular clubs. Though schoolwork had never been hard for her and she was naturally athletic and social, these things had lost their ability to interest her. Since her brother's death, she'd unwittingly built a wall around herself to prevent further pain. If there was no desire for a career in advanced mathematics, there was no loss. No zeal for girls' basketball and the team's success, no loss. No hopeful anticipation of her father's attentive adoration, no loss. That was her current, unconscious mantra in life: expect nothing and thereby lose nothing. She would have pushed her mother away, too, but Serene simply would not be pushed.

Serene gently tapped on Keisha's bedroom door, then entered with her weekday-morning ritual of orange juice, served in a fancy stem glass. Half a toasted bagel lightly spread with butter, no cream cheese, was lying on the tray next to the glass, nestled on a lacey paper doily. Keisha pretended to be nonchalant, although she secretly embraced the security her mother's morning routine provided. She was noncommittal as Mom pursued light conversation about her day. Wasn't Tuesday the day she went to French club before her first-hour class? Would Sondra's father be her carpool ride today? Did she plan to wear her new yellow sweater? The color looked so nice with her iridescent brown eyes and blond hair; the hair obviously came from her dad's side, but the eyes were identical to her mom's own color.

Keisha mumbled the obligatory answers, sipped her juice, and headed for her bathroom. "Has Dad left for work yet?"

"Not yet," her mother answered, "but he's out of the shower." It was safe for Keisha to shower now, without any threat of the hot/cold competition from the other bathroom.

Serene left the tray for Keisha, knowing she'd eat every crumb of the bagel and drink all the orange juice while she was getting ready for school. She heard the sound of the shower water as she closed the door behind her and headed back to the kitchen.

Jason slowed as he passed Keisha's room on the way to the kitchen. He knew he'd probably never see his daughter again, and his throat constricted with the thought. His resolve wavered, but only slightly. He stopped. *I just need an excuse for one last hug,* he reasoned. He turned and knocked on her door. From inside, "Mom, I'm coming! I have plenty of time, you know."

He opened the door slightly. "You decent, Punkin?"

"Oh, hi, Dad." *When was the last time he'd called her by that pet name?* So long she couldn't even remember.

Jason continued into Keisha's room. "I just wanted to tell you I signed that permission slip for your field trip. Your mom's got it." What he didn't say was that her mom always insisted *he* sign these things from the school, for the sole purpose of keeping him somewhat involved in his daughter's life. Today, it gave him the opening he needed to give her one last hug. He drank in that pretty face, those luminous brown eyes, so much like her mom's.

"You look pretty in yellow, you know," he remarked as he noticed her sweater. The comment surprised her. He never noticed what she was wearing—or her, for that matter—so she was totally caught off guard. Before she could respond, he'd set his briefcase down on the end of her bed and had lifted her into a bear hug, planting a kiss on her forehead. Was he misty-eyed when he set her down just as quickly? She wasn't sure, because he'd grabbed up the briefcase and turned to go.

"Have a good day, Punkin. I'll see you later."

What just happened? she thought as she stood there dumbfounded.

Walking on down the hall, Jason paused to compose himself for a moment where the hall opened to the foyer, the kitchen on the opposite side of it. After a couple of deep breaths and a quick swipe at his eyes, he continued.

He strolled into the kitchen dressed in his dark-gray suit, light-blue pinstripe shirt, and dark-navy tie with its tiny muted print. His sandy light-brown hair, still slightly damp from the shower, was perfectly combed into place, framing the broad, masculine lines of the face lit by striking deep-blue eyes. Jason was always impeccably groomed. Even when he was casually attired, clothing graced his muscular six-foot-two frame as though it just plain respected him. He reached across the shiny stainless steel counter for his insulated travel mug, with "Devlin, Burke, and Associates" embossed on it. Although she already knew his answer, Serene asked the perfunctory question, "Would you like some breakfast this morning? I have bagels from Feingold's Deli—your favorite. I could fix you an egg to go with it."

"No thanks. I'll grab something from the cart later. The board is meeting at eight, and right after that is my presentation to the Canter Fitzgerald execs." He had poured his coffee over the ample serving of half-and-half, which had gone in first, and was putting the cap on the mug. Walking back through to the foyer, he grabbed his briefcase off the antique Queen Ann chair, and with his coffee in one hand and briefcase in the other, he headed toward the door. As he knew she would, Serene followed, her champagne-colored silk robe swishing lightly. He gave her a quick smile that didn't quite reach his eyes. As she opened the door for him, she gave him a quick peck on the lips, holding back the tears that now burned in the back of her eyes. He smelled so good, that hint of Icy Blue River Cologne she'd bought him for his birthday. It was outrageously expensive but had such a wonderful, masculine scent. It made her long to just be held by him.

He walked down the plush blue-carpeted hall of their fashionable high-rise toward the elevator with a tight knot in his chest that matched the large lump in his throat. He struggled to catch a breath; he had so wanted to grab her and hold her tight, to drink in the scent of her hair and melt into her softness. But he couldn't. That privilege belonged to another time, another man, to the man he used to be. Last night's physical intimacy had been stolen from her, and he'd never do it again. She deserved better. He knew he was a jerk for taking advantage of her, but hadn't he been cheating her of what she deserved for several years now? The memory of last night had to keep him for the rest of his miserable life; in Jason's mind, it was all he had left. For only a split second, he thought about abandoning this whole plan and just going on to work, and just as quickly, the thought was gone.

He'd blown it. He'd failed to protect their son from that accelerating cab, had pulled back from their daughter as though his incompetent parenting would break her too, and unable to show the vulnerability of mourning in front of Serene, he'd finally turned to another woman for the comfort his soul desperately needed. He'd lost the right to hold his wife two years ago when he began an affair with an administrative assistant. About six months ago, when he could no longer stand himself for what he'd become, even that relationship had gone sour and ended abruptly. Oh, Jennifer still tried to seduce him. She flirted shamelessly, even in front of their coworkers, called his cell phone frequently, e-mailed him, and left little notes in his desk, clearly laying out a time and place to meet. He ignored all of it.

His face was fixed like flint now, toward his plan.

CHAPTER 3

Island of Hawaii, March 2000

Serene came out of the bathroom of their hotel suite to find Jason already dressed in his blue jean shorts, comfortable athletic shoes, and that jade-green brushed-cotton T-shirt she'd bought him for the trip. She loved that color on him. It did something to the color of his eyes. They didn't pick up any of the green from the shirt; it just seemed to deepen their electric-blue color. *How did I ever snag such a good-looking guy?* she wondered, not for the first time.

She was still dressed in the hotel's fluffy terry robe, with her sundress laid out on the bed, purse and sandals that complemented the dress color at the ready. She wondered if their daughter was still sleeping in the adjoining room; she hadn't heard any sounds coming from next door.

As Jason picked up his watch, wallet, and change from the dresser, she smiled his way. "I wonder if Keisha is still sleeping," she pondered aloud. "I haven't heard any sounds of stirring from her room."

"She's up, probably reading that travel book about the islands. While you were in the shower, she and I went downstairs and had some breakfast," he replied. "Their sausage and waffles are great, by the way, served with fresh local fruit. I have to leave in five minutes to catch my flight over to Molokai, but if you'd like, I'll order up some breakfast for you while you're getting dressed."

Turning, she searched the drawer for clean underwear; she had to turn her back on him to hide the disappointment on her face. This extended spring break trip was supposed to be about bonding, as a family, which should include her. Now Jason had booked this trek to Molokai to do the rugged hike down the Kalaupapa Peninsula, by himself, since, he explained, it would be too strenuous for anyone who did not regularly work out. And now, apparently, he couldn't even include her in his breakfast plans.

"Serene."

"Hmm?"

"Shall I call room service for you?"

"Sure. Whatever you had will be fine." She bit her lip to keep from crying, took her clothes, and headed back into the bathroom. She didn't feel comfortable undressing in front of a virtual stranger.

Serene called the front desk and asked for the concierge. The desk clerk advised her that Ms. Temple was meeting with another guest currently, but she could leave a message and he'd be glad to get it to her as soon as she was available. He wasn't sure how long that might be.

She thanked him but said there would be no message. She and Keisha were ready to go shopping now. Perhaps she could just ask a cab to take them to wherever the local boutiques were located.

Serene and Keisha stepped off the elevator into the hotel's plush lobby, the large area visually pleasing with its high ceilings, a water fountain, complete with an elegant dolphin sculpture, spotlighting the space. The centerpiece was surrounded with clusters of neutral-colored, leather-bound seating and lamps casting a warm glow over all. The carpet was a pineapple-patterned bright-teal color, and scattered throughout the room were tasteful planters with live local plants and small trees. Mother and daughter advanced toward the reception desk to ask the clerk to call them a cab. There was one customer ahead of Serene, so she waited at a discreet distance.

"I'll be right over here, Mom." Keisha took a chair in the lounge area and said hello to the pretty Polynesian girl sitting in the next chair thumbing through a magazine. Her long straight black hair glistened in the soft light, and her flower-printed shirt in bright shades of pink and purple complemented her bronze skin. "I like your sandals," Keisha remarked, taking in the local girl's huaraches. "My mom and I are going to spend the day shopping. I'd love it if I could find a pair like them."

The girl smiled back at her. "That's no problem at all. My aunt Miranda is a concierge here. She knows all about shopping. It's her job to be able to direct folks to shopping and all kinds of other stuff on the island. That's her right there at the desk." She nodded toward the reception desk.

Miranda reached out for the envelope the clerk handed her, containing her paycheck. "Thanks, Kevin. I thought since Alani and I were in town to grab a few things, I might as well stop and pick this up."

"Sure thing, Mrs. Salenger." He stretched and looked over her shoulder. "Alani looks very pretty today." The young man smiled, blushing a bit. He was seventeen and working part-time at the hotel that his dad managed.

Miranda winked at him. She was well aware that the young man was crushing on her thirteen-year-old niece, and she was just as aware that it would be allowed to go no further than a crush due to Alani's young age. She turned and smiled at the lady waiting behind her as she began to walk toward the seating area, where she noticed Alani was chatting with another girl. Serene returned the smile and stepped up to Kevin. "I'm wondering if you could call a taxi for my daughter and me. And please inquire if they might send someone familiar with the shops in town."

"I'd be glad to make the call for you, ma'am," Kevin replied, then he nodded to Miranda. "But you might want to ask this nice lady here about shopping. She's Mrs. Salenger, the other concierge employed by the hotel, and would be a good person to ask about local shops."

Miranda, overhearing the conversation, had stopped and turned back toward Serene. Nodding at Kevin, she addressed Serene. "Hello, I'm Miranda Salenger, and I couldn't help but overhear. I'm not on duty today, but I'd be more than happy to direct you to some of the best shopping on the island. Is this your daughter over here talking with my niece?"

Serene introduced herself to the new acquaintance, who had a confident, friendly demeanor about her. Miranda Salenger looked to be in her midthirties, was pretty in what Serene thought of as a sophisticated way, with thick dark-brown hair worn in a slightly wavy bob, sun-kissed with highlights. The dark-brown eyes revealed a genuine smile. Her makeup was flawless, and her attire was well-fitted and classy. It was a look, Serene thought, that would easily fit a snobbish woman, but as they chatted, she found just the opposite to be true. Miranda was open, outgoing, eager to be of help, and showed a sincere interest in becoming acquainted with someone who was a mere hotel guest.

As they conversed, the women turned and walked to where the younger girls were laughing about something.

"Yes, that's my daughter, Keisha. And this pretty young lady, I assume, is your niece."

The feminine foursome spent about twenty minutes discussing what kind of shopping interested them and what might be available to meet the need. At the end of their discussion, they were so taken with their like-mindedness on the topic of shopping that they'd decided to forget the cab and just all go together, with Miranda doing the chauffeuring. Even the younger girls seemed to be hitting it off as though they were long-lost friends.

As they emerged from the boutique where Keisha had, indeed, found huaraches almost exactly like Alani's, along with two new bathing suits and a shorts-and-top set, Miranda pointed out a shop across the street called New to Me. "That second hand store belongs to me and a friend of mine. We take in donations of high-end used clothing, and proceeds from the sales go to women who are in need of a leg up in their lives, transitioning out of rehab or prison, getting out of abusive relationships…that kind of thing. We also help them choose clothing for interviews and new jobs. The first few outfits are free."

"What a wonderful idea for a ministry!" Serene remarked.

"Oh, Mom, can we go in there? Look at the cute yellow sundress in the window! I wonder if it's my size!" Keisha gushed.

Looking at the cute displays in the window of the store, Serene flashed back to the years when she and Jason were first married and she had to do all her shopping at secondhand stores and yard sales. Otherwise, it was a choice between buying retail clothing or the groceries. Jason had been intent on building a nest egg with his investments. He'd said he wanted to be in a position someday where his money would work for him and not the other way around, and to do so while they were still young enough to enjoy it. During that lean time, Serene had become expert at making preowned outfits look fashionable. It pained Serene that even though they had arrived at that place of material comfort now, Jason still hadn't cut back the amount of time he poured into his work. Fortunately, by the time Keisha and Michael were old enough to be embarrassed by secondhand clothing, the purse strings had slackened enough for new clothes, at least for the kids, so they'd never developed any complex about it.

Serene smiled at her daughter. "Sure, let's go in. I'd like to check it out myself."

Later that afternoon, happily tired from a day of power-shopping, the ladies sat in the hotel's poolside indoor-outdoor snack bar, chatting over cool drinks, while the girls sat on the edge of the pool with their feet dangling in the water, enjoying their own fancy tropical drinks. They were still giggling, having hit it off from the beginning of the day, and now appeared to be scoping out some boys who were showing off on the diving board.

"I feel like that was an especially productive day." Serene sighed. "I found gifts for everyone on my list and was able to do it without blowing out my budget. Thank you so much, Miranda. You've not only been very helpful, but you and Alani also provided very enjoyable company for Keisha and me today."

"You are most welcome. I can't imagine you enjoyed it any more than Alani and I did."

"I'm excited about the used-clothing boutique too. As I told you, I volunteer counseling hours for women in much the same circumstances as you mentioned, but to take part in a shop such as yours would be such a great addition to the services our organization already provides. I'm going to look into getting it started as soon as I return home. I'm sure Jason could easily set up the tax-exempt status we'd need. All things money, including taxes and tax exemptions, is his area of expertise."

"Speaking of husbands, I would love it if ours could meet. Perhaps the two of you, and Keisha, of course, could get together with my husband and me for a meal at our home while you're here. How long are you going to be able to stay?"

"We are on our third day of a two-week vacation, so there should be plenty of time for us to get together. We could all go out to dinner if it would be more convenient for you than having to host a dinner at your house."

"Oh, hosting is no problem at all." Miranda waved off the thought. "It's something I love to do. I think the Lord must have graced me with that gift. If you don't have plans for this Friday evening, I'd love to have you all come to the house for dinner. I'd also invite my brother and his wife, Alani's parents. If you'd be interested, why don't you check with Jason and I'll mention it to Wayne? But I'm sure he'll be excited to meet you both."

"I'll do that. You have my number, and I have yours, so we can connect and work out the details." Serene was pretty sure Jason would not be interested, but she'd do her best to talk him into it. At least it would be something they could do together while they were on the island. She didn't often pressure him into anything, so maybe she had one coming. Besides, she knew Keisha would enjoy seeing Alani again, and she could always use that as leverage. As she thought about it, she realized that she and Jason didn't share many friends. She hoped Jason would be willing to meet Miranda's husband and that they would hit it off, because even if it was long distance, she wanted to cultivate a friendship with Miranda; she just felt drawn to her.

As they'd chatted throughout the day of shopping, Miranda had talked some about her church. It apparently was one of those contemporary churches with a worship team complete with instruments instead of hymnals and an organist. Miranda also mentioned a youth group that Alani attended, and Serene couldn't help but wonder if Keisha might benefit from such a group. She worried that Keisha had refused to go to church since shortly after Michael's death. When she'd questioned her daughter about not wanting to attend services, Keisha had responded that she didn't know if she believed in God anymore.

According to Keisha, the pastor in their traditional church had not had a satisfactory answer to Keisha's question as to why God allowed Michael to die. "He said we shouldn't question God because His ways are higher than ours. We just need to accept such things and be satisfied that we will know the answer when we get to heaven. So either I don't believe in God or, if He is there, I don't think I like Him very much." That had been her conclusion, and then she refused to talk about it any further. Jason had been no help when Serene had tried to enlist him to talk to Keisha about it. He'd just said, "You can't make her go if she doesn't want to, Serene." And since he hadn't gone with them in years, he would have been on shaky ground to try to enforce church attendance on his daughter anyway.

After Miranda and Alani left the hotel late in the afternoon, Serene started pondering how to approach Jason regarding Miranda's invitation to the Salengers' home for dinner on Friday. "Help me, Lord. I really want to know these people better." But instead of leaving it there, her mind began scheming ways to get her own way in this. *I don't know how much weight my prayer carries with God, but I do have some tricks up my sleeve that I learned from my psychology training. Maybe I should go with the more sure thing.*

C H A P T E R

Island of Molokai, March 2000

"So let's just get right to the point: you're a drug runner." Jason looked him right in the eye, gauging his reaction to the direct comment.

"Not!" A profanity followed that exclamation. "I'll admit that some things I import and export may be questionable in the eyes of law enforcement, but I'm not *that* stupid." His face looked grave and, Jason thought, sincere, though the eyes were a little glassy from the booze. "You have to stay away from drugs. They'll kill you…and drug cartels, they will too. I'm just a very clever person, Jason. Everybody knows that you find something people want and provide it to them—that's how you get rich. It's figuring out how to do the providing that's the clever part. That's what sets me apart from the pack."

Jason sat on a barstool next to this half-inebriated braggart in a cabana bar. He was relaxing after his long hike on the island of Molokai and nursing a refill on his mango ice tea. He'd sworn off liquor after it had begun to control his life soon after Michael's death. He had realized quickly that with booze, he was on a downhill spiral and would soon be in danger of losing his job, not to mention his wife and daughter. So he'd made the decision that *he* would retain control; guilt, shame, and anger would not ride roughshod over his life. If he couldn't rid himself of those feelings, he would stuff them so far down inside they could never resurface. Work had become his vice of choice to distract him from the emotional dysfunction, and when that wasn't enough, an extramarital affair had made up the difference. Now he was left with only his bitterness and controlling instinct.

Del Mayhew had sat down on the stool next to Jason and introduced himself while Jason had been working his way through an order of nachos and his first mango ice tea. Jason had acknowledged the introduction, providing his own name and nothing more, wondering and more than a little irritated at how forward some people could be. Mayhew began to extoll the virtues of the island, which apparently had endeared itself to him because of its rugged, quiet demeanor compared to the more tourist-oriented larger islands in the Hawaiian chain. Jason begrudgingly agreed with that observation. It had figured into his own decision to book this trip on the Big Island, rather than the more-popular and tourist-saturated Oahu or Maui.

The two men spent some time in discussion of Molokai, with its rain forest west coast, much more arid east side, and on the north, the Kalaupapa Peninsula. Just that morning, Jason had done the hike down the 1,700-foot cliff to the famous former leper colony, joined the tour, then hiked back up the three-mile trail that afternoon. In spite of his being in excellent physical shape, thanks to having access to New York City's fine, state-of-the-art gym equipment, he was still sore from the trek. Mayhew had shared that he had taken the trail once on foot and on another occasion via mule some years back. He admitted he was in no shape to be indulging in that kind of physical activity now, being forty-eight years old and having long neglected any kind of fitness routine. With his thinning wavy black hair, about thirty excess pounds, and a paunch straining the buttons on the wildly colored Hawaiian shirt that was directly related to his affinity for beer, Jason had decided it was easy to agree that such a trek was not in the cards for Mayhew's present or near future.

If not his physical endeavors, Mayhew *was* readily amenable to discussing his current business activities. He painted a vivid picture of a lifestyle rife with intrigue and adventure, arranging for the import and export of that which was difficult to access. For Americans, knockoff designer fashions and accessories and Cuban cigars were popular. For third world countries, American blue jeans were wildly in demand if a clever importer/exporter could provide them at an affordable price. Spices and gourmet foods were also a specialty, again, if their handler could find a way around expensive tariffs. It was at that point that Jason suspected that street drugs were likely Mayhew's cash cow, and had told him so, prompting the quick denial.

The presence of an unremarkable female one table away, who sat nursing a soft drink and covertly listening intently to their conversation, went unheeded by both men. The FBI agent who was currently assigned to monitor the activities of Delwin Mayhew processed and committed to memory the comment about drugs and other contraband, hoping for something more specific to surface.

After his vehement disavowal of Jason's assumption and admission that the law, nevertheless, was not always his friend, Mayhew was now anxious to hear about his teetotaler drinking buddy, ever on the lookout for a potential barter that might profit him in his lust for material things. He had rightly presumed, by Jason's attire and Rolex watch, that he was a man of means. Now, how to make that means mean something to him. As the island breeze cooled the cabana patrons and the ukulele music lulled them, Del inquired as to Jason's occupation.

Perhaps it was pride that had Jason reciting his own exploits in moneymaking through the investment banking skills he'd perfected. Normally, he would be very tight-lipped with someone of short acquaintance, especially someone who was so self-absorbed and not all that likeable. Jason squelched his grin when an inner voice opined that he could be describing himself. When he analyzed it, and he always did, he concluded that he might somehow make use of a man with Mayhew's networking skills, so it was instinctive to share some general info about himself.

The two users sized each other up, and in the end, when it was time for Jason to catch his helicopter ride back to the Big Island, they'd exchanged cell phone numbers and e-mail addresses. Del was pretty pleased with himself as he walked, just slightly wobbly, across the sandy beach, back to his rental car, to go home for the night to his bed-and-breakfast accommodations. Polluting the fresh island air with his puffs of cigar smoke, he thought to himself, *Now that's a guy who could help me erase a great deal of income tax liability.*

Jason watched the changing light show of the gorgeous tropical sunset from the window of the chopper during the forty-minute ride back to Kona and thought to himself, *Now that's a guy who could help me ditch the money-grabbing treadmill and furtively disappear to some remote island paradise.*

CHAPTER 5

Island of Hawaii, March 2000

"I don't know how I let you talk me into this," Jason grumbled as they followed Miranda's directions in their rental car. He had been grouchy all day because Serene refused to allow him to back out of their commitment to dinner with the Salengers at the last minute.

I know how I did it, Serene thought, in silent answer to his question. *I shamed you into spending some of your time here on the island doing what your daughter would like to do.* She wasn't proud of it, but Serene had even recruited Keisha into cajoling her dad, by talking about how she'd made a friend in Alani and wanted to see her again while they were still here. Her manipulative behavior was the kind of thing Serene would condemn to the women she counseled, but she really wanted to establish a relationship with the Salengers, and to go to their home without Jason would have been beyond awkward. So she had justified her behavior by convincing herself that it would be good for Jason to be compliant for a change, good for Keisha to develop a new friendship, and good for herself to befriend Miranda and hopefully find out how she had tapped into a relationship with God, which provided such a peacefulness in her life that it radiated from her very pores, peace that had so far eluded Serene.

Ignoring Jason's grumbling comment, she remarked, "This region of the island is beautiful." Although Serene admitted to herself that she'd yet to see an area of the Big Island that was not. As they approached the driveway to the Salenger residence in the convertible Jason had rented, the landscape was lush and green, with pops of bright color in the various local blooms, set off by the assorted dazzling tones of the setting sun. The warm ocean breeze conveyed a medley of local floral scents across the air. "This is it right here, according to Miranda's sketch."

Jason didn't reply. As they pulled into the driveway and slowed, the sound of waves gently crashing against the nearby shore finished off the peaceful symphony for the senses. *It just feels like God Himself is preparing the evening for us,* Serene thought. *Please, Lord, help Jason to loosen up and enjoy the company of these good folks.*

Wayne and Miranda met them at the door, and the introductions were made, which included Alani and her parents, Derek and Kalena Nolan. Serene looked around at the flowing, open-concept rooms of the spacious home. Miranda's design preference seemed to be contemporary, with the softer, more rounded lines that modern design lacked. Her colors were mostly neutral, earthy tones of taupe and muted shades of gray-blues, reminding Serene of a stormy ocean. Here and there were some pops of bright yellow in small tasteful doses. Some rustic elements were also evident in nature-inspired textures, like the driftwood sculpture and course fabric window shades. *It just feels relaxed and peaceful,* Serene thought, *much like Miranda herself.*

The women congregated in the kitchen to converse over preparation of side dishes as the menfolk gathered on the back lanai around the barbecue grill, where Wayne was in charge of grilling meat and veggie kebabs.

Giddily, the two girls headed to the pool house to change into swimsuits so they could enjoy a swim while they waited for supper to be prepared. Miranda had poured drinks of fruity punch for Serene, Kalena, and herself, and since Serene had been assured that Miranda didn't need help right now with the prep, she sat on a stool at the kitchen island and took the opportunity to pursue conversation with Kalena. "Well, I see where Alani gets her good looks, Kalena. Did you allow her dad to contribute any genes, or is she just pretty much a replica of her mom?"

Miranda and Kalena both laughed at the remark. The pretty, dark-haired, dark-eyed Polynesian woman replied, "You'd probably not be surprised to know that I hear a lot of comments about the resemblance. But yes, she inherited several characteristics from her dad. It's just that they are mostly reflected in personality, not in her looks. The outgoing, friendly, people-oriented thing is definitely from Derek. I tend to be more introverted and task-centered. Now our son, James, looks a lot like his dad. He wasn't available to come tonight. He just recently got his driver's license and had a date—very important stuff." She winked at the other two ladies.

Miranda interjected, "My brother owns his own construction company, and when he was first getting it off the ground years ago, Kalena was one of the first hires. She did bookkeeping and clerical work for him. The poor sap. I knew he was smitten with her long before he ever figured it out himself." Kalena blushed at Miranda's remark.

"Keisha is also a very pretty young lady. Is she an only child?"

There was a slight pause as Serene looked down at her hands, and Miranda, who already knew the answer to Kalena's question, wondered if she would need to jump in and change the subject. But Serene found her voice. "Our son, Michael, Keisha's younger brother, was killed in a car/pedestrian accident a couple of years ago." Her voice was almost a whisper.

"I'm so sorry!" Kalena looked sincerely compassionate. "How awful for you all!"

"Thank you." Serene quickly directed the conversation away from the sad topic. "I guess I haven't asked you, Miranda, if you and Wayne have children of your own."

"I have two stepchildren, Wayne's sons from his first marriage. They're both grown and are living and working on Maui. They're such good boys, and I love them dearly. Wayne and I don't have any children of our own, so I enjoy spoiling his boys."

With the discussion recovered from the sad moment, the ladies continued to cover a variety of subjects of light conversation, such as the Salengers' beautiful home, the striking countryside, husbands, recipes, and other girly topics.

Meanwhile, the men dived right into the first door opener of conversation common to men: occupations.

After pouring the preferred drinks, an ice tea for Jason, lemonade for Derek, and ice tea for himself, Wayne began, "So, Jason, what do you do for a living?"

Should I give him the honest answer? Jason thought to himself. *I line the pockets of greedy billionaires with my investing expertise, while riding the coattails of their sleazy gravy train into my own motherlode of loot, stepping all over the little guy on my way there.* "I'm in investment banking. I work for a firm in Manhattan, Devlin, Burke, and Associates. You may have heard of it." He knew they likely hadn't heard of it. From what Serene had told him, these guys probably had a different and less-cultured focus on life.

Wayne didn't miss the veiled edge in the "you may have heard of it" portion of the remark, but he didn't let on— better to take the high road. "Sounds like interesting work if you're wired for that kind of thing. It's a good thing God made guys like you with a brain for numbers. It's sure not something I could do."

Jason smiled a smile that didn't quite reach his eyes and reciprocated the inquiry. "So what line of work are you in, Wayne, and you, Derek?" he added.

Wayne nodded to Derek to take the lead as he took a sip of his tea.

Derek hesitated from his task of loading squares of meat, veggies, and pineapple onto skewers from the bowls of food Miranda had set out for him and spoke up. "I'm in construction. I own my own company, thanks to Wayne. I was working my tail off for other people, trying to learn all aspects of the business, when Wayne sold me his company and mentored me until I could manage to keep it afloat on my own."

"He's being modest," Wayne interjected. "Derek worked his way up from the bottom of the business, with a work ethic and savvy for all aspects of it that is rare, indeed. I'd just been offered the job I'm in now, commercial building inspector for the islands, so it was an ideal time to sell the business and make the transition. It freed up some of my time, and since Miranda and I had just married, I really welcomed having more free time."

Screams of delight and laughter arose from the nearby pool as the girls enjoyed the curvy waterslide, which dropped them, after all the twists and turns, with a satisfying splash into the temperature-controlled, aqua-reflected water below.

All three men grinned at the exuberant pair. Turning to Jason, Wayne asked, "Does Keisha have any siblings, or is she an only child?"

Serene walked up behind Jason just in time to catch his reply to the question she'd just overheard.

"It's just her."

"Hey, here comes Kalena's yummy hors d'oeuvres," Derek enthusiastically observed, seeing the tray that Serene was carrying. "I was beginning to be concerned that you ladies were keeping them all to yourselves in the kitchen."

Serene swallowed the lump that had suddenly formed in her throat and put on a cordial smile. "I can relate to your concern, Derek. I've had two of these already, and you're absolutely right: they *are* yummy!"

She set the tray down on Derek's work table and turned. "Miranda has decided it would be nice to sit out here for dinner, so I'll be right back with the place settings." She turned and retreated quickly so the tears in her eyes would not be detected, but Jason didn't miss them. He wouldn't talk to her about Michael, and now he seemed to be denying his very existence.

*****

"I don't fully understand why, Wayne, but I just feel drawn to Serene." The evening had drawn to an end, and the Salengers were getting ready for bed. Miranda stood leaning against the bathroom doorframe while Wayne finished brushing his teeth. "We seem to have a lot in common as far as girl stuff, likes and dislikes, ya know? But I think it's more than that. I think God wants me to befriend her for some reason. For one thing, I think she still needs to work through her grief over the loss of their son."

Replacing his toothbrush, he rinsed his mouth and looked over at her, eyebrows drawn together. "Son? When Derek asked Jason if they had children other than Keisha, he replied that it's only her. He didn't mention any other children."

"Yes, they lost their son a couple of years ago in a car accident. Wow, must be he just didn't want to get into it... maybe he hasn't worked through his feelings either. Other than his not acknowledging that they'd even had a son, what other impressions did you get about Jason?"

She turned down the bed as Wayne flipped off the bathroom light and joined her. "Okay, this is just a gut instinct, but I'd be willing to bet he'd probably dug his heels in trying not to even show up here tonight. He was polite and said all the right things, but it seemed superficial, and I detected a little bit of attitude just below the surface." He crawled into bed next to his wife and fluffed his pillow.

"He makes me want to break into song."

"Whaaat?" She dragged the word out. Wayne was not the singing type, but he did have that dry sense of humor.

"You remember that song from a few years back, 'People Need the Lord'? If my instincts are right, sweet pea, Jason Brigholtz could have been the poster boy for that song—just something to keep in mind if you decide to develop your friendship with Serene."

CHAPTER 6

Along with its FAA ID number, *Polytelis Metafora* was emblazoned on her side, in bright navy-blue lettering, enhancing the silvery hue of the elite aircraft.

In the cool early-morning air of September 11, Jason was sitting on a bench just outside hangar 23 at New Jersey's KTEB airport. He perused the sleek, shiny private jet, glowing in the newly risen sunshine, looking very much like an eager thoroughbred stallion, taut-muscled and chomping at the bit to gallop away at top speed, needing to be anywhere but here. He could relate to the feeling, or maybe he was projecting the feeling.

When Mayhew had told him about the plane, Jason had researched it. Per Mayhew, it was a 1998 Malibu Mirage, which made it three years old now. Mayhew had purchased it at a government auction. It had been confiscated from a crook who was doing time for tax evasion, among other white-collar crimes. Jason wanted desperately to disappear but not to die in a fiery plane crash, so he'd done his homework on the plane. The Malibu Mirage single-engine jet held the pilot plus up to five passengers, could ascend to 25,000 feet, and had a top speed of 253 miles per hour. It could travel 1,500 miles before needing to refuel. Mayhew attested to its having an annual inspection, which apparently meant that a mechanic went through the whole plane to make sure it was mechanically safe and sound, and repairing anything that was found to need repair.

Polytelis Metafora meant "lavish transportation" in Greek. Mayhew's mother had been Greek and had left her son with a smattering of words from her native language. When explaining the aircraft's name, he'd told Jason that he used his limited linguistic knowledge when he wanted to be mysterious, and Del Mayhew loved to be mysterious. He had a flair for the dramatic and had even disclosed to Jason that the FBI had an interest in his dealings, though Jason surmised that Del's estimation of his own notoriety was likely overinflated; more likely, he was a small-time smuggler. In the nineteenth century, he'd have been a pirate. But he'd clearly been enjoying his mysterious interaction with Jason, providing the stealthy disappearance Jason required in exchange for Jason providing Mayhew with every legal, and several dubious, tax-evading maneuvers that Jason's financial expertise could produce and help to implement for him.

From all appearances, this was a sweet ride, and the months Jason had spent researching, educating, and executing Mayhew's evasion of the government's hand-in-pocket tactics might just prove to be worth his effort, although he still didn't fully trust the man, whom he fondly thought of as *the little weasel*, and resented having to deal with him. However, here he was with a new identification, papers that supported it, courtesy of Mayhew's sleazy business contacts and what, indeed, appeared to be luxurious passage to obscurity. As well, the secrecy surrounding it meant he could stay gone as long as he chose to do so. And at the present, Jason could not envision ever wanting to return. No family, no former mistress, no employer, and no clients dogging him for his time, attention, money, or anything else he might be able to provide them. He was thoroughly sick of the material rat race and was ready for a simplistic existence, with no obligations to, or expectations from, anyone. Yes, his mighty steed with the weird name was looking better with each passing minute. Hopefully, his pilot would be just as impressive.

He grabbed his briefcase, rose from the bench outside the hangar, where he'd been processing his thoughts, and headed across the tarmac to the terminal, where a locker he'd rented a couple of weeks ago held a duffel bag with the sparse trappings of his future, the new passport, social security card, and driver's license, a few articles of casual clothing, basic toiletries, and cash. If it was true that money talked, then US dollars were the universal language. Where he was headed, the meager ten thousand should last a long time. If he had to do so, he was confident he could get his hands on more without too much effort. He'd left abundant funds for Serene and Keisha to be quite comfortable, but what he'd also set aside for himself could not, by any means, be described as meager.

Inside the terminal, he bypassed other travelers in various pockets of conversation, nodded to the clerk behind the reception desk, and headed to the locker room. Opening the padlock, he retrieved the sturdy canvas duffel bag, placed his wallet in his briefcase, and the briefcase into the locker. He proceeded to the men's room to retire his business attire for the last time. Inside the handicapped stall, he emptied his pockets of the cash that was left after he paid the cabbie, keys, breath mints, four wallet-size pictures of Serene, Keisha, Michael, and one of the whole family taken the Christmas before Michael had died. He paused momentarily to look at each picture. Shedding his jacket, tie, vest, belt, pants, and shoes, he stuffed the expensive garments into a plastic trash bag he'd retrieved from the duffel. When he'd dressed in khakis, navy-blue T-shirt, and athletic shoes, he put the small items back in his pants pocket. He stood there staring at the keys for a few seconds—keys to his apartment, his car, his desk at work, and various lesser things. Not fully understanding why, he dropped the keys into his pocket along with the other items. Now was not the time to analyze why; he could figure that out later. Surely, he'd discard them once he'd thought it through.

With the plastic bag stuffed in the locker along with the briefcase that held no more than a wallet identifying the man he'd previously been, Jason slung the strap of the duffel bag over his shoulder and walked back through the terminal. Acute awareness that he'd just become Jason Barnes descended over him like a shroud. The power of it caused his insides to quiver and sweat to break out on his forehead and upper lip. *Surely, becoming this new man is a good thing. It's just that assuming the identity feels a bit creepy.* Just nerves, he assured himself; he'd get over it.

No time to contemplate it now. As he approached the terminal door he'd entered earlier, Jason spotted his pilot holding a crude sign that read simply, "Barnes." Jason checked him out as he approached—young, mid to late twenties, athletic-looking, blond hair in the latest gelled hairstyle, aviator sunglasses pushed up on his head, faded blue jeans, a well-worn leather jacket hooked by a thumb over his shoulder, and a Guns N' Roses T-shirt. His jaws worked out vigorously on a wad of gum, while bloodshot brown eyes searched all the nearby faces. Jason made eye contact with the young man and hoped their verbal exchange would instill more confidence in the pilot than the young man's appearance had.

"Hello, I'm Jason Barnes." Withholding the typical, cordial smile, he thrust his hand forward, hoping his crisp deportment would inspire consideration of the seriousness of flying a jet plane. "And you must be Dale Fordham, Mr.

Delwin's pilot?" He applied the Delwin alias that Mayhew had instructed him to use.

His serious demeanor seemed to be working, at least somewhat. Fordham wiped a sweaty palm on his pants and shook Jason's hand. "Yes, sir, I'm B.Dale, as Del likes to call me, says Dale sounds too much like Del, so he tacked on my first initial—stands for Bertrand—so of course I never use my first name." A nervous grin accompanied the remark. "But I don't mind being called B.Dale. It's different, so the chicks dig it. But hey, I'm rambling again." With a nervous grin, he pulled the wad of gum from his mouth, stuck it to the crude cardboard *Barnes* sign, and thrust both into the nearby trash can. Motioning to the door, he invited, "Shall we go take a look at the big bird?"

Under the guise of social niceties, Jason quizzed the young pilot as they walked to the plane. Where you from? Where'd you go to school? Married? How long have you been flying? Etc. From Iowa. Couple of years at Iowa State, but didn't graduate. Not married. Flying since he was sixteen, so twelve years. The kid was no dummy. He was aware of what Jason wanted to know: Are you capable of getting me to my destination without dumping me into the Atlantic?

"Look, Mr. Barnes, I get it. I don't look seasoned, like you would expect of an experienced pilot. I'm not sophisticated. Am I a druggy, a space cadet, or a daredevil hotshot? The answer to all those questions is no. I come from farm country. My dad was a crop duster, and like any kid would, I fell in love with his plane. So he taught me to fly. I started out flying with my dad when I was twelve, learned all he could teach me, then with money I saved up from odd jobs and some my grandma left me, I took lessons and got my license, soloed when I was sixteen. I took jobs flying businessmen to their meetings, sick kids to bigger hospitals, and chauffeured bumpkins above the local farms so they could look at their houses, barns, and crops. I spent two years flying in the military, mostly helicopters. I was flying tourists among the islands in Hawaii when I met Delwin, and he offered me the job of being his personal pilot. I've flown almost every small aircraft out there, prop planes and jets, and I'm meticulous about safety—the first lesson my father drilled into my head." They'd reached the plane. Fordham turned and looked Jason right in the eye. "So you can come fly with me or tell Pat Delwin you want a different pilot. I really don't give a flip. But make up your mind, because I've got a preflight check to do, and I don't like distractions. So you need to either walk away or get aboard the plane."

Jason suppressed a grin and got aboard the plane.

B.Dale finished his preflight check and was cleared for takeoff at 8:37 a.m. With his sole passenger, he ascended and headed southeast out over the Atlantic. At 8:46 a.m., the first hijacked airliner exploded through a wall of windows on the North Tower of One World Trade and demolished Jason Brigholtz's workstation. The second airliner hit the South Tower at 9:03 a.m.

At approximately 9:25 a.m., US Secretary of Transportation Norman Mineta ordered all civilian aircraft in US airspace to be grounded. Over 4,500 aircraft complied. The *Polytelis Metafora* did not; flying southeast, it was well out over the Atlantic by then, without having filed a flight plan and without the benefit of its radio, Patrick Delwin's directive. Incognito was the rule of the day since Delwin's private jet, if it could be located, was subject to be repossessed.

CHAPTER

Jack Mason was certain that he'd have to take Keisha's key from her adrenaline-charged, shaking hand to unlock the apartment door. Pent-up apprehension was emanating from the girl like a force field, but to his surprise, she had slid the key into the lock on the first try and opened it in record time, barging in and yelling for her mom. He and his daughter, Sondra, followed Keisha into the apartment. As Serene emerged from the kitchen, Keisha threw herself into her mother's arms and, with a painful sob, let loose the barrage of tears she'd been holding back since the schoolteachers had gathered at the curb to let the arriving parents and students know what had just occurred at the North Tower of One World Trade. There would be no classes at Drake High School today.

Jack could see that he'd have to explain to Serene; Keisha was in no shape to be able to talk. How he dreaded what had to be said, but he plunged ahead. She had to know.

"Serene, a commercial airliner has hit the WTC North Tower, just rammed right into the building!" He noticed the shaking in his own hands as nervous gestures accompanied his words. "People are trying to escape, some heading to the roof, hoping to be airlifted. Others are taking the staircases down. Of course, elevators aren't safe to use in an emergency. Who knows if they are even working." Jack recognized his own edgy blathering. There was a quiver in his voice as he avoided the elephant in the room—Jason Brigholtz was at work in the North Tower. "They closed the school. Some of the students have received calls from parents who work in the building." He hoped Serene would say that she'd received a call from Jason. She did not.

Suddenly realizing what that explosive sound was that she'd heard earlier, Serene addressed her daughter. "Keisha, have you heard from you dad?"

"No," came the choked reply, "and I keep getting a recording when I try to call his cell phone."

"Okay, baby, don't worry. We'll find out what's going on. I'll call his office." She stroked her daughter's hair in a comforting gesture, although she was beginning to feel pretty shaky herself.

Trying to remain composed for Keisha's sake, she asked, "Jack, do you know at what level this plane hit?"

He'd heard an approximated guess by the announcer on the car radio but couldn't bring himself to say anything about it. "I really don't know any more than what I've told you, Serene. I think you should turn on the TV." He quickly added, "I also think Sondra and I should get started for home before traffic becomes so choked that we can't." *And while I still have enough wits to drive,* he thought to himself.

"Yes, of course, Jack. Thank you so much for bringing Keisha home."

"You're welcome, Serene. I hope you hear from Jason soon."

Sondra tearfully hugged Keisha and whispered, "Bye." It was all she could force out as she and her father took their leave.

After settling Keisha in the family room, covered with a soft afghan, two ibuprofen and a cup of chamomile tea nearby, Serene again punched Jason's cell phone number on her speed dial. This was her fourth try; the first three attempts had elicited the same "Unable to complete your call" message that Keisha had gotten. This time it was ringing. Her heart did a little flip; however, in the next moment, she heard a muted ringtone coming from Jason's converted bedroom office, the ringtone she recognized as Jason's cell phone.

*****

John Barbour sat on a stool at the island in his Manhattan apartment's kitchen, holding a bottle of water, as yet unopened. The small TV in the kitchen continued to display the painful newsfeed, now with muted volume. He was quivering inside; he'd never felt anything like this. Unable to sit still, his wife scurried around the kitchen, making fresh coffee and mixing up the dough for cinnamon rolls that neither of them wanted. She was just too nerved up to sit still, so she burned off the nervous energy through the familiar activity.

He'd been unable to reach her by phone when he left the dentist's office, so he'd just driven home, being rerouted a couple of times and held up in traffic. A drive that would normally take him twenty minutes took him three times that long. She'd been frantic when he arrived, for fear that perhaps he'd skipped the dental appointment that morning and gone right to work.

John processed his thoughts yet again: His appointment to get his teeth cleaned and checked had been for Thursday, September 6, an appointment made six months in advance. Then at the beginning of last week, he began hearing in his spirit, *Don't go to the dentist on Thursday.* He tried to brush off the thought the first couple of times, but then he began to feel an apprehension each time the recurring thought came to him. There was never any indication of why he was not to keep the appointment, but he finally conceded that he was receiving a directive from the Lord and needed to obey it and not question it any further.

So on Wednesday morning, he'd called the dentist's office and, apologizing for the late notice, told them that he was not going to be able to keep his appointment for the next day. He asked to reschedule it. Checking their bookings, the receptionist came back to the phone and said that they were booked solid until late in October. They could get him in on Monday, October 29, if that would work for him. He was about to affirm that date when she said, "Wait just a minute. Judy just told me she had a cancellation yesterday for next Tuesday, the eleventh. I know you prefer late afternoons, Mr. Barbour, but if you'd like the September 11 appointment, we can slip you in there. It's for 8:00 a.m." He had affirmed and booked the appointment. He immediately felt peace in his spirit.

John reflected now on how he'd come out of the exam room, running his tongue over his silky, clean teeth and carrying his little bag with sample-size toothpaste, dental floss, and a new toothbrush. He was mentally congratulating himself for no cavities and no need to return for a cleaning for another year. Then he encountered pale, somber faces and even uncontrolled tears at the reception desk. Obviously, something had seriously upset the three gals behind the counter. A patient stood at the counter, who was in the same distraught condition as the dentist's staff. The man had just come in for his appointment and was so shaken that he held on to the counter for support. Then he repeated for John and other staff and patients who'd gathered around what he'd just heard on his car radio.

John had shared with his wife last week what he heard in his spirit about not keeping his Thursday appointment at the dentist's office. Together they had prayed for the staff and any patients that might be there on Thursday, in case the Lord wanted to protect him from something that would occur on that day in that location. They were relieved to find out that it had been a routine day. Now they knew that he had, indeed, been protected, just not in the way they'd anticipated. While John had submitted to the pink minty stuff being polished onto his teeth, a step in the cleaning process that he really disliked, the first plane had hit right at the level of his office, Devlin, Burke, and Associates.

There was no getting through by phone to anyone at the company. He feared the worst. With the impact at that level of the building, how could any of his coworkers have survived that fiery crash? His mind drifted to the familiar setting of the office, and he could see each person with whom he worked every day. Tears slid unbidden down his cheeks as he thought of Zoe, his secretary of the last four years, a pretty young gal in her midtwenties who had married just last year. She had shared a few weeks back that she and her husband were expecting their first child. They were so excited. He couldn't imagine what that young husband must be going through right now. It gave John *some* relief to recall that the couple had recently received the Lord and were regularly attending church. But what about other coworkers?

His thoughts turned to the other three men in his work zone, Grady, Jason, and Neil, and an image came to mind— was it a T-shirt or a bumper sticker? He wasn't sure where he'd seen it, but the caption had read, "Salvation—Don't Leave Earth Without It." How many of those men had stepped out into eternity this morning unprepared? He had tried to be a witness to all of them, but he couldn't help but wonder if he'd done enough. He vacillated between extreme gratitude to God for his own rescue and teary-eyed, queasy mourning for his coworkers.

John had wanted to hurry to the site to see if he could help in any way, but of course, the police were saying that no one except first responders should go anywhere near the scene, a scene that now included the South Tower as well. His wife was fine with his staying right where he was, content to have very little conversation, as long as she could just have him near. She allowed him his pondering.

Being a man of practical and analytical personality, John let his thoughts wander to the information that had been lost; so much of it in his line of work would represent dollars and cents. Computers, floppy disks, hard-copy paperwork. Most of what was saved on computer could be recreated as long as it had been backed up, but perhaps not all. Recovery, of course, would be focused first on people, survivors and then casualties. The secondary logistics of data recovery would be a long-term undertaking, nightmarish in its sheer volume, a task that would be the charge of employees of every company housed in those buildings.

Even as John was processing his thoughts, billions of bits and pieces of papers floated, along with other debris, to the dust-covered ground around the two towers, both of which would soon collapse. One such scrap that landed in the dusty rubble contained the words, "My dearest Serene..." The gangly boy from the mail room ran as fast as he could away from Tower One, thanking God that he had not yet ascended to any of the floors above the mail room when the explosive impact occurred.

*****

Sitting in the family room of her spacious Hawaii home at 5:30 a.m., her first daily cup of Kona Blue Mountain Coffee next to her on the end table, Miranda Salenger hung up the phone from her fifth attempt to reach Serene in New York. She'd never before encountered that strange "Unable to complete your number as dialed" message, and for some reason, it caused a hint of fear to flutter in her stomach. There had never been any problem getting through at their designated time of 5:30 a.m. for Miranda, which was 10:30 a.m. for Serene, a time that worked well for both of them because Miranda was always up early to pray and then do her workout. On the other end, Serene was ready for a break in her morning household routine, and this every-second-Tuesday call was a refreshing anchor to her unsettled existence.

Reann, the Salengers' housekeeper, was also on Miranda's early schedule; it allowed her to be done with her workday early in the afternoon, which suited her just fine, permitting her to be home when her two teenagers got out of school. She had just let herself in to the Salenger home, dropped her purse and keys on the foyer table. She hurried into the family room. "Mrs. Salenger," she blurted anxiously, "turn on the TV. There has been a disaster in New York City. I've been listening on my car radio."

Miranda grabbed the remote and flipped on the TV. The smoking and burning that spread across the large screen was her answer to why New York City phone lines were completely overwhelmed. The whole city of New York was completely overwhelmed, as soon the whole country would be.

C H A P T E R

Jason's insides were still quivering when he felt the wheels touch down on the runway and the plane begin to decelerate, eventually taxiing to a safe stop in the area designated for smaller aircraft. He was inwardly cursing Del Mayhew or Patrick Delwin or whatever the little weasel cared to call himself today. B.Dale had already expressed his opinion that Mayhew had surely not had the last annual done, since it would have undoubtedly found and corrected the small but deadly dangerous problem that had almost killed the two of them and, in Jason's estimation, probably had taken years off his life just in anticipation of dying. He wondered if the man had *ever* had an annual inspection done on the plane. He held out his hands and noticed they were still shaking. In a car, you might have had to pull over to the side of the road, but in an airplane, a stalled engine could quickly become a death sentence.

About fifteen minutes short of the Bermuda airport, the plane had begun to sputter and lose power, which the young pilot had explained could be one of many causes: water in the fuel from condensation, an injector problem, or a failure of one of several sensors—all were possibilities. All these potential deficits would have been easily picked up and corrected during the annual inspection, *if* it had been done.

Once the engine had restarted and B.Dale had been able to talk to Jason—other than to say, "Shut up!"—he'd told him there were crooked mechanics who would sign off on an inspection for half the cost of actually *doing* the inspection. The young pilot, as it turned out, had about as much confidence in Mayhew's integrity to avoid those mechanics as Jason did, which had been very little and now was a whopping zero!

Heat rising from the tarmac in visible waves, Jason looked down at it as he stepped down with wobbly legs that felt like so much jelly. The weight of his bag flung over one shoulder threatened to topple him—he was that shaky. "I don't know what your future plans are, kid, but I sure hope you're smart enough to break off all ties to Pat Delwin, which, by the way, is an alias! The man is a dishonest, self-absorbed dirtbag who cares about no one but himself!" His face had turned red, and his voice had increased in volume with every word as he vented. "He's never going to respect you or pay you what you're worth, or even do the bare essentials to keep his plane from killing you!"

Angry as he was, he still felt compassion for this boy, who'd just managed to save their lives, no thanks to Mayhew. The kid didn't deserve to be put in danger or to be put in a position of being responsible for the danger to Mayhew's passengers.

In a softer tone, Jason tried again. "Look, go find out what you can about booking your own transportation off this island, and if you need money to pay for it, let me know, but don't climb aboard this death trap again. And don't assume responsibility for taking care of the jerk's crippled plane for him either. I'd suggest you find your way back to Iowa and start over from there, cutting off all association with Delwin. If he doesn't put you in danger by not maintaining his plane, he'll do it by getting you involved in smuggling something illegal. You're too young and too smart to let that happen."

Fordham looked pale himself from the ordeal, and humbled, head hanging slightly. He nodded when Jason was done with his stormy rant. "Sounds like a lecture I might expect from my own dad," the kid said quietly. "Good advice."

Jason's expression softened. "And by the way, thanks for keeping a cool head up there and saving both our hides. You're one extraordinary, steely-nerved pilot, kid." That remark earned him a half-grin. He slapped the young man on the back. "Let's go see if we can each find a cold drink and a pair of clean undies."

As soon as they'd walked into the large modern terminal building that occupied the end of a long peninsula, surrounded on three sides by water and on the fourth side by the runways, Fordham had been immediately met and was taken into a separate room by airport officials; it was to answer some questions about the plane, they'd said. After checking his ID, they had waved Jason aside and told him to go on about his business; obviously, they had no intention of involving a mere passenger in the details of their interview with the pilot. Jason assumed it had to do with the less-than-normal landing. What else could they want with the young pilot? His thoughts were more geared to mentally congratulating himself that the first inspection of his false ID had gone well. At least Mayhew had done that right.

Just in case Fordham's little meeting had anything to do with his crooked boss, Jason decided to wait so he could vouch for the kid. Dale had held out his bag to Jason. "Could you hold on to this for me?" His eyes had seemed to be asking more than that. *Wait for me* was the message they really conveyed. Jason sat waiting in the lounge area with other travelers, who were either waiting for their rides to show up or for an outbound flight to be called. Several animated conversations seemed to echo off the high ceilings of the room. Jason sat off by himself in a corner, not wanting to invite any polite small talk with strangers. Still a little unsteady, he did some deep breathing exercises to quiet his nerves and settle his stomach. As he began to calm a little bit, his thoughts wandered to the "mighty steed chomping at the bit to run off." After the proud and impressive mount had soared into the wild blue, it had run out of steam and come close to a disgraceful crash and burn. If Jason were a philosophical man, he might think the whole unsound trip was a metaphor for his own proud and impressive plans. Reflecting on it was starting to unsettle his stomach again.

Get a grip, Brigholtz! What was a near disaster was simply the result of a careless jerk disregarding any semblance of prudence in the care of his aircraft. It bore no reflection on you and your plans…did it?

Clad in Bermuda shorts, the traditional attire of the island, two locals walked by him just then. They caught his attention with their conversation about the fishing boats at the docks that were about to head out to the smaller islands after having stocked up on supplies. *Perfect timing,* Jason thought. *I don't want to miss out on my opportunity to move on.* He wondered how much longer Fordham would be detained. But other than making sure the kid had money to get back to the States on a commercial flight, he decided there was no need to wait around for him.

Spotting a teenager wearing headphones and nervously flipping a pencil over a notebook in which he appeared to be taking notes, Jason approached him and waved a hand in front of his face to get his attention. The boy, slightly annoyed, looked up and removed an earbud from one ear. "Excuse me, but I was wondering if I might bum a sheet of paper from you and borrow your pencil to write a note to my friend? I have to leave, but I want to let him know I'm going and why." He added his kindest smile to the request.

The boy said nothing but flipped back through the notebook and tore out a clean page of paper and grabbed another pencil from his backpack, handing both over to Jason.

"Thanks." He squatted in front of the molded plastic chair next to the boy, and using it as a desk, he began his note. When finished, he returned the pencil to its owner and walked back to his original chair, where he'd left his and Fordham's duffel bags.

Jason trifolded the note, discreetly pulled five one-hundred-dollar bills from the money belt beneath his shirt, and tucked them inside the folds of the note. He unzipped Dale's duffel just enough to place the note and money inside. Zipping it closed, he picked up both bags and walked to what appeared to be an information desk. He turned on the charm for the cute brunette working the counter, who looked to be in her midforties and was wearing her age quite well. "I wonder if you could help me with something, young lady. I have to leave to catch my ride, and my friend is in with some airport officials." He nodded to the door behind which they'd disappeared.

She blushed and smiled sweetly at the flattering attention from this exceptionally attractive man, while cautioning herself to remain professional and be alert to what he might want from her. "What is it I can help you with, sir?" Her reply was heavy with a British accent.

"If it's all right, I'd like to leave his bag with you for safekeeping. His name is Dale Fordham. See, it's right here on the tag." He held the bag up for her perusal of the tag. "He's midtwenties, has spiky blond hair and brown eyes, and he'll be wearing blue jeans. If he asks, just tell him Mr. Barnes had to leave to catch his ride and that I've left a note inside his bag to explain."

Reaching over the counter to accept the bag, she smiled and said, "I guess I can do that for you. Do you know how long he might be?"

"I expect he could be out of there anytime, but just in case it takes another half-hour or so, I really am not able to wait. You are so kind to help me out." He added a wink for good measure, and she blushed again.

Dale Fordham was wide-eyed and slack-jawed. Hands pressed to his temples, he just shook his head, trying to wrap his brain around all he'd been hearing since being taken into this conference room forty-five minutes ago. On the opposite side of the conference table was the airport supervisor, head of security, and a repo agent hired by the bank that had financed Mayhew's purchase of the Mirage. The first topic of conversation had begun with the repo agent, who advised that he was there on an off-the-record tip from an FBI agent that the Mirage would possibly be flown to the island of Bermuda on this date. "Mr. Fordham, let me begin by saying that your employer, Mr. Delwin, is not the owner of the airplane that you flew here today." He paused for dramatic effect. Dale kept a grip on his poker face and just shrugged, waiting for further explanation and hoping the man was not going to tell him the plane had been stolen.

Looking a little bit disappointed that his comment had not resulted in the shock he'd expected, or a sputtering argument, the agent continued, "After the down payment was made on the jet, only one more monthly installment has been remitted—that was sixteen months ago, and it was late, at that! Since then, the lender has received no further payment. The aircraft would have been repossessed long ago, but it seems Mr. Delwin has been hiding the plane in various locations since the first missed installment, making it very difficult to find. You wouldn't know anything about that little game of hide-and-seek, would you, Mr. Fordham?"

Dale was confident in his answer. "I've been responsible for transporting passengers on several occasions. It's what I was hired to do. I don't know anything about Delwin hiding the plane, nor was I ever asked to hide the plane. It's mostly been in the Hawaiian islands." As he thought back, there might have been occasions when a flight destination was a little bit off the beaten path, but always under the pretext of transporting passengers or for some sort of maintenance. He didn't offer any further details about that, but since maintenance had come to mind, here was something he *could* offer. "If you plan to repossess the plane today, you should know that, from our flight in, it has become evident that the plane is urgently in need of maintenance. I strongly suspect the last annual, which was due to have been done in April, was likely *not* done, although I was told that it had occurred while I was on vacation on the mainland. I strongly suggest that you not attempt to fly the plane off this island until you have a mechanic do a thorough inspection of it." He related the problems they'd encountered just before they landed. The other man scribbled notes on a pad of paper. After he assured the repo agent that the plane's log was aboard the aircraft, there was a lull in the conversation.

Thinking that was the end of the inquiry, Fordham assumed he was free to be on his way. He needed to find Barnes and see if he, indeed, could borrow money from him for a commercial flight. He was pretty sure he'd fall short of the full cost of a ticket.

"Well, if that's all…" He began to rise from his chair.

The airport supervisor put the palm of his hand up like in a stop sign. "Not so fast, son." And then began the next topic of inquiry. "Did you fly in from the United States today? And if so, from where?"

"Yes, sir, from KTEB in New Jersey."

"Why did you not file a flight plan or maintain radio contact until you experienced the problem just before landing?"

It didn't make him proud to answer the question, but he did answer, as honestly as he could. "On both those points, I was following the instructions of my employer. Now that I know about the threat of repo, I realize that was likely the reason for his directive."

There was no further inquiry into that, but he knew the flight plan wasn't mandatory, nor was the radio, although it was certainly advisable to make use of both safety options.

The next question, posed by the security officer, caught him completely by surprise. "Why did you not ground the plane when that order was given?"

He was flummoxed, and his expression reflected that. He shook his head. "What order? Ground the plane?" He was clueless. He'd heard nothing about such an order, but then he hadn't had his radio on. "Sorry, I don't know anything about any order to ground the plane."

Looks were exchanged among the three men opposite Dale. The security officer inquired, "What time did you take off from the New Jersey airport, Mr. Fordham?"

"It was shortly after eight thirty this morning, eastern time, sir."

"And you had no further communication with the tower in New Jersey after that?"

"No, sir."

The three men across from him looked at one another and said nothing for several long seconds. The security guy was the first to breach the awkward silence. The story he related was almost too wild and too horrible to believe.

But none of the three smiled, snickered, or tried to hide an amused expression. They weren't kidding around; they were deadly serious.

Once they had decided there was no reason to hold him, Dale was dismissed and left the room in a stupor. He walked into the lounge area to locate his duffel bag and the man to whom he'd entrusted it. Barnes was *from* New York City. Dale needed to find him and see if anyone had told him about the attack. "Excuse me, sir. Would you be Mr. Fordham, by chance?"

Dale looked over at the attractive brunette who'd addressed him. "Um, yeah. I'm Dale Fordham."

"Sir, your friend Mr. Barnes left your bag with me. He asked that I give it to you when you were out of your meeting. He said he had to leave to catch his ride and that he'd left you a note inside your bag." She lifted the bag from behind her reception desk and held it out to him.

He took possession of his duffel without breaking eye contact with her. "Did he say where he was going, a hotel or something?"

"No, sir. He didn't say anything about that at all. Perhaps the note he left you will have more information."

He thanked her.

Sitting down in a nearby chair with his duffel, Dale took a few seconds to compose himself and then looked down at the bag on his lap. He reached for the zipper and slowly opened it. Right there on top of his clothes was a folded sheet of lined notebook paper. As he opened it, currency began to drift to the floor. He quickly grasped for the bills, making sure he'd caught all of them. He counted five in all; each one was a hundred-dollar note. He breathed a sigh of relief. Added to what he had in his wallet, he could get home, that is, when the secretary of transportation allowed flights to be resumed. Stuffing the bills back into the bag, he turned his attention to the note.

Dale:

> *Sorry I didn't get a chance to say good-bye. I have an opportunity to catch a boat to my destination island and a limited window to make that connection. Never let it be said you don't provide an exciting ride, kid! Take care of yourself. Hope this "tip" is helpful in getting you home.*
>
> *Jason*

CHAPTER

At her home in Indiana, Calleen Revelle arose from kneeling at her bedside. She'd been fasting and spending time in prayer, seeking the Lord about her brother, Jason, who was presumed dead in the 9/11 attack in New York City. For almost two years now, she'd been skeptical that he had really died in the attack. It wasn't anything in particular, just an unsettled sensation in her spirit.

Her husband, Keith, walked into the bedroom. "Your one hour is up, babe. Have a good prayer time?"

She heaved a deep sigh and sat on the edge of the bed. "I still have no peace over Jason, Keith. It was a good prayer time, in that I am really feeling God's arms around me in comfort, but I still can't shake that questioning of whether Jason was in that tower when it was hit. You know, I've wanted to bring it up to Serene, but I'm concerned about giving her false hope when I can't be sure if the Lord is trying to tell me something or if it's just my own wishful thinking."

"No, I agree, you've been wise not to bring it up to her, and I think you still can't say anything, not unless the Lord gives you peace about telling her. Besides, she and Keisha are leaving for Hawaii in a couple of days. She doesn't need something to stress about with that trip pending." He sat down next to her on their bed and rubbed small circles on her back. "On the phone the other day, she sounded tired. I think she needs this time away, and certainly nothing more to worry about. By the way, when she called, she said she'd leave word with the building super that we might be visiting." He picked up her Bible off the bed and set it on the nightstand. "So if you are interested in a New York City vacation, maybe for our anniversary, it's something to keep in mind."

"That does sound good. Maybe by August, I'll be a little more settled in my spirit."

"So Bella is going to stay over at Sherrie's tonight. They just picked her up. And the boys and I are planning to indulge in pizza and watch that *Chicken Run* video we rented. I want you to go ahead and go to the women's retreat. Everyone's talking about the speaker, mostly about her prophetic gifting. It will be interesting, I'm sure, and you need a break, to take your mind off things."

"I don't know, Keith." She crossed her legs and, pulling them up onto the bed, leaned into him. "I don't feel like getting ready for it, and I probably wouldn't even be able to concentrate. Can't I just stay home and eat pizza with you and the boys? I think I'm ready to break my fast."

Keith rose, reached for her hands, and pulled her up and into his embrace. After a firm squeeze, he kissed her softly on the lips. Then with lips hovering over her ear, he said softly, "Get in the shower, babe. By the time you come back through the kitchen, the pizza will be here, and you can grab a slice on your way out to the car. Seriously, Callie, I think you should go." He slid his hands into the golden-blond locks on each side of her face and leaned in for another gentle kiss. His smile was loving but firm as he nodded toward the master bath, took ahold of her shoulders, and turned her toward it, gently slapping her bottom as she moved away from him.

*****

The church building was abuzz with excitement when Callie walked in. She chugged the last of her Vernors and dropped the can in the nearest receptacle. A couple hundred females chatted and moved about between the ladies' room, the book table in the foyer, and the sanctuary. Several of her friends welcomed Callie, some with hugs, some with quick greetings as they moved on to find their chairs in the meeting, which was to start in just five minutes. Callie made her way toward the bathroom; she wanted to give herself some time so that she could slip into the meeting and sit in the back by herself. She just wasn't in the mood for discussing the guest speaker or listening to sympathetic remarks regarding the loss of her brother.

"And now, without further ado, let's welcome Deirdre Farnsworth to the pulpit." Applause broke out as Callie slipped into a mostly vacant pew at the back of the sanctuary. Two ladies Callie didn't know sat on the platform with the pastor's wife and worship leader, off to the right of the speaker. Deirdre spoke for about ten minutes; her observations on familiar scripture were encouraging and insightful. She then moved into the operation of the gifts, speaking words over the pastor's wife and worship leader. She and the two ladies who'd been on the platform that Callie didn't recognize came down the stairs then and stood at the front of the pews. Deirdre introduced them as Maddie Denning and Joan Middleton. They were apprenticing, as Deirdre put it, in the activation of the gifts of the Spirit. The three then spread out across the front of the sanctuary, so there was enough distance between each of them, so that they would not be distracted by each other as they ministered. The worship team began to play softly.

Men from the church's ushering team organized the ladies who wanted to receive ministry into a line, and as the line reached the front of the sanctuary, each lady was directed to whichever of the three ladies was available to minister to them. It kept a nice, smooth flow to the process. Behind each of the three ministers, there was a female volunteer who held a cassette recorder; a fresh supply of tapes covered a small table next to her that the ushers had quickly set up. Callie got in the line without giving it much thought. She had a sense that it was why she'd come tonight in spite of her reluctance. As she slowly neared the front of the sanctuary, her spirit began to get excited. Those coming away from the front were very animated about the words Deirdre had spoken over them. She was obviously very experienced and anointed in her gifting. Callie began to be hopeful that when she reached the front of the line, Deirdre would be the one available to minister to her.

Joan was beginning to relax. This was only the second time she'd been with Deirdre, ministering at a women's conference, but she grew more comfortable as the ministry continued and the Holy Spirit always came through. Early on, as she was first learning, she would get just one or two words and not know what to do with them, but she gradually learned to just begin to speak, in faith, about the words, and immediately the heart of the Lord for the person would come through.

A woman was moving toward her now. Joan had noticed that she looked a little disappointed that Deirdre hadn't been open, but she had quickly put on a smile and headed toward Joan, as she was being directed to do. Joan returned her smile. She had learned to ignore that disappointment she saw on so many faces because they were being directed to the *newbie*.

She didn't allow it to distract her. The pretty woman with dark-blond hair and deep-blue eyes stepped up to her and said hello.

"What's your name?" Joan asked.

"Callie."

Joan smiled. "Pretty name for a pretty lady." She laid a hand on Callie's shoulder and quietly prayed, "Show me Your heart for Callie, Lord."

Joan stood quietly with her eyes closed for a few seconds. She smiled. "You have been a precious daughter to Him for a very long time. He wants you to know that He appreciates your faithfulness to love Him and to love others on His behalf."

A moment's pause, and she continued, "You have three children, a daughter and a set of twin boys."

Callie's eyes got big, and she nodded.

"Your daughter has a gift for singing and will use it for His glory."

Callie got misty-eyed. Nine-year-old Isabella was always singing around the house.

"Don't be overly concerned about the twins' frequent spats. They are exploring their individual personalities, which are very different in spite of their identical looks, but it will not affect their affection for each other. That mutual love will be a strong, lifelong bond between them."

Callie relaxed, pleased that the Lord knew her and Keith's concerns about their five-year-old twin boys and would want to bring them peace about it.

Brother. Reckoning. Hug.

"I'm seeing that your brother is on your mind...that you have some deep concerns in your heart for him."

A sudden gasp sucked air in through the lips of the pretty blonde, who clapped her hand over her mouth. Profuse tears soon flowed unchecked.

"Don't let your heart be troubled. He has some reckoning to do. He's in a process right now of setting some things straight. The Holy Spirit is working with him in that process. When that is all settled, he will be restored to you. I see a reunion hug, with much love passing between you."

Callie had slipped to her knees, with deep sobs freely flowing now.

*****

Keith had put the twins to bed with two stories, hearing their prayers, speaking a blessing over them, and coming back into their room after several minutes with a stern warning to stop the giggle fest and settle down. He had cleaned up the bathroom after their rather-rowdy bath and was just beginning to attack the mess in the kitchen from the ice cream sundaes, letting his mind drift to tomorrow's deposition; he needed to go over his notes one more time before he went to bed. Oh well, the night of domestic duty, rather than working on office work, was well worth it if tonight's women's meeting had been therapeutic for Callie, as he was hoping it would be. As though his warm thoughts toward his wife had conjured her up, he heard her car pull into the driveway and the garage door opening. His heart did a little flip. *Please, Lord...*

As Callie walked through the back door from the garage into the kitchen, Keith looked up from where he was mopping up the counter with a dishrag, to find a warm glow on his wife's countenance and a cassette tape held up between her thumb and forefinger. Tears glistened in her eyes, and a full, peaceful smile possessed her pretty features.

CHAPTER

Jason stretched out on his hammock. He had completed his hut, using the materials and methods the locals had shown him—not all that different from the first island he'd lived on. He had gathered or purchased supplies and food and had gained some knowledge of cooking, even though some things on his menu were completely new to him. He was learning new skills to survive his newly sought-out digs, and although he couldn't describe himself as happy, he was certainly content to have an existence that was basic simplicity compared to the rat-race world of investment banking that was a thing of his past.

Jason had always thought of himself as someone who had a talent for making money—an instinctive ability was a better descriptor. However, it had become a beast in his life that had driven him. He'd gotten to a place where he was never satisfied, never at peace. There was always a nagging feeling that whatever he achieved, it just wasn't quite enough. Trying to maintain relationship with a family with whom he no longer had connection was also in the past, though not as simply forgotten. He was all right with calling himself a failure with the latter. The only mentor he'd ever had, his father, had also failed to produce a happy, cohesive family unit, eventually walking away from the responsibility and the family, seemingly resigned to the failure. Jason had been twelve when his father filed for divorce and never looked back, not to his ex-wife and not to his children. Perhaps it was to be expected that the son would do the same. Then to compound his misery were the feelings of guilt and shame for failing to protect his son, but he never allowed his thoughts to go there. It only produced immense pain.

He'd been more than a year on the first island he'd adopted as his home but became dissatisfied when the locals were determined to include him in their little society. He even suspected that a couple of the families were trying to marry off a daughter to the tall standoffish foreigner in their midst. So he'd packed up his meager belongings and hopped on the next fishing boat that came through. This current island had been the boat's next stop to drop off supplies and pick up the touristy trinkets that would go back to Bermuda for sale in the shops there. It was a barter system that seemed to work well for both sides. The fishing boats also proved to be a good taxi service for transporting and relocating people.

Now, if only the locals on this new sanctuary would just get the idea that he did not wish to become a member of their little social circle but just wanted to be left alone. He thought he'd built far enough away from their village to identify himself as willingly reclusive, but bored children still sought him out as a curiosity, and the witch doctor, who called himself David, also seemed intent on continually coming around to impress him with his prestige in the tribe and his business acumen. He had proved to be a good source for most of the things needed to establish a household. For the right price, *always*, he was willing to make himself available as Jason's grocer, pharmacist, bartender, doctor, handyman, interpreter, and handy-dandy agent in procuring anything else that might not be included in the other categories.

He lay back on the hammock, large-brimmed straw hat covering his face and shaggy hair, wanting nothing more than to enjoy the sunshine on his bare arms and legs and relish the breeze that was just robust enough to keep the insects at bay. He was on the verge of napping when David's opportunistic voice stirred him.

"Joe-son! Joe-son! This your day of fortune, mon. I have for you today, at very low price, very beautiful woman for companion, one day only. No other to available such beauty. No other to available such good price. You are surely be thrilled. At no extra cost, you look first. Definite to be undamaged. Still very young," he professed. "Show to customer, Meelae. Show yourself."

Thoroughly irritated, Jason roused himself and removed the straw hat to rudely dismiss the witch doctor's solicitation when his eyes were confronted with a curvy young native girl, probably no older than his own daughter, with her sarong flung wide for his perusal. Her smile was innocent and without shame. He was so shocked it took a minute for the curse word to form in his mind, and before it could pass his lips, another raised voice filled in the blank.

"I have one word of advice for you, mister: *syphilis*!" The shout had come from about twenty yards off to his left, on the dusty trail from the river, a white man walking along with four native boys, each youthful pair carrying a pole of dangling fish between them.

The man, American by the sound of his voice, spoke to the chuckling boys sternly. The boys continued on with their catch, while the self-appointed adviser turned off the path and headed for the witch doctor, the naive lass, and the still-stunned new guy to the neighborhood.

"Meelae, close your dress." It was not a harsh command, just a matter of fact instruction. She quickly complied and was then instructed by the man to go on back to her mother's hut.

"Okee, Mr. Thud." And she skipped away, smiling.

The man was tall, Jason guessed maybe six feet, slender, and probably in his midfifties. He had dark hair and deep-brown eyes and wore cargo shorts, a T-shirt, and sturdy sandals. He had a certain presence, a charisma that probably had attracted women in his younger years.

"David, what have I told you about selling favors from these poor young girls? It is sinful, unhealthy, displeasing to the Lord, and generally harmful to everyone involved. We'll have to go over this again at our next Bible study session. Now, would you be so good as to introduce me to our new neighbor?" The man's demeanor remained pleasant.

At first looking shamefaced at the berating, the witch doctor, at the last remark, perked up; apparently, it pleased him that he knew someone that the missionary did not. With his chest puffed up, David replied, "Mr. Thud, this Mr. Joe-son, my customer friend."

"How do you do, Mr. Joe-son? I'm Thurston Judd, Christian missionary to this region, here with my wife, Rae Jean, for about three years now. Thud is a nickname I picked up back in college—e-mail address, first three letters of the first name and last two of the last name—a handle the natives seem to enjoy using as well." The chatty missionary offered his outstretched hand.

"Jason Barnes," Jason responded succinctly, begrudgingly stretching out his hand while eyeing Thud warily. "So his name really is David?" He nodded toward the panderer. "I didn't know whether to believe him on that or, for that matter, on pretty much anything."

Ignoring the reference to David's character, Thud explained, "I've done pretty well learning local names, but some are just too much for my Oklahoma dialect to pick up and pronounce." Smiling at the native as he affectionately clamped him on the shoulder, he continued, "There is a D in his name somewhere, so after trying and failing several times, David has graciously allowed me to Americanize his name for the sake of convenience. I think he kind of enjoys the distinction of being renamed." David childishly grinned back at him, revealing a few gaps where teeth would normally reside. "Happily, David has recently received the Lord but is still in the process of learning. His entrepreneurial gift sometimes prevails over the leading of the Holy Spirit."

"Must to be excused, misters. Will now buy fish for my customers at very good price." This parting remark came as he trotted off, calling to the lads with the fresh catch.

As he watched the expressive witch doctor leave, Jason asked, "So is that young girl really infected with an STD?" It sickened Jason to think it might be so, her appearing to be so close to Keisha in age.

Thud openly studied him for the meaning behind the question.

Under Thud's scrutiny, Jason realized how his question must have sounded. He immediately took offense. "I was *not* thinking of purchasing her services! Not that it would be any of *your* business." Contempt at being suspected of lusting after the child filled the remark. "It's just that she's so young she could be my daughter!"

As a matter of habitual kindness, Thud thought to, once again, neutralize the tenor of the conversation. "Sorry, I should have realized that was your concern. I'm not sure about Meelae, but some who are no older than her have been thusly diagnosed. And you are correct, Mr. Barnes, in that how you enjoy your leisure time is not for me to police. But I do love these villagers, and I am very concerned about their Christian growth. It's my life's work to help people to be found of the Lord as He seeks them out and then to help them grow up in His nurture and admonition."

Not giving the other man the opportunity to respond, Thud continued, "But where are my manners! Mr. Barnes, please join Rae Jean and me for dinner tonight. We have plenty of fresh fish, Rae Jean is a fantastic cook, and she will have my hide if I do not insist you come. She'll want to meet the new American on the block for herself and will be just as eager as I, myself, to hear the story of how you came to be on this no-name island, here at the junction of nowhere and not much else." He grinned at his own attempt at humor.

Jason quickly did an inventory of likely excuses with which to decline the invitation. The only thought that came, however, was that there must be a better way to cook fish than what he'd found, so he heard himself reply that he might be able to work it into his schedule. He'd just have to find a way to escape as politely as possible, or impolitely, if necessary, when the preachy reproaches were worked into the conversation, as they surely would be. And he certainly had no intention of letting the Judds, or anyone else, in on the story of how "the new American on the block" had come to be there. It was time to invent his backstory.

"I'll check my planner. If I don't have any other pressing engagements, I might stop by."

"Very well, then, schedule allowing, please arrive around 6:00 p.m., third hut on the left past the market pergola. You can't miss it. It's a little bigger than the other huts because we have a closet-size guest room, and Rae Jean's flower garden out front will make it stand out. Her garden is the envy of the community."

Jason strolled through the village, the evening breeze providing a refreshing respite from what had been a hot, humid day. Half a dozen small children ran circles around him, giggling at the tall, intriguing, light-skinned man, probably expecting him to act like Thurston Judd, hoping he'd want to play or, at least, pass out treats for them. He ignored them. He knew he was being rude as their parents looked on, but he didn't want to encourage interaction. He was not here as a missionary, to befriend them and win them over to a new religion; he just wanted to be left alone. He would initiate as much friendship as he cared to at some later date, and then only if he needed something from them.

A parent or two called out to the children, and they reluctantly began to retreat from him.

Counting huts as he passed the market pergola, he easily picked up on the garden Thud had described to him. There was a riot of color as blooms of all shades, shapes, and sizes graced the yard in an orderly fashion. There was even a meandering path to the door of the hut, strewn with dried palm fronds and complemented with a crudely fashioned bench, in case you needed to rest on your way to the bamboo-framed entrance. Jason wondered how many trips had to be made from the nearby creek each day to keep the garden sufficiently watered. He noticed the Judds had a rain barrel similar to the one David had procured for him. No doubt that helped somewhat with the garden's thirst.

Good smells wafted from the hut, making his stomach growl in response. "Hello, anybody home?" Jason called. Thurston himself appeared at the door and greeted him.

"Jason, so glad you could make it! Come in, come in. Rae Jean, our guest has arrived. Step away from that stove and come meet him."

As he stepped across the threshold, Jason took in his surroundings. The stilted bamboo hut appeared to be stoutly built and enjoyed the inclusion of strips of dried bark from the local neem trees, woven into floor mats and into the walls and wherever else they'd imagined to put it. A wooden bowl of leaves and nuts, also from the local neem trees, sat on the small table in the room's center. Jason had been told that the neem tree had properties that were a natural bug repellent. He made a mental note to include more of it in his own hut.

In response to Thurston's callout, a willowy woman turned from what looked like an outdoor pizza oven built into the wall of the hut, chimney jutting out the crude roof. Rae Jean Judd was pleasing to the eye. He guessed midfifties, like her husband. She still had a nice figure, slender and tall for a woman, maybe five foot nine or ten. She had a pretty face, even free of makeup, with classic lines and clear green eyes. Her hair was medium brown, streaked with gray, slightly wavy in a bobbed length, just above the shoulder. She was dressed in a loose-fitting cotton print skirt and sleeveless blouse. Jason's first thought as she came and shook his hand with a warm smile and friendly greeting was that she must have been a looker when she was younger.

Rae Jean had cleared the table after the meal, and they now sat on the primitive chairs around the small table, chatting amiably. Jason never had to pull out his excuses to leave, rude or otherwise. No preachy remarks had ever surfaced. Nothing of their religious beliefs was brought up, with the exception of the prayer over the food prior to the meal. Jason had sat through that with respectfully downcast eyes, about all the meekness he could muster. He certainly didn't have enough respect for that kind of thing to close his eyes and bow his head. The evening's conversation ran from the food, which had been delicious, to the preparation thereof; to the island, including the culture and superstitions of the people, geography, and weather, which apparently didn't differ that much from Bermuda's; and finally, to how the Judds had come to be there. That topic, of course, brought up the question of how Jason happened to be there.

He'd given them a version of vague half-truths. A businessman acquaintance had told him of the place. He was a single man who had accumulated enough wealth to live his life the way he wanted, and what he wanted was a simple, frugal lifestyle. After some wandering, he'd managed to book passage to this place the same way as the Judds had—hiring the fishing boats to transport him. He was purposely ambiguous, other than to say that, at one time, he'd been in investment banking in New York.

Jason left his hosts that evening with a gift of leftover fruit compote in a wooden bowl that had been hollowed out from a burl cut and fashioned from a local tree, an invitation to raid veggies from their garden at will, and a committed-to-memory recipe for the fish they'd enjoyed.

"What did you think of him?" Thud asked his wife as they stood and watched through the rustic, glassless window of their hut as he walked away, out of earshot now.

"Well, two things came across clearly: he's lying and he's hurting."

"You're very astute, my dear. He's probably lying because he's hurting. I'm curious, though, What do you believe he's lying about?"

"Well, for one thing, there's a very slight indentation on his left ring finger, evidence that a wedding band at one time resided there. And he's a dreamboat, Thud! That man could not have lived in New York City, or any other place, for long without most of the female population targeting him as husband material. It's unlikely that not even one of them could have bagged him."

"Ha! Is that what you did to me, my gorgeous? I've been bagged?" He wrapped his arms around her from behind and squeezed.

"True enough—and don't you *ever* forget it!" She turned her head to him and planted a sound kiss on his lips. "Now, help me wash up our fine china." She gestured to the tin plates sitting next to a wooden bucket.

As they worked, Thud continued to speculate. "I don't sense anything devious behind the lies. He's probably just being secretive to avoid dealing with something in his past. Life has a way of disbursing its agony to all of us. I wonder what kind of a blow *he's* suffered. Do you think, perhaps, the 9/11 attack might be a source of his pain?"

"Mmm. I don't know," she remarked. "But I don't think we need to suggest anything to him. It might make him crawl deeper into his protective cocoon."

"Lord, show us how to pray for Jason." As was her habit, she talked to the Lord just as she did to her husband, like He was also standing right by her side.

It came as no surprise to Thud, who was just as assured of God's presence in the room as his wife. And confident of the answer to her prayer, he added, "Thank You, Holy Spirit, and until we receive more specifics from You, we speak blessing over Jason and release him to fulfill Your destiny for his life."

CHAPTER

Keisha was just beginning to come out of her funk. She'd been depressed for well over a year now, ever since her dad had gone missing on 9/11, presumed dead. Her mom had tried to be strong for her, but Keisha could tell that Serene was also struggling to keep it together. Serene had wanted them both to go into counseling together, but Keisha had adamantly refused. She'd had enough of "And how does that make you feel?" after Michael's death. They'd made her explore her feelings, validated them, and then did nothing to resolve them. Oh yeah, coping methods. Well, Keisha didn't want to cope anymore. She wanted to be angry. And she couldn't help but be afraid. Everyone she loved was being systematically taken from her. She feared her mom would be next.

But the despondent feelings had abated somewhat here in Hawaii. The vitamin D probably helped. There was never this much sunshine in New York. Also, this beautiful, breezy island lacked the frantic pace of New York City. But the restoration of her feelings of well-being came mostly when she was in church services or youth meetings. The people were nice and were not overbearing. They all seemed to have a kind of peace that she couldn't understand, peace that didn't come from coping methods. She loved the worship services. The atmosphere seemed to fill the whole room—they called it a sanctuary—with love so thick you could actually feel it.

She had been attending the midweek youth group functions with Alani, Wayne, and Miranda's niece, who was two years older than Keisha. That could be a big gap with teenagers, but Alani had accepted and befriended her immediately. They had actually met a couple of years ago, when the Brigholtzs were in Hawaii as a family. The two girls had hit it off then and were happy to pick up their friendship where they'd left off. At first, Keisha had put on her best snobbish attitude with the church youth group, but everyone treated her like she was their best friend, anyway, totally disarming her. Dropping the superiority thing, she next tested the group through flirting. There were some really cute guys in the group, and she wanted to see how much of their attention she could draw. That failed to have the desired effect as well. The guys just treated her like a sister, and the girls refused to get mad at her.

Finally, one evening after a meeting, Keisha was thinking about how the other kids were resistant to being provoked. She was spending the night with Alani, and they were kicked back, relaxing to soft praise-and-worship music, in Alani's bedroom. "You're being awfully quiet tonight, Keish. Is something on your mind? You know you can talk to me about anything, don't you?"

"Yeah, I know. I'm just sorting through some things." There was a pause, and Alani kept brushing her long black hair, quietly waiting, believing Keisha would talk when she was ready. "You know how everyone seems so nice to me...do you think they are being real, or is that some kind of act? I mean... you've probably noticed I haven't exactly been nice to them."

Alani said a short silent prayer that the Lord would help her say this in a loving way. "All the kids are aware that you've had some tough things to overcome in the past few years, Keish. I think they realize that when a person is hurting, they can use attitude as a way of venting that emotion. Some of them have been there—with pain in their lives, I mean. They're trying to give you the benefit of the doubt and just love you anyway. If you let us all be your friends, Keish, it may help you to heal."

Keisha was quiet, so Alani took the opportunity to go on. "I could pray with you if you'd like. It's always been helpful to me when my friends agree with me in prayer."

"I'm not sure about prayer. It feels awkward to me. I guess I'm not sure about God. I mean, I think He might be real...or the worship service wouldn't feel so good. But it's hard to believe He loves everyone, like Pastor Eric says. If He's God, then He must know everything, yet some people are left hurting and have no answers to why bad things are going on in their lives. If He's so loving, why would He do that?"

Alani knew Keisha was talking about herself. *Help me say the right thing, Lord.* Her request was silent, but she pressed on, trusting He'd lead her. "I know you've said it feels awkward for you to pray and that you're not confident that He's real or that He loves you. So let's try an experiment. For the sake of argument, let's say He's real. You don't have to believe He loves you. And you don't have to decide how you feel about Him. Just think of Him, like you said, as someone who knows everything and ask Him for the answers to what you want to know. If He's real and He cares about you, He should be able to get some answers to you. What do you think?"

There was almost a spark in the air as the reply came quickly: "I've got just three questions for Him: Number 1, Why did You allow my brother to die? Number 2, Why did You allow my dad to die? Number 3, Are You going to take my mother away from me too?" Her voice choked a little on those last words. "There. If your God is real, surely He can handle just three questions."

Besides the tears brimming Keisha's eyes, Alani read the pain and fear in her voice, though it was trying, desperately, to hide behind the defiance. "Well, I believe He's real and that He loves you. I also believe that He can handle three questions, so here goes."

The prayer sounded just like Alani was talking to a good friend who was right there in the room with them. "Lord, Keisha has questions for You. I believe You are real and that You *can* handle her questions, so I am agreeing with her that You will get her some answers, and I want to also ask that You will show her that You love her. I thank You in advance for the answers we want, in Jesus' name. Amen."

Keisha was surprised that Alani had addressed God so boldly, but she was also relieved that her comments hadn't triggered a debate. She didn't feel like she had the energy for that. But Alani let the whole thing drop then. Discussion after that was on how to make a facial scrub using ingredients typically found in your own kitchen. The mood lightened significantly as the friends laughed their way through making and applying the concoction.

Four days later, on Sunday, Serene tapped on Keisha's door and made her way, softly, into the room, one of the guest bedrooms at the Salengers' luxurious home. She carried a tray with Keisha's fresh pineapple juice and a buttered bialy, which would have to pass as a bagel since that was what had been available in Miranda's kitchen. She set the tray down on the dressing table, sat on the edge of the bed, and gently rubbed circles on her daughter's back. "Time to get up and get ready for church, Keisha," came the gentle, singsong wake-up call.

A moan, muffled by the pillow, was the response.

"I think you said it's a beautiful morning…and I certainly agree with that!"

"Mom, you're incorrigibly cheerful. Can't you just let me sleep in, just this once?"

Incorrigibly. Serene had to smile. That learn-a-new-word-by-using-it-frequently-for-one-week game she'd played with Keisha for several years now had worked to increase her daughter's vocabulary. However, she would not allow it to distract her from the task at hand. "The Salengers have been incredibly generous hosts, Keisha. For four weeks now, they've opened their home to us and made sure we both have had opportunities to do fun and interesting things. I think the least we can do is show our gratitude by attending services with them. I can give you slack in a lot of areas, but being rude to good people who are hosting us is not one of them." It was spoken softly, but firmly.

"Your breakfast is on the dressing table, and you have about forty-five minutes, so don't dawdle." Confident that would be the end of it, Serene quietly left the room.

Keisha might have been rebellious in some ways, but she loved her mom and believed her to be one of the most gracious women she'd ever encountered. She wouldn't embarrass her by defying her in front of the Salengers. Keisha commanded her reluctant body to roll out of bed. She rubbed her eyes and caught sight of the breakfast tray. In spite of her grumpy self, she made her way to the tray, picked up the bright-pink plumeria blossom, and deeply breathed in the scent of it. Her stomach, however, growled for the warm, buttered bialy. She decided she might like these better than bagels. And they went so well with the amazingly sweet, fresh pineapple juice, also a new favorite.

Keisha had been allowed to sit with Alani and a couple of the other youth group kids, so she was on the aisle seat about three-quarters of the way back in the large sanctuary, with Alani directly on her right. Her mom and the Salengers were closer to the front and two rows left of Keisha's group. She was once again feeling that wonderful warmth as the worship segment of the service came to a close. A glance at Alani revealed that familiar glow on her face; she was also sensing it. Alani referred to it as the Lord's manifest presence. In the order of the service, the greeting of your neighbor and receiving of the offering had taken place earlier, because the pastor liked to move right into his message while the anointing that descended in the worship service remained. He believed the people were most prepared for receiving the Word in that atmosphere.

"Precious Holy Spirit, we welcome your manifest presence and the tangible love of our Savior, so obviously here with us this morning." Pastor Dawson began his prayer as the eleven members of the worship team quietly made their way off the stage. After a moment, he pronounced the "Amen," and it was echoed throughout the crowd of worshippers.

"I will be continuing my message this morning on the God Factor, His hand at work in various situations, in the lives of His people, as well as in the lives of those who *will be* heirs of salvation. Last week, we explored several instances where God's unseen hand was at work in people's lives, while going unnoticed or unacknowledged by the world."

A pause. He seemed to be gathering his thoughts before he went on, but then the pause itself went on and on, until it became awkward. Keisha felt bad for him, wondering if he'd spaced out on what he wanted to say. The silence from the pulpit arrested the room, but the people remained still and quietly waited. This happened occasionally, not that their pastor had forgotten his message; rather, they knew he was hearing from the Lord. He paced as the silence continued, then from his mic could be heard the incomprehensible, muffled words of his prayer language.

"The Lord is saying, 'Your questions are flawed. You want answers from Me, three answers, but how can I give you answers when you are asking the wrong questions?'"

A shiver went through Keisha's body, from the top of her head to the soles of her feet. In her peripheral vision, she saw Alani slap her hand over her mouth to hide her gasp. Keisha was reeling. He couldn't be, couldn't *possibly* be speaking to her. Her heart pounded, and she was afraid to breathe, for fear that the sound of her own breath would prevent her from hearing what he would say next. She was on the edge of her seat now and trembling all over.

"Here's a lesson for us all, folks. Whenever you have asked and asked God why something happened and there seems to be no answer but only silence from Him, you might want to consider that you aren't getting any answers because you are asking the wrong questions." Slowly spoken and individually emphasized were the last four words. "Here's a word picture that might help. An innocent man on the witness stand is asked, 'Do you beat your wife daily or just on weekends?'" A few chuckles could be heard. "He just sits there with his mouth closed because he has been sworn to tell the truth, and neither of those options is the truth!"

Another pause, this one not quite so long. "Trying to receive answers to your three questions is like trying to follow the instructions to operate something, but the instruction sheet you have begins with step 2. If you are even able to follow the steps, you will have dysfunction in the end because you did not have a known, truthful beginning premise. *Here* is your step 1. *Here* is your known, truthful beginning premise: I am love, and I have made a covenant of love with my people, sealed in the holy blood of Jesus Christ, my Son. Jesus is the personification of My love for you. Learn of Him in My Word, and with knowledge of Him, begin every quest. Jesus Himself said in the twelfth chapter of Mark that erroneous questioning will result from not knowing the scriptures or the power of God."

"I may not be real swift, but I've been taken deeply enough into this diversion that even I can discern that today's sermon is intended to take a different direction than I had planned. There is so much to be said on the question of whether God causes or allows suffering. We'll get back to my series next week. But for now, let's check into some of the many scriptures on this."

Keisha's brain was soon on overload, and her eyes began to glaze over. Alani, who had been taking copious notes, whispered in her ear, "Don't worry, we'll get the cassette tape of the message." Forty-two minutes later, clarity once again returned to Keisha when Pastor Dawson concluded with these comments: "The God of love suffers our ignorance and questioning for a long time and remains loving and kind in His demeanor toward us. Young lady, don't *ever* doubt the Lord's love for you. There are approximately four hundred people in this room, and He interrupted the message I had for them today to speak *directly* to you."

After being dismissed, with people beginning to move about and the drone of voices all around them, Miranda leaned over to Serene and said, "I don't know about you, but I doubt that anyone was disappointed in the direction Pastor took today. I think that message was awesome!"

Reflectively, Serene replied, "It could have been for me, Miranda…except for that last remark directed to a *young* lady." They looked at each other, as if it dawned on both of them at the same moment, and said at the same time, "Keisha." Both women looked around, but so many people were moving about, some making their way to the exits, others milling around and conversing in small groups, that it was almost like looking for a needle in a haystack. Then Wayne, taking his wife by the shoulders and turning her, pointed them to the front of the room, in the direction of the altar. Sure enough, Keisha was standing there with Alani's arm around her. They were listening to one of the altar workers. "Should I go to her, Miranda?"

"She's in good hands, Serene, but would *you* like to go down and receive prayer too? I'd be happy to go with you." Suddenly, Serene couldn't speak for the lump in her throat. With tight lips and tears overflowing her eyes, she simply nodded at Miranda.

Wayne smiled at them both, gently touching each on the shoulder. "I'll wait right here for you ladies."

C H A P T E R

Jason was seeing the chairs again, the chairs in primary colors—yellow, red, and blue adorned each chair. The seats, legs, backs, and cross slats were all painted in those three attention-grabbing colors, but randomly applied so that no two of the eight chairs were just alike. The table which the eight chairs surrounded was wood-stain-finished, but with the top all beaten up. Scratches, stains, and graffiti added plenty of history and character. The table's legs had been cut down to accommodate the small chairs with their small occupants, and a folded piece of cardboard from a cereal box was wedged between the tan looped carpet and one table leg as a leveler. He couldn't shake that scene from his aching head. It was the neighbor's paneled basement rec room in Michigan, where he and his younger-by-one-year-and-one-week sister went once a week during that one fall season when he was five and Calleen was four. Even at that tender age, and although she was younger, Calleen had mothered him. In this setting, when he was called on to answer a question or offer a comment, Callie would advise the adult that he was shy and didn't like to talk. Therefore, he didn't need to talk if he chose to remain silent. He wasn't shy or intimidated; he just chose to let Callie protect him while he sat back and observed. He liked her mothering. It was pretty much all he got of feminine nurturing attention. Both of their parents worked, and interaction with their mother was more intellectual than affectionate. If Callie spoke up on his behalf, it gave him the opportunity to take in and analyze what was going on around him. Even at five years old, all things needed to be analyzed. He didn't know why, but it made him feel safer if he did that. All his growing-up years, and even into adulthood, Jason had been accused of overthinking things.

His analysis of Mrs. D, as the children called her, was that she liked him. She looked hard at him to try to understand what was behind those deep-blue eyes, some smoldering hurt or perhaps an unmet need? But she wasn't ever pushy about it. He also knew instinctively that she was a casual person in his life, so it was not safe to allow himself to respond too much to her kindness. She always served good snacks, though. His favorite was the milk and graham crackers with frosting sandwiched between them. They were especially good dunked in the milk. But she had an agenda, Jason had figured out; this Sunday-school-type stuff she was teaching was her ulterior motive. He just hadn't been able to analyze yet why it was so important to her. Callie drank it all in. She answered the questions about the Bible stories, colored the pictures with gusto, and giggled girlishly with the Devareau twins and other neighborhood children who attended the Thursday *fun times*. For two hours every Thursday afternoon that fall in 1969, Mrs. D eagerly offered to watch the neighborhood preschoolers at her home to give the other moms a break. She made it clear to the parents that she would be sharing her Christian faith with the kids, as she also did with her Sunday school class. The Thursday venue was to take in those children that weren't allowed to ride with the Devareaus to their Sunday church services. It gave the neighborhood moms a nice weekday break and therefore was well attended.

Groaning, Jason concluded his head probably throbbed so much from trying to determine why the aged scene was so clear to him, and yet what Mrs. D had taught them would not come through his muddled brain—and why did it matter, anyway? He felt like his very life depended on remembering the lessons from those Thursday afternoons of so long ago. But the pain was way too bad; he decided living wasn't worth it. Instead, he embraced the oblivion that was once more encompassing him. And so the hours of the third day of the fever slid by with no further cognizant thought.

*****

Rae Jean lifted his head slightly and forced another teaspoon of tepid water between his lips. "Come on, Jason, God loves you and still has plans for your life. You've got to help us fight for this. I, for one, want to hear the scoop on those multicolored chairs you've been going on about."

What was it Mrs. D just said? Something about a plan? Yes, that was it. *God loves you and has a plan for your life.* What was the rest of it? Oh yeah, Callie had explained it to him while they were on the swing set, that bright-yellow swing set. Who had picked that color? *Focus, Jason.* Callie had said, "You have to ask Jesus into your heart, then He shows you the plan." She had done that and promised to tell him as soon as she knew her plan. She said he should ask Jesus into his heart, too, because she wanted to hear about his plan as well.

From far away, a voice was calling his name.

"Callie, is that you?" It came out in a croaked whisper.

"Well, well, look who's trying to open his eyes. Welcome back to the land of the living, Mr. Barnes. We were pretty concerned about you there for a while. But praise God! He's so good to us. I'll go get Thud. He'll be so pleased to see you rallying."

*****

Jason sat steeped in exhaustion while Thurston sat across from him at the small table. Thud had helped him bathe and dress in clean clothes. That task ensued under the threat that if he didn't submit to it, Rae Jean would be summoned to take over and get it accomplished. He now sat in the hard chair pulled up to the small table. He was there only because the Judds had assured him he needed to make some effort toward normalcy, such as sitting up, in order to help facilitate recovery. He was completely drained of any energy, so he just watched as Thud happily went on about how so many were finally recovering from the mysterious fever and how David's herbal concoction seemed to be the Lord's means of delivering that recovery. That had bolstered the man's faith, since the newly saved "witch doctor" had specifically asked the Holy Spirit to show him how he could help the locals, so many of whom had been sick with the unidentified debilitating fever.

With undisguised gusto, Thud devoured his stew, the base of which was some unfamiliar, exotic jungle creature, which concerned the missionary not at all. Jason had barely survived the last four days, felt queasy from the smell of food, and was weakened to complete frailty from the effort of bathing and dressing. He was in no mood for Thurston Judd's undying optimism. Mustering a small voice laced with large attitude, Jason laid it out for him: "Ya know, Judd, I'm sick of your peppy happiness, thoroughly ticked that you and your wife didn't just let me die, and I'm really tired of your phony God and His bogus plan for my life!" He had no energy left for any type of pretense. "Some plan! He let my son die right in front of my eyes, and I hate Him for it!"

Walking into the hut just then, Rae Jean overheard the feeble-voiced, venomous tirade. She exchanged looks with her husband over Jason's shoulder, shook her head, and mouthed, "I've got it," before Thurston could verbalize his reaction.

Rae set the cup of the medicine man's healing broth in front of Jason. "I know you still have no appetite, but try to take a few sips. Every little bit will help build your strength." Jason glared at her. Thud bristled. Rae acted as though it was just another day in Mr. Rogers' neighborhood.

Sitting down next to the little table, Rae began, "While you gentlemen finish your supper, I'd like to respond to your comments, Jason. Jesus used to talk to His followers in word pictures, called parables. So if it's all right with you, let me tell you a parable." She didn't pause for a response, knowing it wouldn't be affirmative. "It's about a wealthy man named… oh, for the sake of our story, we'll call him Jason. He lived in New York and lacked for nothing. The other character in our story, we'll call Tommy. Tommy was orphaned, impoverished, and lived in…umm…Nevada. He'd been in several foster situations, boys' homes, and is now on the street, lying and stealing in order to survive. He's about ten years old, eating out of dumpsters, exposed to the elements, and in constant danger due to his street existence. One day, Jason found out about Tommy's plight and was moved with compassion. He undertook to adopt Tommy, and pretty soon a social worker hunted Tommy down and told him about the wealthy man in New York who wanted to help him, indeed, wanted to become his new father. Tommy was skeptical but decided he had nothing to lose, so he agreed to the adoption. After several days, the social worker again hunted Tommy down and told him the paperwork had gone through and that Jason had sent a plane ticket for Tommy so he could go live with his new father in New York. Tommy took the ticket and left the social worker's office."

"Yeah, like they'd allow a kid to just walk out the door with a plane ticket."

Okay then, he was *listening.*

"Track with me here, Jason. It's a word picture. Tommy kept the ticket but wasn't fully convinced that someone else could do a better job of running his life than he could himself, so he went back to what he knew—the streets. He was, once again, dumpster diving for meals. One night, he was beaten up by thugs and seriously injured. Even though his every need had been met, provision, protection, and plenty were his, along with Jesus' unconditional love, in his doubt and determination to take care of himself, harm had come to Tommy. His benefactor could only mourn the fact that His loving-kindness had not been received and enjoyed."

She continued, "Now, sometimes Jesus would even further explain to His disciples what He was saying, so let me just say, in case you hadn't already picked up on it, Jason, in this story, you are Tommy and Jason is God."

Jason glared at her. Thud bristled. Rae Jean began to pick up the dishes from the table. Jason feebly rose and made his way to his cot, which sported freshly laundered bedding. "Excuse me a minute while I overthink this *parable.*" Sarcasm laced the comment. He collapsed on the cot and threw his arm up over his eyes. Breathing heavily, and with his heart pounding from the minor exertion, he began to seriously contemplate Rae Jean's story.

*****

Holding his wife close in their small bed, Thud whispered to her, "So God sends us to this hot, dusty, underdeveloped island to minister to impoverished, oppressed, superstitious, indigenous people, but no, my sweet Rae Jean snags herself an arrogant, self-centered, self-indulgent New York millionaire! Great job today, babe! I think you actually penetrated his armor. Good thing, too, because one more of his dirty looks aimed at my wife and I was going to have to mash his melon!"

Rae tried, in vain, to stifle her giggles.

"But seriously, babe, I love you so much right now I can hardly contain myself."

"So don't contain, my melon-mashing hero."

Early the next morning, Thud woke her with a question: "Rae, do you believe the Holy Spirit gave you that parable?"

"Good morning to you too, darling."

"Sorry, my lovely. It's just that I can't stop thinking about your parable, and something about it is bugging me."

Rolling over and contemplating his question, she replied, "Well, to answer your question, yes, I know it was the Lord. You know how sometimes your spirit gets ahead of your brain and you just know you have the answer before you know what the answer is? That's how it was yesterday. I mouthed to you, 'I've got this,' before I knew what He'd have me say, and then it just began to pour out of me. Why do you ask?"

"Did you notice that, in your story, the adoption papers were completed and Tommy had accepted the adoption? If this parable is specific to Jason, then is the Lord telling us that Jason is saved? Completed adoption papers could be indicative of Jason's name being in the Lamb's Book of Life. Possibly, he's a heart in the thorny ground that's been so choked by the weeds of everyday secular life that he's unable to function like we'd expect of a Christian."

"Wow, I hadn't thought that through. You could be right." It was a quiet minute as they both contemplated it. Fixing her husband with eye contact, Rae spoke. "If the opportunity opens up, I think we should ask him outright."

"Let's pray about it before we do anything more." And they did.

C H A P T E R

Serene had set the tray of appetizers on the coffee table and started back to the kitchen to get the drink tray when the doorbell chimed. Miranda raised her voice from the kitchen. "Serene, could you get that, please? My hands are in the dishwater."

"I've got it." Serene made her way to the front door and opened it to find Luke Vaughn, sporting a bakery box, his Bible, and his usual handsome smile. A clean, manly scent wafted into Serene's nostrils, and her eyes quickly did an appreciation sweep of the broad chest and muscled arms extending from his fashionable Hawaiian-print shirt. And old-fashioned or not, she noted that he was rocking that flattop haircut.

"Hello, Serene." His gaze lingered. "You look lovely this evening. That's a good color on you."

"Thank you, Luke." She couldn't stop the self-conscious blush that rose to her cheeks. "Come in. I assume you've brought treats for us." She indicated the box he held.

He couldn't seem to tear his gaze off her eyes. That yellow sundress seemed to bring out their color even more, if that were possible. How did God manage to create eyes so beautiful that they looked like clear whiskey in a faceted crystal glass? "Uh…oh yeah, it's my turn to bring snacks, so I

slaved away all day preparing these, uh, whatever is in here."
He winked.

Wayne walked through just then with the drink tray
on his way to the family room. "Hey, there, Luke. Quit
your flirting and come on in here. Miranda's in the kitchen.
Whatever you've got in the box, she'll want it on a platter of
some kind."

"Yes, sir." With a parting smile for Serene, Luke headed
to the kitchen.

Serene backtracked to the family room and busied herself rearranging chairs to form a roomy circle around the designated snack area. The routine would be snacks and light
conversation, then an opening prayer, followed by an inter-
active Bible study, and more prayer to wrap up the evening.
Wayne set his burden down and grinned at her. "I think Luke
may have a little crush on you." He crooned. She just gave
him a mock glare, which prompted a laugh.

Ever since the Sunday that Serene and Keisha had
both gone to the altar and received ministry, Miranda had
started up this midweek Bible study for the adults, on the
same night that Keisha attended youth group. Several of
the Salengers' good friends from church had been invited,
making a nice-size group of ten to twelve people. They were
mature Christians who could bring helpful observations to
the topics being discussed. Most were couples, but some were
singles. Miranda was mindful of helping Serene, a single, to
feel comfortable in the group.

It had been four weeks now since that Sunday, and
Miranda wanted to be sure she helped Serene grow in the
Word as much as she could before she and Keisha had to
return to New York. That would happen the last week of
August so that Keisha would be home to begin the school
year; they had about eight weeks to go.

The group had been going over a teaching their pastor had developed and used on a rotating basis to help new believers get a healthy start in their walk with the Lord. He called it the Three Rs: repent, release, renounce. The repentance was for the believer to recognize and repent of their own sin and receive the forgiveness that God had already made available to them. The next step was to release others by forgiving any sins or perceived sins another person had committed against them. The third step consisted of renouncing any demonic activity that had resulted from the sins of the first two categories.

Serene had been receiving a lot of freedom during their sessions, both in the teachings and the ministry of prayer afterward, surprising herself by the sheer volume of issues that she had apparently stuffed down inside in order to survive the pretense that her life had become. Each time the Holy Spirt brought something to the surface that was causing her to be unsettled, she would deal with it, using the method of releasing the other person involved, usually Jason, repent of harboring offense, and then renouncing any evil spirit that had settled onto her dysfunctional life, closing the door, soundly, on the heaviness that had been oppressing her soul. She was surprised to find that she even felt better physically as her thoughts were taken captive to God's Word and her emotions were not allowed to run amuck.

Although Jason was gone, Serene still felt a loyalty to his memory and protective of their daughter, who didn't need to hear any possible gossip about her late father's shortcomings. For that reason, Serene kept detail to a bare minimum during their times of ministry. She did, however, unburden some specifics when alone with Miranda.

She couldn't remember when she'd felt so free. She found that, on Sundays, she wept all through the praise-and-worship portion of the service for sheer joy over what the Lord was doing in her life.

The study part of the evening was complete, and the wrap-up prayer time was winding down. Several of the attendees were quietly moving about, taking dishes and leftovers to the kitchen, while others were gathered around Serene, still praying and ministering to her. Luke had just taken a platter to the kitchen when Miranda cornered him there and insisted that he take some of the leftovers home with him. As usually happened, they'd had more food than the small group could consume, so Miranda insisted some of the folks take something home. Luke, being a widower, was always on the list of those who were in need of mothering, so Miranda always asserted that he take what she called a care package. He stayed in the kitchen and chatted, quietly, with those who'd gravitated to that room, in deference to those who were still involved in ministry in the family room.

Wayne entered the kitchen, carrying a tray of cups and snack plates. "I think this is the last of the dirty dishes, babe. I'll rinse them and load the dishwasher while you finish putting the leftovers away, if you want."

Before Miranda could reply, Luke interjected, "When you're done there, Wayne, I was wondering if you'd loan me your chain saw to clean up that tree that blew down in my backyard last week during that crazy windstorm we had. I'd be willing to share some of the firewood with you for your fireplace." By now the whole group was milling about, saying their goodbyes and starting to leave.

Serene had also come into the kitchen to help with the cleanup. Overhearing Luke's remark, she offered, "Go ahead, Wayne. I can help Serene with the cleanup. You guys go do your guy things." She quipped, grinning at Wayne and Luke.

"You don't have to tell *me* twice." Wayne squeezed Miranda's shoulder as he made his way to the door connecting kitchen to garage. "Come on, Luke, before they change their minds and put aprons on us." The two made their way to the garage to retrieve the chain saw.

Shuffling a couple of lawn implements, Wayne made his way to where the chain saw hung on a large hook. He lifted it down and handed it to Luke. "I don't use much firewood. It just doesn't get cool enough to build a fire that often, but I wouldn't mind a few pieces if you have them to spare when you're done." Luke took the saw Wayne was handing to him.

With a sheepish look at his friend, Luke changed the subject. "I could take the saw to my car and put it in the trunk, but then I'd have to make a second trip to retrieve my Bible, which I left in the kitchen, along with my sack of leftovers." Wayne looked confused. "What's the big deal? I'll take the chain saw, you go get your other stuff."

"How about I take the chain saw and you go ask Serene if she would please bring out my sack and Bible?" He raised his eyebrows in a "Do you get it now?" signal.

Wayne grinned. "You dog! I'll see if I can round her up to help you with that little chore." With a conspiratorial grin, he socked Luke on the shoulder and started back to the kitchen, hesitated, and turned. Pointing his finger, he warned, "You watch yourself, brother. If Serene ends up hurt, Miranda will make sure you are dead meat, and"—he poked himself on the chest—"I'll be collateral damage."

Luke closed his trunk lid to find that the beautiful redhead was standing near the passenger-side door of his car with a bag of plastic food containers. "Your Bible is on top of the fruit salad container." She smiled sweetly.

"Thanks. Here, let me take that." He took the bag she handed off to him and opened the door, depositing it on the passenger seat. As he closed the door, he seized his opportunity. "Serene, I was wondering if you'd like to have a cup of coffee with me later in the week. We don't get too much of an opportunity for one-on-one conversation in the group, and I'd like to get to know you better." He gave her his best come-hither smile, trying not to look as desperate as he felt, to have some alone time with her.

Serene did a quick search of her mind for a reasonable-sounding excuse when she suddenly realized she really wanted to say yes—and why not? This was an attractive, intelligent, dedicated Christian man, and she had no reason to deny herself the pleasure of his company. So she met those expectant blue-green eyes with her own smile, not coquettish, just honestly pleased, and said, "Well, okay, then. What day did you have in mind?"

*****

On that first lunch date, Serene learned a lot about Luke, and vice versa. She found out he'd been widowed for almost four years and that his wife's death had been sudden. No kids. He owned a private investigation and security company with his brother and had Friday afternoons off, as long as there was no big case requiring immediate attention. Thus, Fridays became their day to get together.

Luke had learned that Serene had lost her son over five years ago to a car/pedestrian accident, and then her husband had died in the World Trade Center attacks on 9/11, coming up on two years ago now. She and her daughter, Keisha, were trying to put their lives back together. Serene had been a stay-at-home mom, other than some charity work, so she was now praying about what to do for a living, although he got the impression that money was not an issue for her.

Today was their fourth Friday together, and they'd just eaten lunch at a local place that the tourists, for the most part, hadn't discovered. The fish tacos were delicious, and the atmosphere was quaint in the small diner with a rustic cabana bar vibe. They lingered on a shaded bench in the little park adjoining the diner's property, drinking cool mango smoothies from disposable cups. Though a few others enjoyed the little beachfront park, no one was close by.

Luke had been thinking that before this date was over, he'd ask her to dinner, instead of lunch, someplace nice, with a walk on the beach afterward. A slow, moonlit stroll would present the perfect atmosphere to move things in the romantic direction that he had in mind. In the years since Caroline's death, Serene was the first woman to make him feel like he was ready to move on from the memory of his wife.

When they'd finished their cool drinks, Luke grinned and offered, "I'll do the dishes today." Reaching for her cup, he took the empties to a nearby trash can. Sitting back down beside her on the bench, he smoothly took her hand, interlocking their fingers. The physical contact felt good, Serene decided, as did the direction their relationship seemed to be taking. Keisha had been watching the relationship develop as well. Just yesterday, in her youthful candor, she had asked her mom if she was falling in love with Luke. Unprepared for the direct question, Serene was forced to examine her feelings more closely. "I don't know, Keisha," had been her honest response. "But I do, very much, enjoy spending time with him. I guess the best answer to your question is that it could possibly come to that."

"What do you think of him, Keish? I mean, how would you feel if I did, you know, get serious about Luke?"

"I like him, Mom. He's nice. But like you told me last year when I had that crush on Mark Hennesy, there's lots of time for that kind of thing—don't get in a hurry."

Serene had grinned and hugged her daughter then, happy that they were regaining their ability to talk to each other, and very pleased with the maturity Keisha displayed on the topic of Luke Vaughn. With tears in her eyes, she had told her daughter just that.

*****

Sitting here on the park bench with Luke as they listened to the birds sing and enjoyed the sweet scent of the Hawaiian breeze, Serene pondered if she was ready to move on from Jason. That caused her to think about Luke's prior marriage. She wondered if he was ready to move on from the loss of his wife.

There had been a comfortable lull in the conversation; she broke it now with her inquiry. "Tell me about your wife, Luke. What was she like?"

He looked thoughtful for a moment. "Caroline had black hair, gray-blue eyes, and clear, porcelain skin. She was tall and slim, beautiful, smart, and sophisticated. We met when I was a detective with the police department in Denver and married after eight months of dating. She was a pianist, taught lessons to children mostly, and before we married, she played in a hotel lounge on weekends. That was how we met. We had been called in because she had a stalker from that gig. We caught the guy, and he did time for it. He's still locked up. He'd been seriously obsessed with her and was very dangerous. It was a relief to put him behind bars."

Serene watched as sadness took over his countenance. "We'd only been married three years when she passed away."

"How did she die, Luke? If I'm prying, just tell me to back off." She spoke gently.

He didn't hesitate to answer. "It was a brain aneurism. We were getting ready to go out for the evening. One minute she was blow-drying her hair, the next she was lying on the bathroom floor, gone. From the other room, I heard the dryer crash to the floor, then her body right after. The ER doc told me that he suspected she died before she hit the floor. The autopsy proved him right.

He paused, then went on, choked up now. "We had decided to use birth control the first year we were married, but after that first year, Caroline went off the pill. We had hoped for and expected a pregnancy during those last two years. About six weeks before she died, we had started researching fertility clinics." Barely audible now. "The autopsy report showed she was pregnant, just a couple of weeks along. She probably didn't even know it."

Now Serene was as choked up as he was. She couldn't stop herself. She wrapped her arms around him and squeezed. "Oh, Luke, I'm so sorry."

A moment passed, then he settled his arm around her shoulder. The close contact was pulling his thoughts away from his past pain. "I've dated casually in the last couple of years, but finally I realized I was only doing it because everyone said it was time I 'got back out there,' as they put it. I really wasn't interested in women…that is, until I recently met a beautiful redhead with eyes like clear whiskey in fine crystal cut glass."

That last comment lightened the mood, as he hoped it would. She grinned up at him. "You are such a smooth talker. You know that, don't you?"

"I'm glad to hear it's working." He slowly lifted his hand from her shoulder and lightly grazed her cheek, close to the hairline. His aqua gaze had deepened to a deep teal; that gaze now left her eyes and drifted to the luscious pink lips a few inches below. He slowly inched his head closer, allowing her plenty of opportunity to pull back. She didn't. Her eyelids drifted closed, and her breath caught in her throat in anticipation.

He was close enough that a tissue paper would not have passed between his lips and hers when he heard the audible voice from inside his head, *You do* not *have permission to do that!*

Luke moved so quickly he almost leaped from the bench. A stunned second later, he began stuttering. "Uhhhh…I…I…I'll get us another round of smoothies." With that deer-in-the-headlights look still in place, he turned toward the diner and began to walk away.

Her mouth was open in overt shock as unbidden indignation welled up inside her. "Hold it right there, mister! Don't you dare just walk away from me!" She was on her feet now, her heart thumping, not with arousal, but with pure anger. Without giving it a thought, she felt her legs slowly move toward him, like they had a mind of their own. Within a couple of feet, she stood, fuming for a moment, and then…

"I have had all I can take of communication-stunted little boys in men's bodies, passing themselves off as the strong, silent type!" She was poking her finger at his chest now. "I don't want another smoothie, I want an explanation!" Pinching her forefinger together with her thumb, she advanced even closer. "You were *that* close to kissing me and then jumped like a scalded cat." She nailed him with her glare. "And you *will* tell me why!"

The blood that had flooded to his face when she'd begun her angry rant now drained to his toes, leaving his face deathly pale as he realized he *was* on the hook to be completely open and honest with her. "Okay, you're right. I do owe you an explanation. Come on." He gestured to the bench. "Sit back down." He again gestured toward the bench and attempted to take her elbow to guide her.

She shook off his hand, and shakily she sat. Her face now suggested that tears were close to the surface, her anger having given way to hurt and humiliation. She trembled in the aftermath of the confrontation. This whole scene had triggered too many memories of Jason's perpetual reticence.

He sat with a respectable distance between them. "I'll have to go back a ways to make this clear."

Sitting stiffly on the edge of the bench, arms folded across her chest and eyes straight ahead, she barked, "Go!"

"Okay, to condense it as much as I can, when I first got out of the service, years before I'd met Caroline, I got radically saved and wanted nothing more than to serve the Lord, but I was having trouble with old habits." A slight pause. "Womanizing and drinking mostly. One day, on one of those *mornings after*, in self-disgust and desperate, I set two chairs opposite each other. I sat in one and invited the Lord to sit in the other. I confessed my sins to Him and asked for forgiveness. Then I asked Him to, in the future, please show me plainly when I was veering off course, so I could live before Him in an honorable way. It has only happened a couple of times, but believe me, when you get jerked up short by the Lord, you don't forget...and you certainly don't proceed."

"Is that what just happened? You were...what, womanizing again?" A measure of disgust was evident in her voice.

"No!" He looked pained. "Serene, I have nothing but respect for you. Well, okay, it wasn't respect that made me want to kiss you. I'm really attracted to you, but I would never take advantage of you. That was the old me. I'm not that guy anymore."

Looking at him now. "Then what just happened, Luke?"

Resigned, he just came out with it. "This may sound crazy, but I literally heard the Lord tell me that I don't have permission to kiss you."

She was quiet. She was trying to understand, he knew. "I don't understand it myself, but I have a feeling that I should have prayed about this attraction before I ever asked you out, or, more honestly, before I ever began flirting with you. If I'm being candid with myself, I probably, subconsciously, didn't want to ask His opinion, for fear I'd get a negative response. I'm so sorry, Serene. The last thing I'd ever want is for your experience of knowing me to be hurtful for you."

It came out very softly. "Take me back to the Salengers', Luke. Suddenly I'm exhausted."

C H A P T E R

"So, Rae, the flight, what does that look like?" It was four days after the day of the parable, and Jason had been steadily regaining his physical strength, while mostly avoiding Thud and Rae Jean. He now stood at the edge of her garden as she plucked away at the stubborn, recurring weeds.

As Rae looked up from the row of vegetables she had been weeding, her brows drew together in confusion. "I beg your pardon?"

"The flight, from Nevada to New York. Say, Tommy is considering taking it. What does that look like?"

Oh yes, there it is! She wanted to stand and do backflips but managed to hold it to a slight grin, one that didn't go unnoticed.

"Well, Jason, it's got to be getting close to noon, and I could use a break. I'll send one of the boys to fetch Thud, and I can make us some tea while we wait for him." Looking right at him now, she continued, "We'll talk about it."

"So the orphan now has a Father," Rae Jean began, "and must get to know Him in order to enjoy the benefits of that relationship, and there are a lot of benefits." She poured tea into the three cups that she'd set out on the little table. As she gathered her thoughts to go on, Thud had finished washing his hands and joined them.

He inserted himself into the conversation. "So, Jason, may I ask you a few questions to pinpoint where we should begin?" Another wife might have been miffed to have her husband just take over the conversation she'd begun, but Rae was not just another wife. She waited patiently.

Jason looked confused. "I don't follow. What exactly do you need to pinpoint?"

"To use Rae's parable again as a reference, Tommy had accepted the adoption, although he continued to be self-dependent. To be blunt, I guess I'm asking if that accurately describes you, Jason. Do you recall a time in your past that you've accepted God? I ask because Rae Jean and I wouldn't counsel an outsider in the same way as we would a son of God."

Thud glanced at her, and Rae Jean held her breath, as well as any telling expression. She hoped Thud's direct approach didn't bring out the defensive anger they'd been witnessing all along in Jason. To her surprise and delight, the countenance her gaze fell on as she ventured a glance at him could be better described as meek.

"When I first began to emerge from that miserable fever, I heard the voice of a lady from my past. She said, 'God loves you, Jason, and has a plan for your life.' That triggered a memory." Rae Jean remembered saying almost those exact words to Jason as he was coming around, but she kept that to herself. The Holy Spirit was obviously working here.

"I was, oh, maybe five years old. My sister and I attended an afternoon kids' group at a neighbor's house. Mrs. D. She had games, snacks, lots of stuff kids enjoyed, and Bible lessons. That was her motive. It was okay with the moms because they got a free babysitter for a couple of hours, once a week. Callie, my sister, was a year younger than me, but she was much more outgoing. She grabbed onto the lessons right away. It wasn't long before she had 'asked Jesus into her heart,' as she put it. I was still trying to figure out if it was some kind of a scam." He paused, took a drink of his tea. "Analyzing was always my thing. I wasn't sure if I could trust Mrs. D, but I loved and trusted my sister, and the way she put it made sense to me. Callie and I were at the swing set in Mrs. D's backyard, waiting for Mom to pick us up." With a faraway look in his eyes as though he was picturing the scene, Jason paused and then went on. "That swing set was such a bright-yellow color that it made me crave a banana every time I saw it." He grinned. "Anyway, Callie explained, you ask Jesus into your heart, then He tells you your plan. She promised to let me know her plan as soon as she got it and wanted me to get a plan too."

Jason heaved a sigh. "My dad was a realtor. Mom was a claims manager for an insurance company. I didn't know how to define it then but realized later that they were both workaholics, and although we had everything we could want in material goods, neither of my parents was what you could call affectionate or hands-on with their parenting style. Their only plan for us was babysitters, housekeepers, and day care. So I figured, if there was someone who wanted to show me a plan for how I could have a life, I was in. Callie's prayer wasn't eloquent, but it was honest and innocent. She had me repeat, 'Jesus, come into my heart and show me my plan. Thank You! Sincerely, Jason.'

"When we got home that evening, Callie cheerfully announced at the dinner table that 'Me and Jason got Jesus in our heart today.' Before she was done speaking, I knew instinctively that she should have kept quiet. Dad pounced. 'What kind of a place have you been sending the kids to, Darlene? You should have known that Bible thumper would try to indoctrinate them! Well, that's enough of that nonsense.

Telling them a few Bible stories is one thing. Brainwashing is something else entirely.' We weren't allowed to go back.

"Mom got on the phone with Mrs. Devereau and explained, very politely, that she and Mr. Brigholtz had misunderstood her intent. Now that they were better informed, they would, themselves, retain control of our religious upbringing. Translation: our little family would go to church on Easter and Christmas, give enough to the church to keep the pastor from complaining, and that would have to be enough to justify us all in God's sight."

"Brigholtz?" Thud asked.

"Hmmm?"

"You said she and Mr. *Brigholtz* had misunderstood the intent."

"Oh, yeah. I lied to you." It was a matter-of-fact statement. "My name isn't Barnes, it's Brigholtz. That's another whole story.

"Anyway, you asked if there was ever a time I said yes to God. That was it. I guess my five-year-old self thought I'd dream about some great plan. No dream came. No plan emerged. My dad became my example of what the plan was like—play up to people and use them. Make as much money as you can. Never let anyone really know you. I didn't hear any plan from God, so Dad's plan is the one I adopted. I guess five years old is just too young for the God thing to take."

"What happened with your sister, Jason? Did her relationship with the Lord also get derailed by your parents' reaction?"

"Callie is a saint. She never gave up on loving Jesus and was convinced that He'd never give up on her. She must be some kind of aberration. Four years old. Can you believe it? She learned to keep quiet around Mom and Dad, but the

Devereau twins were in her preschool class and it was evident to me that they still talked God things with her. She was twelve years old before the folks allowed her to go to church regularly and have her own Bible. She made the most of it. Today, she's happily married, with kids, and is so involved in her church she probably single-handedly keeps it afloat."

"That's great! And no, your sister is not an aberration. Not all children are mature enough at that age to realize what's being asked of them, but some are. Callie, even as young as she was, had ears to hear. She had a propensity to recognize the truth of the gospel and receive it. Scripture tells us that the just shall live by faith. Literally, they shall live by their faithfulness. Callie was faithful to keep seeking out the Lord in His Word, and so more revelation was given to her."

"Tell me, when Callie wanted to lead you in a prayer to receive Jesus into your heart, were you thinking, 'Okay, I'll do this so she'll back off and I can go get that banana I've been wanting,' or did you really mean that prayer?"

"Oh, I meant it. Remember, I'm a thinker. It wasn't a means to a snack for me. I don't know why she got it, and I didn't. Maybe she just wanted it more, like you said."

"Jason, there is such a thing as being offended for the word's sake. In other words, you tripped over a stumbling block when persecuted. Your father didn't realize he was persecuting you. He was parenting the only way he knew how, but he was a major role model in your life, and his rejection of your experience caused it to wither in your estimation. Later in your life, distractions, like the desire to make money, anxieties, and stresses of life, choked out the message the Holy Spirit was speaking to your heart."

Rae Jean looked thoughtful. "Perhaps your sister has prayed for you. That may be what brought you to this place, where distractions are few and the gospel message is prevalent."

"Are you saying that all these years of living like a heathen, I've been *saved*, as you call it? And I'm here now because of some greater plan?"

Thud responded, "Let me put it this way, Jason. A seed needs four things to germinate: soil, water, sunlight, and warm temperatures. It can lie dormant for years if all these necessary elements aren't present, only to spring to life when they finally are."

A beautiful little native girl stepped into the hut just then. "Mrs. Rae Jean, the ladies are waiting in the church for their Bible study." She opened her hands and shrugged her shoulders, nonverbally saying, "What's up?"

"Oh my! I've lost track of the time, Sulee." She smiled sweetly at the child. "Go tell the ladies that I'm coming. I'll be right behind you." The girl grinned, nodded, and ran off.

"Gentlemen, I feel you are making great headway, and I'd love to stay and take part in where this conversation is going, but a prior commitment is calling to me," she said. "So…"

Walking to the door, she paused to kiss Thud's forehead and took one last long drink of her tea. Exchanging her teacup for her Bible there on the little table, she said, "I'll be off."

Thud smiled and bade her farewell. As she took her leave, he then turned his attention back to Jason, whose countenance, he noticed, had drastically changed. His eyes were almost glazed over, with deep, obviously agonizing thought. "You don't understand what a colossal ass I've been, Thurston. There's no way a seed of anything Good is inside of me. I've lied and cheated in business. With my wife and kids, I've been selfish, controlling, manipulative. I've been unfaithful to Serene. I virtually ignored my kids, just like my dad did with my sister and me. Does that sound like someone with the seed of God on the inside of him?"

Thud was impressed with Jason's observance. He was quickly picking up on the *new life* aspect of Christianity, or he had unintentionally absorbed some Christian teachings somewhere along the way—perhaps from his sister. He seemed to know there should be some fruit if Christ really lived inside him.

"Jason, Christianity is not about what you've done, it's about what's been done *for* you. I don't mean to excuse your past conduct. A sin is a sin, but when someone is *in Christ*, God is not keeping track of their sins. Just like the New York millionaire in the parable. He didn't expect good works from the orphan boy. What the Lord wants is to develop a close relationship that will result in the child wanting to please his Father and accept the Holy Spirit's help in becoming that obedient child."

Heartbreak twisted Jason's countenance. The tea long forgotten, he held his head in his hands, his eyes downcast. "But I killed him, Thurston. *I'm* responsible for my son's death."

C H A P T E R

The agony of Jason's thoughts was evident in his facial features. Thud didn't have to ask him to expound. "It was my wife's day to carpool the kids to school, but she had left for an early appointment with a charity board that day—a meeting I had forgotten about—so I had to fill in for her. I was already mad because of the interruption to my schedule. The valet had brought the car around, and the kids were out in front of me, about to get in, when I heard a couple of the young valets talking about Twenty One Twelve." His voice rumbled on in monotone-enforced numbness, masking his deep emotion. "There was this very sexy blonde who lived in number 12 on the twenty-first floor. She didn't need a name. She was Twenty One Twelve, the always provocatively dressed, hot trophy wife of an older rich guy, and not a man within drooling distance would miss the opportunity to gawk at her. So I indulged myself in a lustful look and that's all it took. I looked around when I heard them say she was coming. Next thing I heard was Keisha's scream, a car horn, and the screeching of brakes. I turned just in time for the impact, just in time to see my eight-year-old son bounce off the hood of a cab and fly through the air, hitting the pavement." Jason's voice had choked on these last words. "He'd run out after a paper that had escaped Keisha's notebook and was caught up on the breeze." Tears streaked his face.

"I've blamed God for over four years, but all the time I've known it was my own fault. I couldn't admit it, even to myself. I'm a wretched man and a coward!" He rose from the chair, took a step away from the table, and dropped to his knees. Grief and guilt poured forth from him as Jason released a careening cry, followed by agonized weeping. As he bent over and covered his head with his hands and arms, as if to protect himself from God's wrath, or from his own self-loathing, his anguish poured forth.

Thud knelt next to him, placing a hand of comfort on his shoulder, and silently allowed him to bleed out the pain through his tears. After several minutes of intense weeping filled the little hut, Thud began to pray in tongues under his breath. After a few minutes, he began to minister to Jason's needs, first praying for healing for the emotional pain, asking the Lord to help him by removing the pain from the memory; the memory was not going to go away, but God was able to lift the pain out of it. Jason's sobs began to abate, and Thud addressed repentance next.

"Jason, you've just confessed several sins to me. That is most of the battle in receiving release from them. Would you like me to lead you in a prayer of repentance, asking the Lord's forgiveness?" There was a small nod in response. Thud began, and Jason repeated the prayer in a hoarse, broken voice, after which Thud assured him that the God of mercy and forgiveness most certainly had heard his prayer and had forgiven him.

Jason felt more wiped out than he had when he first woke up from the fever he'd endured for days. He shifted positions; moving from his aching knees, he now sat on the floor and leaned against the wall of the hut, feeling as wrung out, as if he'd just run a marathon. Thud offered him a chair, but he just shook his head. He was quite sure he didn't have enough energy to get up into it.

"Jason, you've just made a major breakthrough, and I don't want to press you beyond what you can handle, but I'd like you to be able to sleep tonight with complete peace, and in order for that to happen…" Thud paused and took a deep breath. "I'd like you to go back in your mind to the scene of the accident, to look on it from the *outside*."

Jason looked up at him, red swollen eyes filled with misery. "How can you ask me to do that?" he moaned.

"So many people, when something horrific happens, ask the question, 'Where was God?' If you can do this, Jason, you can have the answer to that question. I'll help you. I'll go through it with you."

He thought there could not possibly be any more tears in his body, but one lone tear made its way down his cheek. He gave another small nod.

*****

Drawing on Holy Spirit strength from within, Thud began, "You and the children have just come down from your apartment. You are exiting the building. Look at the children and yourself and tell me what you see."

Within a few seconds, the hoarse, gravelly reply came. "We're walking out the exit nearest the parking garage. Michael has on a red-striped shirt, short-sleeved, and blue jeans. It was unusually warm for October. I wondered if he would need a jacket later, but I didn't mention it. He has his backpack, a bottle of water sticking out one of the pockets." Jason was as surprised as Thud that he was recalling—no, was *seeing* so many details.

"Keisha is in a bluish-green jumper and white T-shirt with long sleeves. It's her school uniform. Her hair is in a ponytail. She's carrying a windbreaker and wearing her backpack.

"We're walking out into the courtyard, where others from the building are also waiting for their cars to be brought out. Some are leaving in taxis, which are always in the area, anticipating fares.

"It was a sunny day, breezy and mild."

He was quiet for a minute.

"What are you seeing now, Jason?"

"The kids are talking to each other. Michael's being silly, trying to get Keisha to laugh. She's more serious, steering him to our car, which she's spotted at the curb. I'm lagging somewhat behind. I have a frown on my face. My thoughts are already on my busy day, and I'm resentfully trying to figure out how to juggle tasks and meetings." Jason shook his head. "Pitiful man."

Thud marveled at how detached he was, but he knew God was helping him to observe, without the emotion.

Jason continued, as though he was narrating a silent movie. "The conversation about the woman is going on now, just a few feet to my right. My attention gravitates to it, and away from my kids. Then I turn to where one of the valets is subtly moving his head to indicate *her* hip-swaying advancement."

"What's happening with the kids at this point, Jason?"

Looking through a window to which Thud had no access, he continued, "Keisha is kneeling and rearranging something in her backpack. The breeze catches a couple of her papers—no, three. She grasps and is able to catch two of them, but one is off with the wind, tilting this way and that, like the feather in *Forrest Gump*. Michael has opened the car door, but when he sees the paper, he leaves the opened door and goes after it. It's fun for him. You can see it in the look on his face. Keisha yells at him to stop because she sees the cab coming. He turns, with a big smile on his face, and tells her, 'Don't worry, Keeshee. I've got it.' Keisha screams. The brakes squeal, just as Michael leaps out from between two cars, reaching for the paper."

Jason's breath was coming in short spurts now, and he began to tremble.

"Take a deep breath, Jason, and try to relax," Thud instructed. "Lord, open the spirit realm to Jason now and show him what is happening there."

Jason's breathing visibly calmed then, and his eyes grew wider. "There are two angels kneeling over Michael, one on either side of him. They are there before anyone else reaches him." He leaned forward a bit, as though eager to see through his invisible opening into the spirit realm. "They're so big, strong, and beautiful! All the people are around Michael now, but we aren't seeing *them*." A look of amazement came over Jason's face as he continued, "Michael's spirit is rising up out of his body. The angels are helping him to stand. He is looking at them with awe, and they are just smiling at him, as happy as he was just a moment ago. They are motioning him to come with them, and he does. He's hesitating, looking back at Keisha and at me." Deep emotion occupied Jason's countenance now. "He loves his sister so much! And he loves me too!" Jason's glazed eyes registered some surprise. "He's not sure if he wants to go with them, but they tell him it's time to go and that we will be all right. He turns and goes with them. He's not afraid. His carefree, little-boy smile is back."

Without any prompting from Thud, Jason closed his gritty, bloodshot eyes and took a couple of deep, cleansing breaths. When he again opened his eyes, seeing nothing of the little hut, he continued, "There's an ambulance there now, and police cars. Hernando, the cabbie that sometimes picks me up in the mornings, is pacing back and forth. He's frantic and apologizing. He's going on about working a double shift, and maybe his reactions weren't as fast as they should have been because of fatigue."

"I'm sitting on the curb, Keisha next to me. She's crying, inconsolable. I've got her caught up in a hug, but my eyes look vacant, like I'm in shock or something." With a ragged intake of breath, Jason looked wide-eyed. "I see Jesus!" His throaty voice grated. "He looks so sad. He's behind us, on one knee, bending over us, with a hand on Keisha's shoulder and one on mine. He's weeping with us!"

Jason turned his head at this point and looked straight into Thud's eyes. "Thud, I can see the nail holes in His hands." Jason's voice was no more than a pathetic rasp by this time. "I know He would have stopped it from happening if He could have. I don't understand it, but the knowing is just there. And His love is so overwhelming, Thud, I can't even describe it!"

By this time, Thud was almost completely overwhelmed himself by the heavy anointing in the little hut. Jason lay back fully on the floor now, limp as the proverbial dishrag, speaking praise to God in a volume too low to be discernable to human ears.

*****

With the one-hour afternoon women's Bible study complete for the day, Rae Jean walked back to her hut. Thinking about how much the women were growing in the Word, she was oblivious to what she was about to find at home.

When she was within twenty yards of her and Thud's hut, she noticed a hazy glow surrounding it. She had no uneasiness at the sight, only peace, which assured her that this was a manifestation of God's glory and not something ominous. She looked around to see if anyone else was observing this sight, but she saw no one nearby. Moving closer now, she attempted to walk to the door, but it was like she was hitting an invisible shield that prevented entry, so she backed up and went to the nearby well, got herself a cool drink of water from the tin cup that was always kept there, came back, and sat down on a bench in her flower garden to wait.

Rae thought about praying for the ministry sure to be going on inside, but she couldn't. It was like she knew God had this. So she spent some time softly singing praise songs. It felt like a very short time but was actually about twenty minutes when Thud came to the door, saw her there, and motioned with a drunken-looking smile for her to come in. This time, when she tried to enter, she was able to, but with a definite weakening of the knees.

She clung to her husband for support. As they entered the hut, she whispered, "Thud, what's happening in here?"

He just looked at her with that dreamy smile. "Help me get Jason to bed first, and then I'll tell you all about it—if I can even talk." Together, they were able to lift him to a sitting position, and from there Thud took him by the wrists and pulled while Rae Jean pushed, until he was standing—if you could describe a wet noodle as assuming a standing position. Thud then half-carried, half-dragged him to the tiny guest room and poured his limp frame onto the cot. They pulled the makeshift curtain closed across the doorway, leaving him in there, in the expert hands of the Lord.

Thinking he would be hungry or at least in need of hydration, Thud or Rae checked periodically on Jason throughout the rest of the day, but each time they found him sleeping. They went to bed that night without his having roused. He would sleep through the night as well, for the most part, that deep and dreamless, restorative sleep—for the most part.

But there was one dream. In it he was walking through heaven, observing and analyzing sights that amazed him, some of which he would remember, some he would not. He pulled bright, colorful, ripe fruit from a tree and bit into its delightfully refreshing flesh. Juice dripped down his chin and arm, only to dissipate right away with no sticky residue. The grass and flowers underfoot sprang back, good as new, after being walked on. When a question arose in his mind, he sensed, more than saw, Jesus before him. "Lord," he asked, "how can I ever live with the guilt of being the cause of Michael's death?"

"Would you want Keisha to bear the burden for her lifetime of opening her backpack at the wrong time? Or the cabbie—should he endure the blame due to slow reflexes because he'd worked a double shift to make extra money for his family? Should the valet carry lifelong punishment for distracting you? Even as they were putting Me to death, I forgave My executioners. There's power in forgiveness, Jason, power to be free, and I want My children to be free. Forgive yourself, Jason."

Michael was the other visitor to Jason's dream. As he walked over a rise in the landscape, Jason saw a group of boys playing a game that looked similar to soccer. They were laughing and joking around, thoroughly enjoying themselves, while angels looked on from the sidelines. Though they were yet a ways off and Jason had done nothing to prompt their attention, one of the boys turned to look at him, and he recognized that it was Michael. As soon as Michael saw him, he left the other boys and ran up the slight incline with absolute ease, to meet his dad. As Michael embraced him, Jason noticed how healthy and happy Michael looked and also noticed that he'd grown taller, had filled out, and his face had matured. There were so many things he wanted to ask his son, but he suddenly sensed he couldn't stay there. "Michael…"

"I know you have to leave now, Dad, but before you go back, I want to tell you that I'm happy here. I've met lots of our relatives, and I have a lot of new friends. Mostly, I want you to know that I love you and Mom and Keisha, and I don't want you to be sad anymore. We'll all be together again someday. Please be happy, Daddy." Michael hugged his father fiercely, and Jason returned the embrace with just as much fervor.

Love for his son consumed and overwhelmed him, but before he could reply to Michael, Jason felt himself being drawn backward at a very fast rate of speed, and then he suddenly awoke in the little hut, with the first rays of dawn barely beginning to peak in through the edge of the curtain on the small window.

CHAPTER

The drive back to the Salengers' was quiet and awkward. Luke had attempted to apologize again, but Serene cut him off, not wanting to discuss it any further. After dropping Serene off at the Salengers', and waiting in the driveway until she was safely inside the house—not that there was any danger, but he thought it was the least he could do since she was in no mood for him to open the passenger-side door and walk her to the house—Luke started back to his office. He hadn't made it two blocks, reflecting on the disturbing incident with Serene, before remembering Wayne Salenger's threat not to hurt Serene, and decided that some damage control was in order.

With that in mind, he detoured to the construction site, where he knew Wayne would be doing inspections today. Maybe his longtime Christian friend and mentor could take a short break and listen to a confession.

He pulled into the site, through the open gates, stirring cement dust into the breeze. Pulling off into the area designated for employee parking, where his pickup would not be in the way, he spotted Wayne talking to one of the foremen. Their voices were raised to be heard over the heavy equipment in operation nearby. Wayne saw Luke approaching, gave a quick wave, and continued conversing with the foreman. As Luke closed in on the hard-hat-topped pair, Wayne laughed, slapped the other man on the back, and walked toward Luke as the foreman turned and headed in the other direction. When Luke asked Wayne if he could take a short break, he was only too happy to accommodate.

Removing his hard hat, Wayne wiped his face and neck with his handkerchief and retrieved a couple of bottles of cold water from the small fridge in the site's construction trailer. The two settled into folding chairs in the air-conditioned makeshift office. "What's up, man?"

Knowing Wayne would listen with an open mind, Luke just laid it all out. "It's about Serene. Remember when you basically threatened to toss me to the sharks if I hurt her?" Wayne's face took on an "Oh no, you didn't" look. Putting his hands up in a defensive manner, Luke continued, "Let me tell you what happened before you lay into me." He started from the beginning, and in as much detail as one of the masculine gender was capable of conveying to another, he explained what had happened.

Wayne took it in stride. "Well, I didn't expect you'd deliberately do anything to hurt her, but *wow*, I sure didn't see that coming!" His facial expression confirmed his surprise.

"I'm telling you, Wayne, I felt like a bulldog being jerked up on his haunches by a choke chain. I gotta tell you, I wasn't feeling nearly so amorous after that." That elicited a hearty laugh from Wayne.

"I felt so bad for Serene. She obviously has had some bad experiences in her past where open communication is concerned. And she surely wasn't going to put up with it from the likes of me!"

Wayne looked pensive. "Without getting into detail, you're right about that. She's shared some things in that regard with Miranda. I'm glad you stopped to talk. Thanks for that. At least I won't be going into a minefield unprepared tonight when I get home. And don't beat yourself up, brother. Go talk to the Lord about it. That's your next step in making amends. I'll see what I can do on the other end to smooth things over, with Miranda's help, of course."

Serene let herself into the Salengers' house and listened for Luke to leave the driveway. She hadn't seen Miranda's car when they pulled in, so she didn't expect her to be home. She called out a greeting. "Hello, is anyone home? Miranda? Reann?" She didn't call Keisha's name, knowing that her daughter was with Alani today at the beach. Apparently, Reann was gone already too. She usually did leave early in the afternoon. As she continued through the kitchen, she noticed a note lying on the counter addressed to her:

Serene,

I'm running some errands. I should be back no later than 4:00 p.m. Make yourself comfortable.

M

So she had the empty house to herself. That realization brought on tears, and she let them fall. She headed to the guest bedroom that she'd been occupying, closed the door behind her, kicked off her sandals, dropped her purse on the dresser, and fell on the bed, releasing the sobs. Serene was so accustomed to keeping her emotions in check that, even now, she was reasoning with herself: *I'll just take fifteen minutes to feel the hurt, then I'll pull myself together and put a cool washcloth on my face. I should be presentable by the time Miranda returns.* She thought back over the encounter with

Luke while she cried it out. He had been so fun while they enjoyed their lunch; their conversation was light and witty. She'd been thinking how much she liked this guy and would not mind if they allowed their mutual flirtation to grow into something more. Even Keisha liked him. Then he had blown the whole thing up!

She was just beginning to learn about the counsel of the Holy Spirit, but could it really take the form Luke had described, the Holy Spirit speaking forcefully to him at such an intimate moment? "Lord, if Luke was right about what he said, I certainly don't want to go against Your will. You can have him, even if I don't understand what's going on. I won't be offended and will even try to maintain a casual friendship with him, but if that's what You want, I'll need Your help with it." Amazingly, she felt a release from her emotional upset with this short prayer. She felt no more need for tears and relaxed so much she thought she might nod off. Her thoughts drifted to Luke's comment about her eyes; it certainly wasn't the first compliment she'd gotten on her eyes, but the way he put it was a first, like whiskey in a faceted crystal glass.

That thought circled her back to a memory of Jason, to the first time they'd met. She and her friend had been in the college library at Michigan State. They were getting ready to leave, gathering up their things from a table where they'd been studying, and Serene had picked up her books to put them into her backpack when someone bumped her shoulder, knocking two of her books to the floor. Apologizing, he bent to pick them up at the same time she did. Their fingertips touched, and electricity shot through Serene. Kneeling there on the floor, she looked up to check out this electrified presence; their gazes collided, and she was looking into the most handsome face she'd ever seen. Those deep ocean-blue eyes fringed by thick lashes, chiseled, masculine features, with some end-of-the-day scruff on the jaw and sandy, light-brown hair slightly mussed. The ruddy complexion and mas-culine scent of him mingled with the cold Michigan evening air that had entered with him and still clung to him. He met and matched her perusal, and soon those perfectly shaped lips lifted slightly in a devastating smile.

"It's okay," she managed to squeak out as she stood and fumbled to put the books in her backpack. Turning her back to him, she mouthed to her friend Ardith the word *wow*, her expression undeniably expressing her positive appraisal of the shoulder-bumping offender. What she didn't realize was that the nearby window, with nothing but darkness outside, also reflected her appraisal, causing a smirk to emerge on the very-referenced handsome features. As Serene caught sight of the reflection of his smirk, her face flamed red. But she was nothing if not quick-witted; she immediately turned to him. "Oh dear, I'm so sorry for inflating what's, undoubtedly, already a very large ego!" Her lame attempt to defuse the faux pas with humor summoned a muffled snort of laughter from behind Ardith's hand.

First winking at Ardith, he leaned in closer to Serene and softly spoke. "That's all right. The feeling is mutual. Wow!" He had softly exhaled the word. "I have never seen brown eyes so translucent, like a pair of rare jewels perfectly positioned right there in the middle of that gorgeous face, haloed by shining hair the most beautiful shade of burnished crimson I've ever seen." As he spoke, he was doing an overt visual appraisal of all he described.

His remarks had caused her knees to go weak, and remembering it now brought the tears back to Serene's eyes. The memory had just summoned to her attention that Jason had once been just as sweet and charming to her as Luke, when they were first dating, and even in the early years of their marriage. She missed *that* Jason, still loved *that* Jason, allowed herself to cry now for the loss of *that* Jason. It was a confession to herself that she'd been mourning that Jason for years before the flesh-and-bone embodiment of him was actually gone. She wasn't even sure she knew the Jason who had walked out the door on the morning of 9/11 and never returned. Without her being aware of it, her tears of mourning well outlasted her fifteen-minute allowance. Her eyes were swollen and red when Miranda, hearing the muffled sobs, tapped lightly on her door and entered the room.

*****

When Luke had arrived at his office, he asked Margo where everyone was. Margo, the receptionist / secretary / technical assistant for all four of the guys, rattled off the answer to his question: "Allen and Drew are out on the Maui surveillance assignment and won't be back in the office until Monday. Caleb is doing on-site interviews on the Dillard case and might be back in before closing time, but he didn't know for sure."

"Put the phones on automation, Margo, and take the rest of the day off. I'm going to be here. I have some praying to do, but I don't want to be disturbed, not by the phones or otherwise. If one of the guys phones in, they all know the alternative numbers to connect, so it won't be a problem. Have yourself a good weekend."

"You got it, boss, and thanks." Margo was good help and well paid for it. She knew not to ask him for more details. She set the phones to answering-service mode, gathered her things, and left the building, putting out the Closed sign and locking the door behind herself.

Luke went to his office, grabbing a bottle of water on the way through the break room, and closed his office door behind him. He watched Margo's sporty little coupe exiting the rear parking area, then drew the blinds so he wouldn't be distracted. He sat down in his desk chair, tipped it back, and put his feet on the desk. He started by confessing that he'd been insensitive to cautionary signals the Holy Spirit had sent his way about proceeding with his flirtation with Serene and apologizing for that. He'd been praying, mostly in tongues, for about forty minutes when he heard muffled sounds in the next room, his brother Caleb's office. What sounded like a recording came through the walls, muffled at first, then he clearly heard, "It won't work. She's a married woman." The voices continued, but again muffled, so that he couldn't make out what was being said.

Assuming that Caleb was reviewing an interview he'd recorded, Luke left his office, walked down the hall to his brother's door, and knocked lightly. He turned the knob and let himself in. Caleb was watching a video on his computer of an interview. "Hey, bro," Caleb said when Luke walked in. He paused the video.

"I saw your truck when I came in. Your office door was closed, so I didn't want to bother you. Looks like everyone else has closed up shop for the weekend, so what are you still doing here?"

"I just had something I needed to take care of, so I told Margo to get started on her weekend a little early. What are you up to?"

"Just reviewing my latest interviews on the Dillard case." Gesturing toward his computer, he continued, "This bartender is a piece of work. Don't know if we can believe anything he says. Look at that shifty face—it's got deceit written all over it." Caleb hit the Pause button again and, while Luke looked on, Shifty continued his contrived discourse about some doper he'd ejected two nights ago for making a scene with a female customer. The customer was the object of their investigation; her husband was their client.

When Caleb again hit the Pause button, Luke verbalized his agreement that Shifty's testimony was useless, other than to confirm his own unreliability.

"I was hearing some of that through the wall. It was muffled, but I thought I heard him say something about 'it won't work, she's a married woman'?"

Caleb looked skeptical. "What? Come on, our sound-proofing isn't that bad. You couldn't possibly have made out what the guy was saying. And no, he didn't make any such comment. Nothing in the context of what he's telling me here fits with that remark. Seriously, man, I can't believe you would be able to make out words through these walls. We paid dearly to soundproof this place so that clients would be comfortable with their privacy when talking to one of us about their case."

"Turn this character back on and back it up some," Luke suggested. "We'll go into my office, with the door closed, and see if we can make out what he's saying."

Caleb put the cursor in place and backed up the video. He pushed Start, and the two headed for Luke's office. They listened closely, but the sound was so muffled they could barely be sure it was a voice they were hearing and not some other sound. Caleb looked at his brother and waited for him to concede. "Huh, I must have fallen asleep in my chair and dreamed it." Luke didn't really believe that for a second, but he wasn't ready to tell his whole story to Caleb.

When Caleb had gone back to his own office, Luke allowed himself to realize where that voice had come from. His gut clenched, and he felt light-headed. *Holy Spirit, does*

*this mean what I think it means? If her husband was lost on
9/11, maybe he was just that, lost, not dead after all, but where?
Why has he not contacted his family? And where do I go from
here?* He couldn't stop thinking about it, and by the end of
the weekend, he'd decided that, for Serene's sake, he'd go after
the truth.

Monday morning, Margo sat down across from Luke
with her pad and pen. He'd called her into his office to give
her an assignment, and she was ready—and excited. She considered every aspect of her job an adventure. These guys were
so savvy about digging up information and never failed to
provide an interesting work environment with the cases that
came through here, so she didn't even mind that she couldn't
talk about any of it outside the office. The confidentiality
made it all the more thrilling to her. Her shrewd computer
skills were greatly appreciated by the group; she received
plenty of accolades and a good salary and benefits, so need-
less to say, Margo loved her job.

"Margo, this assignment may end up being frustrating
for you. I'm not sure if there is any info available to be had
out there, but if there is, I surely want to know about it. And
this is for a friend, so I want no *office* records kept on it. It
needs to be a confidential file." He looked her in the eye. She
was nodding.

"I want you to dig up anything you can on a guy named
Jason Brigholtz from Manhattan, New York. He possibly grew
up in Michigan. He's an investment banker, about thirty-five
to thirty-eight years old. Wife's name is Serene, a daughter
named Keisha, currently about fifteen years old, and there
was a son, who was killed in a car/pedestrian accident about
three years prior to the 9/11 attacks. Jason himself worked
in the Twin Towers and is presumed to have died on 9/11 in
the attacks. I have reason to believe he may have somehow

survived, so what we're looking for is any record you can find associated with his name on or after that date. I don't have his SSN, but hopefully you can pinpoint him with what I've given you. It's not a real common name. And this part is very important. Besides the usual confidentiality, there's to be no sharing of the info even within the office."

She'd been taking notes ever since he'd started talking and was now nodding.

"The spelling would be B-r-i-g-h-o-l-t-z?"

"Yup. How much time can you dedicate to this? I'd like something on him ASAP."

"I've done about all I can for Caleb on the Dillard case, so I'm freed up from that, but Allen and Drew need some computer help on this security gig they just picked up in Maui. I should be able to dedicate an hour, maybe two a day, to do some digging for you."

"Thanks, Margo. Keep me posted."

CHAPTER

Thud and Rae Jean continued to be amazed at Jason's voracious appetite for the Word. He had joined the men's Bible study the day after his painful recollection of the day his son died. At first, Thud had to school his features, so as not to show his amusement at Jason's white face among all the brown native faces, intently listening, constantly asking questions, and taking profuse notes on the lined tablet Rae Jean had given him. He'd begun taking most of his meals with the Judds as well and continued his quest for spiritual knowledge every moment he was with them.

Thud finally had to tell his student that he needed some time to interact with the local converts, as well as some alone time with his wife. He suggested, strongly, that Jason use his new prayer language prior to his Bible reading each day and then, specifically, ask the Holy Spirit to help him to understand what he was reading. He should write down any questions and observations he had for Thud, and then they'd set aside a regular time that they could review them. The two men were having this discussion just outside of Rae Jean and Thud's hut, sitting on a primitive bench among Rae's flowers, the hum of the local bees, who were also enjoying the garden, accompanying their dialogue.

"Yeah, okay. I guess I have been monopolizing a lot of your time. Speaking of time with your wife, I've noticed you seem to enjoy spending time with Rae—I mean, besides the obvious physical affection." Jason looked apologetic. "Sorry, man. You just told me to back off. It can wait until later." Jason stood to leave.

"Wait, Jason, Rae just left to work on the community vegetable garden with the ladies. She'll be a while. Sit down."

Jason sat back down.

"So you've noticed that I like my wife, like being around her, like talking to her, like doing things with her—other than sex. It's a given that I like that. You have a wife, Jason —at least you did have before you came here. Am I to take it that you did not have that kind of relationship with *your* wife?"

Jason looked grieved, slowly shook his head. "My wife is a beautiful woman. Not just beautiful to look at, although she is that. She's a beautiful person, kind, generous, supportive, giving, in a proactive way. But no, to answer your question, I did not have the kind of relationship with her that I see between you and Rae Jean. In retrospect, I'm sure the fault lies with me. I've been such a selfish jerk. I know I don't deserve to have her back. She probably doesn't ever want to see me again. But I guess watching what you and Rae Jean have has made me wish, and even hope, that I could have that, that I could have another chance with Serene." He looked like a kid in the schoolyard frustrated by being pronounced the loser of a kid's game. "I want a do over, and if my wife and the Lord were to allow me that chance, I want to know how to do it right, how to not mess it up again." His eyes glistened with unshed tears.

Thud felt strong sympathy for his spiritual son. The new man that Jason had become was anxious to live life right, to make amends and enjoy the benefits of right living that the Lord had always intended for him to enjoy. With kindness in his voice, Thud responded, "Serene sounds like the kind of person I would like to get to know. From what you've told me, Jason, about how you left her and your daughter, you need to prepare yourself for the eventuality that she may have moved on—that desired reconciliation may never happen. But if it does, or if you are blessed with another marriage at some time in your future, here are a few rules that will serve you well: Grab that pencil and notepad that seems to be an extension of your right arm."

Jason quickly picked it up from the bench beside him.

"First of all, it's not your business how your wife treats you, it's your business how *you* treat her. *Always* hit yourself over the head with that one when an argument occurs." He paused, until Jason was finished writing.

"Next, God is the one who thought up the institution of marriage. The physical aspect of it is for procreation *and* for pleasure. The soul aspect of it is for bonding. You will need open, honest communication here. If you are withholding thoughts or feelings from her, the devil will be only too happy to tell her what's going on with you. He has a whole arsenal of lies from which to draw. The third aspect of marriage is the spiritual aspect. The Lord's spiritual purpose for marriage is that it would reflect Jesus' unconditional love for the church. He was willing to die for the church so that He could present it to Himself without spot or wrinkle. We love Jesus because He first loved us. Your wife will respond to you in kind when you first love her, and you show her that by being willing to die to self. That last one, the spiritual aspect, is the God factor in your marriage, the factor the world is unable to duplicate."

Jason hastily scribbled his abbreviated notes.

"What a man needs out of a marriage relationship is respect. He is bound by covenant to his household and carries the responsibility for it. He's wired to protect and provide for his family, and he naturally needs to be respected for that. The woman needs to feel secure and cherished. That's how she's wired. When we are told to treat her as a weaker vessel, it does not mean that she's weaker. It means she is to be treated with tender care, as you would handle a precious, breakable vessel. Her emotional makeup is fragile. Be careful with it."

He continued, "Rae Jean and I have been married thirty-one years. We work at it every day. If you feel there is a strain in the marriage at any given time, ask yourself, What have I done lately to enhance the health of this relationship? Then deal with it, right away. I'll get together some scripture references for you tomorrow."

Thud laid his hand on Jason's shoulder when the scratching of notes had stopped. He bowed his head and prayed, "Father, I love this man, and I love what You are doing in his life. In Your grace and mercy, I ask that You touch the hearts of Jason's wife and daughter, bring them healing for the hurts that have scarred them, and implore them, Lord, to find forgiveness in their hearts for Jason, at the very least. Restoration of the family unit would surely be some tasty icing on that cake. You are a good, good Father, and Your arm is not shortened. We trust You for the healing of this family. In Jesus' name. Amen." They both swiped tears from their cheeks.

A deep longing was evident on his face. "I want to go home, Thud. I need to go home. I've left behind so much pain. I want to apologize and beg my wife's forgiveness, my daughter's forgiveness. With all the bridges I've burned, I don't know how I can pull it off, but I need to go home. Every minute that I stay away, their hurt is just being perpetuated."

C H A P T E R

It was 7:40 a.m. on Monday. As was usually the case, Margo had been the first one into the office. She'd found that at least twenty minutes before the office was officially opened was what it typically took to accomplish first-one-there status. She wasn't obsessive about it, but she did enjoy the bragging rights of being first one there. And today she couldn't have done otherwise. She was ultracharged about the outcome of her Frasier Crane research—so antsy to talk to Luke about her findings, she literally pranced around her reception desk and filing area. If anyone saw her acting this way—she smiled to herself—they'd think she needed to relieve her bladder.

Frasier Crane was the pseudonym for her Jason Brigholtz file. She'd come up with the idea of giving a celebrity or fictional character's name to any case an associate brought in, which required complete confidentiality. That way, it could be referenced in the office without giving anything away. At the meeting where she'd suggested the idea, Allen, Drew, Caleb, and Luke had all grinned and taken it lightly—sweet little Margo playing the detective game with relish. It had since proved to be a valuable tool, and she no longer had to endure smirks and wisecracks when a reference was made to the Billie Jean King project or the John Grisham case or, currently, her Frasier Crane research.

She'd been spending no more than two hours a day on Frasier—that is, two office-time hours. However, as she worked on it, she had become almost obsessed with getting results for Luke, so some days she'd spent twice that many hours of her own time, per day, on the research, some of it while in the office, some at home, using her personal computer and phone. The islands being behind the mainland by several time zone hours was good for her evening connections to the continental states. Luke's main concern seemed to be whether Brigholtz was alive or dead. With the date of death, if there, indeed, was a death, being established as September 11, 2001, and the place of death being the North Tower of the WTC, it didn't seem to Margo that it would be that difficult to determine. Either he'd died that day, in that place, or he hadn't. How hard could it be? *Hard!* She'd been so close yet so far from the answer so many times that she felt like a pit bull with her jaw locked in place and unable to bite down, unable to let go.

Another thing that had been extremely hard, and which she hadn't anticipated when she began her research, was the brutal horror of that day, the details of which came up during her investigation. On more than one occasion, she'd had to stop and pray to keep from getting mired down in the despondency of it.

All four of the guys had been extremely busy on a new case they'd recently received, or she was sure Luke would have been asking her about her results by now.

Having pulled into the lot at virtually the same time, Allen and Luke were chatting and walking across the parking lot toward the door, each carrying their polystyrene Kahlua Koffee cups and their briefcases. Seeing them approach, Margo postured herself to pounce.

Luke entered first. "Good morning, Luke. I know today is going to be busy, but I really need to conference with you on the Frasier Crane case." Coming out fast and continuous, like one run-on sentence, her obvious vigor spilled out all over the words.

Before Luke could even respond, Allen, who'd entered right behind him, offered, "Good morning to you too, Princess. Remember me? Chopped Liver?" Allen, being the eldest of the team, though at fifty-three, hardly old, always related to Margo in a "patronly" manner. He grinned at her, bringing out the crinkles at the corners of his kind brown eyes. "I just hope both Luke and Frasier Crane appreciate your enthusiasm."

Smiling back at him, she deliberately softened and slowed her tone. "Good morning, Al. How are you this morning? I hope you enjoyed your weekend."

After a bit more friendly banter, while Luke just watched, grinning at the two of them, Al proceeded on to his office. Luke set his briefcase next to her desk, lifted one hip onto the edge of the desk, and removed the lid from his coffee. As steam and an aromatic scent wafted into the room, he gently blew over the rim of the cup and took a small testing sip. It was his move, so she waited, albeit impatiently. "Okay, Sparky, you seem pretty excited about the Crane case. Would that be a fair assessment?"

"Yup. You'll have to be the judge, but I'm pretty sure I've got it nailed down." Bouncing on her toes, she couldn't have veiled her grin with a paper bag over her head.

He was anxious to hear her feedback immediately, but he had to maintain his professionalism. In another few minutes, Drew and Caleb would be in, and they absolutely must do their debriefing first thing or they'd lose ground on this new case, and they couldn't afford for that to happen.

But his insides churned with the excitement that Margo openly portrayed. He'd seen Serene a few times since *that* day, but never alone, and the conversation was always at a superficial level. He was relieved that she didn't seem to be harboring any resentment toward him, but he wanted the air cleared between them, and his having the answer to Jason's demise, or lack thereof, would be a giant step in that direction. "Okay, you know the Steele case is our hot potato right now, right?" She nodded. "As soon as Caleb and Drew get here, we'll be heading to the conference room on that one. It can't be hurried, so let's plan to devote the morning to Steele, and you and I will put our heads together on Brig—uh, Frasier Crane—right after lunch, in my office. One o'clock work for you?"

"I'll plan on it. By the way, do you think I should get a phone temp in here for today, since I'll be in conference one way or another for most of the day?"

"Good idea." He picked up his briefcase and headed to his office.

"Stop in the break room on your way through," she called after him. "I got sweet rolls from Lailani's."

"Oh, you heaven-sent angel!"

Luke was sorry he'd ordered the pastrami sandwich for lunch. It sure had sounded good when they ordered lunch in, because they were still brainstorming on the Steele case, and in order to get everyone's assignments in place to move it forward, they'd worked through lunch. The heartburn he was experiencing attested to the fact that you shouldn't eat and work at the same time, or maybe you just shouldn't east pastrami. He chewed on a chalky antacid Drew had produced from his desk and grimaced at the taste. It was a good incentive to stick with his normally healthy diet.

Expecting Margo any minute, he straightened the mess on his desk that represented his portion of investigative notes on the Steele file and shoved them all into a manila folder.

He needed a clean desk to shift his attention to the next item on the agenda—Frasier Crane, a.k.a. Jason Brigholtz. A tap on the casing of his opened office door announced her timely arrival, 12:57 by his digital watch. "Come in, Margo. Your timing is perfect, as always."

She entered with a tray, balancing two tall glasses of ice tea, and a file folder under her arm, gently kicking the door closed behind her. "Caleb just made a fresh pitcher of ice tea, so I snagged the first two glasses." Ice cubes clinked as she deposited the tray on the one clean corner of his desk. Two tall sweating glasses held the tawny refresher, translucent and swimming in ice cubes.

He looked at the cold brew with enthusiasm. "Bless your snagging skills. No one makes ice tea like Caleb. There's some kind of spice in it that I can't quite identify, and he's not talking. Someday I'll get him in a headlock and wrestle out of him what he uses."

"Well, my goodness, no need to hurt the boy! It's pretty simple, really. He blends 80 percent Earl Grey and 20 percent Constant Comment. The spice is in the Constant Comment—orange peel and cloves, I believe."

He shook his head and reached for one of the frosty glasses. "Margo, you amaze me. Nothing gets past you." Taking a long pull on the tea and swishing it around his mouth to rinse out the chalky taste, he went on, "Please tell me that tendency has served you well on this Frasier Crane matter." He nodded to the folder she held.

"I believe the research material will speak for itself. Do you want the longer, raw data version, or shall I bottom-line it for you?"

"Bottom-line. I want both," he quickly corrected, "but before we move into the details, let's start with the crux of the matter. Dead or alive?"

C H A P T E R

It was four months since Jason's conversation with Thud about marriage and his desperate confession of his need to get home to make amends. And now it was finally going to happen. Thud had poured tireless energy into convincing the missionary board through which the Judds worked to also include Jason in the travel plans that would achieve the furlough that was due Thud and Rae Jean.

Jason was elated yet nervous as a teenager with complexion problems about to go on his first date. He could hardly believe that he was finally going to get to go home, to be able to tell his family about his transformation, about what the Holy Spirit had been doing in his life, teaching him, revealing truths to him in the Word, changing and maturing him. Yet he knew he was in for an uphill battle, with Serene especially, and also Keisha. Although he'd left them financially sound, even affluent, he *had* abandoned them. His letter explaining that they would be better off without him had left Serene without any say in the matter. She certainly had no obligation to him now, and no reason to excuse his callous actions. Though he hoped he had no right to assume that anything good would come from that reunion. He encouraged himself by picturing his eventual reunion with Callie. He knew that no matter what, his sister would be overjoyed to see him.

She would hug him fiercely and forgive him for abandoning his family because she was just such a good Christian and forgiveness was requirement number 1 for a good Christian.

His gut knotted up when he thought about how Serene might already have divorced him, that she might even have already remarried. He pushed that thought down; he couldn't bear to dwell on it. He knew it was what he deserved, but he had to hold on to God's merciful nature and hope that He'd preserved at least a chance for Jason to try to save or re-establish his marriage. If he didn't have that hope, he couldn't bear the thought of returning. *All right, I could bear it, Lord. I can do all things through Christ, who strengthens me,* he corrected himself at the Holy Spirit's prompting. *It's just that I don't want to cross that bridge unless and until I have to. After all, love hopes all things, so for now that's what I'm going to do.*

Rae Jean poked her head in the doorway to his hut. "You all packed? You were traveling so light when you arrived here I can't imagine there's much to throw together now. Thurston's arranging for the Jeep that will take us to the coast. There might be some negotiations going on. It seems that one of the most difficult things to break the locals of is living day-to-day life in the practice of bribery."

"I'm not sure American money is even something they value all that much, but if it helps, I can produce some. And yes, I'm packed, pretty much as lightly as I was when I arrived. What this island has given me is not something that can be arranged neatly into a duffel bag."

With said duffel in hand, he ducked out of the doorway and joined her as they began the walk back toward the village. The missionary, approximately twenty years older than him, had no problem keeping pace with Jason's long strides. This lifestyle kept both her and her husband in good physical shape. "David has graciously agreed to house-sit for me and to make himself at home if I don't return with you and Thud. Making that arrangement was easier than saying a permanent goodbye to him. He'll probably become a slumlord and get rich renting out the place." They shared a laugh over that observation.

Walking in silence for a few minutes, Rae Jean looked over at him. "You clean up nice, especially with that great haircut someone gave you."

He grinned. He hadn't wanted to arrive home looking like some scruffy hermit, and he noticed that Thud's hair was always nicely trimmed. He'd known for a while that Rae Jean cut her husband's hair, so he'd asked her to do his too. "I do believe you could open your own barbershop, Rae— that is, if you ever decide to give up your day job." A pause. "Scratch that. What your day job provided me is worth vastly more than a lifetime of haircuts." She smiled; his comment warmed her insides.

Jason looked around with fondness one last time at the familiar scenery of his own personal back side of the desert, the tall brown grass waving in the breeze, worn sandy paths, and hearty trees that thrived in spite of the mostly dry climate. Turning once again to his companion, he asked, "Are you looking forward to your sabbatical back home?"

She smiled up at him. "You know, Jason, I am greatly looking forward to seeing our children and grandchildren, but I know that at the end of the six months, I'll be just as anxious to return here. The folks here are as much family to me as my own flesh and blood."

"Well, I'm eternally grateful to you and Thud for arranging for me to travel with you back to civilization. I know it wasn't easy to convince your organization to allow that, but I would have been forever trying to get off this rock without any connections, not to mention trying to get any farther than the next island in my attempt to reintegrate the more technically advanced world. I owe you both so much I can never repay you."

"Just pay it forward, Jason." She shrugged. "Or not. Thud and I are so overjoyed with what God has worked in you that we already feel like we're well paid."

*****

"So you folks flying out of Bermuda, are ya?"

"Yes, that's the plan, from Bermuda to Atlanta," Thud answered the fisherman.

The burly man with rugged features was the captain of the third boat they'd hired to ferry them from island to island. This largest of their water conveyances had been located and hired to take them directly to Bermuda, thanks to Jason's available cash. The boat's captain, known locally as Captain Clay, had mentioned, in casual conversation, that he had been born and raised in Florida. When asked to go out of his way to taxi the trio directly to Bermuda, this American was found to have a healthy respect for American dollars, unlike some of the small islanders.

The three had been booked by the Judds' sponsoring agency on a direct commercial flight from Bermuda to Atlanta. Thud had finally convinced the missionary board that Jason had undergone a major transformation but needed to make amends at home in order to complete God's work, necessitating his return home. They also had the promise of Jason's healthy donation to more than repay the expenses of his plane ticket. From Atlanta, Jason would split from the Judds, who were headed back home to Tulsa via car, as they had family to visit on the way. Jason planned to board a flight in Atlanta to New York City.

Jason and Thud now stood in the boat's wheelhouse with Captain Clay, watching the wings of water shooting up from the sides of the vessel and enjoying the fact that their journey had finally picked up some speed. Rae Jean was below, taking advantage of the opportunity to grab a nap.

"I assume you know that you need to arrive at the Bermuda airport at least three hours before your flight is scheduled to take off. They're very particular about security, you know, since 9/11." The captain's raised voice projected over his shoulder.

"Yup, we are aware of that, but our flight isn't until tomorrow, so it shouldn't be a problem," Thud replied. Gripping the back of a chair that was bolted to the deck to steady himself, he turned to Jason. "I hope your papers are all in order, Jason." Recalling that Jason had been traveling under the name Barnes. They had discussed the necessity of his retaining the false ID until Jason could return to the States and reclaim his true identity. Right now, his false identification papers were all he had with him and were thus his only means of traveling by air.

"I'm pretty sure there won't be any problems with my papers. They're pretty high quality, by forgery standards." He said that last part in a lower volume and behind the captain's back. "But what's that reference to 9/11? What's that all about?"

"It's just a catch phrase people are using to reference the terror attacks."

Jason cocked his head slightly; his eyebrows came together in a look of continued confusion. Thud elaborated, "You know…the New York City and Pentagon attacks back in September of '01. Had you left New York prior to that?"

"Apparently. I certainly would have remembered a terror attack in the city. What do you know about it?"

Moving out from under the canopy of the boat's wheelhouse and away from the captain, Thud sat on the bench along the boat's railing. Jason settled next to him. Thud provided the condensed version of the events. "Radical Islamic terrorists hijacked four commercial airliners. Two were flown into the Twin Towers of the WTC in New York, the third was flown into the Pentagon building in DC, and a fourth, which they suspected was planning to hit the White House, crashed in a Pennsylvania field when the passengers took control away from the hijackers. The towers in New York both collapsed. Thousands died. Altogether, it was about 2,700 people." He realized this was a heavy disclosure for someone who'd heard nothing of it previously, especially when that someone was a New Yorker. He watched the blood drain from Jason's countenance.

The captain's attention was on steering the boat, and the engine noise prevented him from hearing their conversation. Jason's pained expression scrutinized Thud. "The Towers? Thud, I worked in the North Tower. The company I worked for is on the ninety-sixth floor, Devlin, Burke, and Associates." Just speaking the company's name brought up the memory of his one-time ambition to hear it called Devlin, Burke, and Brigholtz."

His fingertips pressed into his temples as he tried to process all that Thud had just told him. "Both towers collapsed?" Thud nodded. How could he not have known? He continued to rub his temples in an attempt to extract the information he needed. "When did you say this happened?"

"September 11, 2001, 9/11. Our national emergency code, thus the 9/11 moniker that has attached to the event."

Jason was praying in the spirit now, under his breath. *Come on, remember!* His departure had been early in September that year. It had been, what, maybe a week prior to that date?

Wait. A thought was pushing its way to the surface now. His last intimate night with Serene, the night before he left, the small talk he'd initiated that would open the door for sex. He'd asked about carpool; she'd said, "What's tomorrow?" And he'd replied, "Tuesday, the eleventh." *Oh my God!*

Thud looked on helplessly as Jason quickly leaned over the railing and threw up his lunch into the Atlantic.

*****

Atlanta's airport was bustling with busy people, as usual, all hurrying to get to somewhere they considered important. It reminded Jason of everything he had wanted to escape two years ago. He sat with Rae Jean and Thud at the small round table in a little airport café. They wanted to relax over coffee a few minutes, real coffee. It had been a while. Also, they wanted to allow Jason some time to unwind before the Judds headed to the car rental area and Jason to the gate for his New York flight. Thud and Rae Jean hoped to be a support system for him as long as they could before they all moved on in their different directions.

They had prayed together in Bermuda and on the plane, and he was beginning to settle somewhat. After all he had come through on their little island, the revelation of the 9/11 attacks had sent him, once again, spiraling off another emotional cliff. He had been able to read some old newspaper accounts of the attack online while they waited for their flight in Bermuda. From what he'd read about the level where the plane had hit, it was unlikely that there could have been many survivors from his company, if any. Upsetting as this was for him, there was also the realization that Serene and Keisha would almost surely have assumed that he was dead. His stupid plan of abandonment had inadvertently resulted in faking his own death, potentially causing untold pain to his family!

"Will you call them?" Thud's question interrupted his thoughts.

He looked up. "I don't know. I've been thinking about it, but how do you greet someone who has believed for two years that you are dead? 'Surprise, I'm not dead! Hope to see you soon'? There's so much to explain I almost think it would be better to do it in person. It will be a huge shock either way. If I'm right there, I just feel like I will have a better chance of controlling the situation." He shook his head, disgusted with himself, realizing what he'd said. "God, help me," he choked out. "I still want to control things."

The poor man looked so forlorn; the Judds didn't have the heart to lecture him on turning the control of it over to the Lord. His eyes were red and puffy. They knew he hadn't slept and had probably spent the night sobbing out his sorrow over his colleagues, as well as remorse for the pain he'd caused his family.

"I just keep thinking my family would be better off if I'd just gone to work that morning."

Rae Jean was instantly incensed. "Now that is *not* true! I won't berate you over the control thing, but I don't have to sit here and listen to you pretend that it would be better for *anyone* if you had died that day! For one thing, I would have been denied the pleasure of meeting you and watching the miraculous metamorphosis the Lord has worked in you." Rae had tears in her eyes by the time she'd finished her short rant. Thud reached for her hand and squeezed.

A small weak smile broke out on Jason's features. "Only you, Rae. No one else would have put up with my miserable, pain-in-the-butt attitude and self-serving behavior and still been able to focus on the miraculous." He looked her square in the eye. "I love you for it, you know." His smile might have been weak, but the sentiment was solid.

"Hey, watch it, buster! I'm sitting right here. If you want to declare love for my wife, at least have the courtesy to do it behind my back." They all laughed, breaking the tension for a few minutes.

Then Thud interjected a thought. "You may have devised an ill-conceived plan, one that the Lord would not overrule because of your free will, but He did work out the timing so He could use the circumstances to save your life. And I think that same God will do what He can to help you reconcile with your family."

There were more tears and lots of hugs as they parted ways half an hour later in the car rental area. "I don't know what I'll find in New York or where I'll eventually land residence-wise, so I won't try to give you guys contact information, but I promise I'll be in touch to let you know how things turn out for me." He patted his shirt pocket. "I have all your contact info and the ministry's, so I can repay the travel expenses. So long, my dear friends."

"We won't stop praying for you, Jason, and your family." Rae had called it over her shoulder as he was walking away from them. "God still has a plan for your life, no matter what you find in New York."

He looked back, smiled, and nodded. There it was again, another reference to a plan, a plan that had been put on hold since he was five years old. *I want that, Lord. Help me to find out Your plan for me and to live it out for Your glory.*

C H A P T E R

"Alive."

He sighed deeply, seemingly oblivious that his young associate was watching his reaction. *But you knew that, didn't you, Luke?* Had she told him the man had died, *that* would have surprised him. This didn't.

Margo had looked him in the eye and responded to his question with that one word. She now watched Luke's eyebrows draw together, immediately going into pensive mode. She knew he would already be thinking ahead to, "What does this mean going forward?" She had a strong sense that Luke carried a robust, vested interest in this answer to the dead-or-alive question. She would never directly ask him, but she suspected there was a woman involved. She had no evidence to support her suspicion; it was just feminine intuition.

As he gathered his thoughts, she went on, trusting that he would by listening or that he'd stop her if he needed more time. "At least, from the evidence I've turned up, that's my conclusion. I guess the details will govern whether you agree. Shall I get into the longer version?"

He tipped his head and gestured toward her file folder, a go-for-it signal. She opened the folder and began to tell the story of her research, referencing her notes as she went.

"The first thing I discovered was that Jason Brigholtz *is* listed among those who died in the North Tower that day. Not surprising, even though my other evidence contradicts that. In most cases, only small fragments of remains were found of the victims in those towers, with chemical and bacterial contamination making it even more difficult to identify the remains by DNA testing. With the number being in the thousands, it is slow, tedious work, with minimal positive results, to date, on the remains that are still being tested." Her voice held a certain reverence now. "Of those presumed to be in the building that day, they've had to, for the most part, go by whether they were otherwise accounted for when compiling the casualty list. Jason's company, Devlin, Burke, and Associates, was right at the level where the plane hit. And 72 percent of their workforce is presumed lost. Of the remaining 28 percent, some survived because they were out of the building for some reason or were in other locations inside the building.

"So if Brigholtz somehow survived, I asked myself why he hasn't come forward to correct this assumption of his death. It stands to reason that either he's unable to do so or he doesn't want to be found. Then I remembered my Vaughn and Associates training—don't ask why until you've thoroughly researched what." She looked up and caught his half-smile at that observation. That little bit of encouragement made her think, once again, *Oh, how I love my job!*

She did a quick check of her notes and continued, "Using my superpower of computer manipulation, I hacked into the Devlin, Burke e-mail account, which had been methodically backed up, and found that Jason Brigholtz was actually communicating via e-mail right up to and including the tenth of September. Indeed, his last e-mail on the tenth went out at 8:47 in the evening. All his e-mails seemed to be job related—investments, what's hot, what's not, buy, sell, tax loopholes. That sort of thing. I didn't follow up on the content since my purpose was to track his movements on the tenth and early on the eleventh. I wanted to determine if he ever walked into that building on the fatal day."

Luke's attention was rapt, even though he didn't comment.

She continued, "Next, I contacted his condo building, Morgenstern Towers, to inquire about cab service in the mornings when so many of their residents would be going off to work. Traffic is horrendous and parking essentially impossible to find in Manhattan, so I was presuming that Jason would not regularly drive his own vehicle to work, even though there was a vehicle registered in his name. Also, from the Morgenstern's location, subway doesn't get you that much closer to the Towers to make it worthwhile as a means by which to commute. I found out that two cab companies regularly sent cabs that way every weekday morning, since fares were virtually guaranteed, with drivers from other companies also showing up on a more occasional basis. I contacted both of the companies that regularly sent cabbies, but I hit a dead end with both since they don't keep records of who was in a cab when it went from point A to point B. Although both companies did confirm their drivers had regularly transported fares from the Morgenstern to the Towers prior to 9/11, it appeared to be a dead end, or so I thought. We'll come back to the cab element later."

She flipped a page in her notebook. "Phone records: Jason's cell phone, one that his company provided, revealed no activity after September 10. I checked his phone records, staying close to our date in question—within four months prior. Most calls were business contacts, some calls to or from his wife, daughter, and coworkers. There was one name

I couldn't place, and so it piqued my interest. In that four-month period, there were a total of six calls to and from a Del P. Morrison. And how's this for intriguing? The number had an area code..." Her voice lilted on the last word, followed by a dramatic pause. "Wait for it...808. Yup, right here in the good ole Hawaiian islands."

Luke had been listening attentively. Now he leaned forward in his swivel chair and cocked his head slightly. Laying his forearms on the desk with his fingers slightly entwined, tapping his thumbs together, he watched her intently, waiting expectantly for her to continue.

"So I did a local search on this Morrison person and came up with an arrest record for running out on a dock fee on a rented yacht in Maui. It seems the local police also confiscated several boxes of contraband spices from the yacht, spices that had originated in the Orient. The case was concluded with a hefty fine, no jail time."

"This is where I took it upon myself—I hope you don't mind—to call your friend Jerry at the FBI. I figured, if this guy, Morrison, is on the shady side, Agent Ballard could perhaps save me a lot of digging." She looked a little sheepish, waiting for a possible reprimand.

He interjected, but it wasn't a reprimand. "I'll admit, I was surprised when Jerry called me on my cell to see if I had an associate named Margaret Garrison, and if so, was it all right to give her info that would pertain to her *Frasier Crane* investigation?" He was trying to stifle his smile, failing. "You can assume it was all right, or he wouldn't have gotten back to you."

A little timidly, she went on, "Well, he wouldn't give me anything unless I told him what it specifically pertained to, so I had to give him Jason Brigholtz's name. Jerry—uh, Agent Ballard—said they have a file on Del Patrick Morrison, who also goes by two other aliases: Delwin Mayhew and Patrick Delwin. Apparently, he has a girlfriend on Molokai, and eighteen months prior to 9/11, Del Mayhew was there on Molokai. Brigholtz was too. Jason Brigholtz's name appeared in the FBI file because he spent about an hour talking to Morrison, a.k.a. Mayhew, in a little cabana bar on the north side, near Kalaupapa. Seems Mayhew was under surveillance at that time, so the FBI investigator took it upon herself to find out Jason's identity. Nothing more came of it, at least as far as the FBI was concerned. Agent Ballard told me they suspected Mayhew of transporting artifacts that had been stolen from an excavation site in Egypt, but no hard evidence had ever been established, and Brigholtz's name never came up in reference to that investigation."

Luke was processing. Eighteen months prior to 9/11 would have been about March of 2000, the time the Brigholtz family was vacationing in Hawaii. He knew that Serene had met Miranda while shopping here on the Big Island. Miranda was working as a concierge at that time. Apparently, Jason had also made an acquaintance for himself.

Reading that contemplative demeanor on his face again, Margo paused and took a long swig of her ice tea—cool tea was probably a better descriptor now, since the ice was history. It still refreshed a throat that was parched from nonstop talking. There was the muffled sound of the phone ringing out in the reception area. She turned and looked at the office door. It was a natural reaction to want to pick up the call. It was a part of her job, and Margo loved her job.

Luke noticed her distraction. "The temp will get it. So did you find anything more about Jason's association with this Mayhew character?"

A slight grin. "All right, here is where it gets juicy." She bounced a little in her seat. "When I mentioned to Jerry that we were interested in the 9/11 date, as it pertained to Jason's whereabouts, he plugged in that date in their records and provided me with our bombshell!" Her face was animated now. "It seems a private jet, titled to Patrick Delwin, flew into KTEB airport in New Jersey on the tenth of September, with one passenger, said Delwin. According to FBI records, he has another gal friend in the Bronx and is known to fly in to visit her occasionally. His aircraft, flown by Delwin's contracted pilot, Dale Fordham, flew out again early on September 11, with one passenger, a Jason Barnes. A coincidental similarity to our subject's name—perhaps too coincidental to be a coincidence."

Luke noticed that Agent Ballard had become Jerry again in her reference; he made a mental note of it. Was there an attraction developing between his administrative assistant and his FBI buddy? He did recall Jerry asking if she was single when he'd checked in with Luke on whether or not to share information with her. It didn't surprise him that Jerry had an interest, even after just one phone conversation. Margo's personality was that effervescent. Maybe a cautionary talk with Jerry was in order.

She continued, "So I wondered if a cabbie might remember taking a passenger from Morgenstern Towers to KTEB on 9/11. Seems like the long drive and that particular date might jog someone's memory. So I got back to the two cab companies, totally struck out with the first one, but I was able to bond with the secretary of the other company over how unappreciated we gals are who make up the support staff in these big companies. After Trixie and I trashed our bosses for a few minutes, she went the extra mile for me, checked the records and found that, although there's a lot of turnover with cabbies, they still employed two that had been with the company on 9/11. She wouldn't go so far as to give me phone numbers for them but promised to ask each of them my question: Did they drive a fare from Morgenstern to KTEB on September 11, 2001? Sure enough, she called me back just two days later and had found a cabbie named Jose, who had, indeed, driven a fancy-dressed big shot—his words—to the New Jersey airport. He hadn't wanted to, citing the money he would lose from other potential fares. Seems the big shot offered him a tip that would match the fare to the airport, even showed him the cash up front to prove he was able to pay it. After dropping the guy at the airport, Jose was driving back into Manhattan with his fat tip when he heard about the attack on his radio."

"Um, about trashing your boss…"

"I'm so sorry, Luke. You know I love my job, and my boss—uh, in a completely platonic way, of course!" Her cheeks were blooming again; she fanned herself with a napkin.

Luke held up a hand. "I was just going to say, even though I think we treat you quite well around here, and certainly depend heavily on your computer skills, we definitely have underestimated your talent for the investigative side of things. You've done an excellent job on this, Margo!" He made a mental note to speak to Caleb, a full partner in the business, about promoting Margo to investigator. And she would definitely get a bonus for this research.

She sighed her relief, delighted with the compliment and so flushed that she was now pressing the cool tea glass to her cheeks. "Oh yeah, I just remembered, since I'd spun a story to Trixie about trying to track down a deadbeat dad, she had tried to get a description out of Jose, the cabbie. All he remembered was that the guy was tall, was good-looking, and appeared to be as fit physically as he was financially. That meager description definitely gelled with a couple of pictures I'd seen of Brigholtz on his employer's website—a real looker, by the way.

"Also, Jerry had told me they didn't track where the private jet headed that day when it left KTEB since Patrick Delwin was not on it. Apparently, the FBI had pretty much concluded that this Morrison/Delwin/Mayhew character was a small-time smuggler, with no evidence of drug dealing or drug cartel ties and, therefore, not worthy of the resources of the bureau. That was especially so after 9/11. They had much larger and more lethal fish to fry. He also said that it would be virtually impossible for me to get flight plan info from the airport, if one had been filed, and if they even still had a record of it."

Luke leaned back in his chair, pursed his lips, and slowly blew out his breath. "Wow!"

She postured for the finale. "I have one more piece of circumstantial evidence. I mentioned that I didn't look closely at the content of Brigholtz's e-mails, but there was one that got my attention. No names were used when Brigholtz e-mailed the guy, or when there were replies. This addressee, 1wheelerdealer, an AOL account, had received a lot of tax info from Jason: deferments, shelters, etc. The last communication, Mr. Dealer to Brigholtz, late on the tenth of September, simply said, 'Your *metafora* awaits.' I stored it on my mind's back burner for a long time while I worked on other areas, but I couldn't get the word *metafora* out of my mind. I had a hard time tracking down the definition of it, a word I'd never heard before. I finally found it, a Greek word that means 'transportation.'" She paused, then said, "It's not like I actually watched the man get outta Dodge on the morning of the eleventh, but I can't imagine coming any closer to it."

"And I'd have to turn in my private investigator license if I disagreed with that. Well done, Margo!"

He didn't verbalize the rest of his thought: *So the mystery man lives...and I've been dating his wife!*

CHAPTER

It had seemed like a very short flight to LaGuardia; Jason got more nervous the closer he got to home and the anticipated encounter with his wife and daughter. He'd been doing a lot of praying on the flight, seeking God about the impending meeting, but he hadn't gotten any instinctive sense of what he might expect when he arrived.

From LaGuardia, he rented a car and drove to KTEB in New Jersey, where he retrieved the briefcase that held his ID and very wrinkled business attire. He doubted the expensive suit would ever be usable again, even if sold secondhand. He thanked the Lord for giving him the foresight to pay five years of rental fees on the locker before he'd left—a just-in-case gesture. The clothing didn't matter, but having his true identity verified by the cards in his wallet gave him as much peace now as the false identity had produced a chill of discomfort two years ago, the day he'd walked out of this same terminal.

He drove the rental into Manhattan, turned it in, and took the subway to the stop nearest the Ground Zero site. Ascending the subway steps, he walked from there to the remains of the former locale of his all-consuming occupation. What an eerie feeling to be standing there, looking beyond a fence at the graveyard of what was so monumental to him two years ago, both architecturally as well as being symbolically reminiscent of financial accomplishment—his own, America's, and even the world's. Though it was not his intention to judge others, nor did he mean to philosophize about the event, he knew this picture was an appropriate rendition of the homage he himself had paid to the spirit of mammon.

No point in asking why—Jason could almost hear Thurston Judd assuring him it was a spiritual battle that had played out in the natural realm, just like the battles of strife in man's soul played out their devastation in the natural body. Evil would always attack the human population, whom Jesus loved so much, wherever doors were left open to it. Jason stood quietly and mourned for those he'd known, who'd undoubtedly been killed that day, along with the thousands with whom he wasn't acquainted, who either worked in the buildings or were just at the wrong place at the wrong time. He grieved also for all the first responders who'd lost their lives heroically trying to save others.

There were several other visitors to the site, standing around with gloomy faces, looking at the devastation that they couldn't fix, at the loss they couldn't recover. More than one glanced at him, as though they'd like to engage in conversation about what the rubble meant to him and share the stories of their own sufferings. But he avoided eye contact, hoisted the strap of his duffel bag over his shoulder, and turned away from the dark shroud, walked away from it, back toward the thriving, bustling city. He'd paid his respects. Wallowing in the sorrow would serve no one except the spiritual enemy who'd perpetrated the horrific event. *Think on that which is just, pure, lovely, of good report, virtuous, and praiseworthy,* Jason reminded himself. He walked a couple of blocks in the city's August heat, then stopped at a little café. Over a tall cool drink, he reminded himself again, and then again, of that wisdom from the book of Philippians.

Callie and Keith exchanged pleasantries with Abel, the friendly senior doorman at Morgenstern Towers. "It appears your shopping trip was successful, Mr. Revelle. You look pretty laden down with packages there. Would you like me to get someone to help you carry them?"

"Thanks, Abel, but with Callie's help…" He indicated the few small shopping bags he'd allowed her to carry. "I think we can manage." They got on the elevator with their newfound treasures from the day's bargain hunting. Juggling his burdens, Keith pressed the button for the fifteenth floor, turned, and smiled at the pretty woman who'd dragged him all over Manhattan, draining his wallet as she went. And he begrudged it not at all. In fact, since they were alone on the elevator, he leaned in for a quick kiss, and she obliged, returning his smile. Callie did not fit the profile of a shopaholic wife. She was so practical with their finances that he often had to urge her to let loose and buy herself something new. Their occasional trips to New York were her exception. She especially loved finding great deals for the kids, stocking up on unique gifts for birthdays and for all those on her Christmas list, as well as finding little keepsakes by which to remember the trip.

"Thanks for being my shopping buddy today, hon. You were no Serene, but hey, that's a pretty high standard for anyone to meet. You held your own pretty well though," she kidded.

He mocked a serious attitude. "It had to be done. I couldn't let you out there on your own. You probably would have put a twenty-dollar cap on your spending."

She playfully swung her purse at him. "Very funny."

Callie and Keith were so in love it was blatantly evident to everyone who knew them well—for that matter, to anyone who just casually encountered them. They had met when Callie came to the city to help Serene, who was close to her delivery date with Michael. Two-year-old Keisha needed some assistant-mothering from someone not laden with a late-term pregnancy, to keep the busy toddler in check. The plan was that Callie would stay for a couple of months after the baby was born, to help out her sister-in-law.

Keith Revelle, fresh out of law school and having recently passed the bar, had been assigned by his new firm to represent a group of tenants of the building where the Brigholtzs resided at that time against the corporation that owned the property. The suit had to do with the corporation's neglect of maintenance and safety issues. Callie was instantly beguiled by the young lawyer, who came to interview each of the tenants regarding their complaints.

That was how it happened, that with Jason at work, as was most always the case, it was Keith who came to the rescue the day Serene went into labor. He had come to the Brigholtzs' apartment to interview them and walked in on two women in a near panic and a two-year-old in a meltdown of tears because of a puddle of amniotic fluid on the kitchen floor. He began by picking up the toddler and soothing her. A surprised Keisha looked up into his face, her teary, big-eyed expression saying, "I don't know who you are, but I'm pretty sure you are going to make everything all right." So she plopped her thumb in her mouth and laid her head on his shoulder. His calm, take-charge manner greatly impressed Callie as well, but only secondarily to his ruggedly handsome face, which had been the first attraction to pull her in like an irresistible magnet. A couple of months later, she was completely hooked after watching that calm, confident demeanor displayed in the courtroom with prevailing results. Kind, caring, handsome, and brilliant in his profession. Her hero.

The lift of the elevator slowed, and her smile for her husband took on a measure of sadness. "I'll bet Serene and

Keisha are having a great time hitting all the stores in Hawaii. At least I really hope they're enjoying the trip."

"I don't think we need to worry about them, babe. You know the Salengers will take good care of them."

*****

They exited the elevator, walked down the plush carpeted hallway, and let themselves into the Brigholtzs' apartment. Keith took their packages into the guest bedroom they'd been occupying. Callie followed. She dropped her purse and packages, kicked off her comfy walking sandals, and flopped, contentedly, onto the bed. Stretching out like a cat, she murmured, "Mmmmm, it feels so good to be off my feet and back in the air conditioning."

Keith sat down on the edge of the bed and, claiming a bare foot with bright fuchsia toenails, massaged it for a few minutes, then lifted the other one and repeated the service, receiving groans of pleasure for his efforts throughout the process. "Want a cold drink, sweetheart? I'm headed that way." He smiled sweetly at his wife.

"I'd love a ginger ale, thanks." She sighed. "I'll try to stay awake until you get back, but that foot rub was so relaxing I can't promise anything."

Turning with eyes squinted in mock seriousness, he eased himself up her prone frame and positioned himself over her, face-to-face, balancing on his forearms. He was met with her answering grin. He proceeded to kiss her soundly.

Running her fingers through his short-cropped hair, she whispered in a husky voice, "Well, then, get our drinks and get on back here. I'll be the one wide awake and waiting for you."

Jason had caught a cab to the Morgenstern. He paid the cabbie, got out, and stood looking at the thirty-story deep-gray-colored stone-and-glass building with mixed emotions. This place had been his home for eight years before he left it on September 11, 2001, planning to never return. Coupled with the traffic sounds, the hustle of busy Manhattanites hurrying into and out of and all around the structure was just a reminder of his stressful previous life and made him want to run the other way. At the same time, there was the pull toward the building, the knowledge that his family made their home here and were likely inside right now. That thought was accompanied by so much love and longing it brought a lump to his throat and constriction to his chest.

He slowly approached the front entrance, his focus already beyond it. He could picture the few modern pieces of furniture in the high-ceilinged lobby, pieces that were left mostly unused as tenants hurried past them. There was the bank of mailboxes covering most of one wall, the cool green wall color, and the tall tinted windows that allowed a view of the Manhattan streets while filtering the sunlight. The doorman's counter and hallway leading to the garage that never failed to remind him of *that* morning.

He could picture his apartment door, number 1508, and see himself turning the key in the lock. His ears could hear the ringing of Keisha and Michael's joyful, childlike voices laughing and teasing each other; this memory brought familiar stinging to the back of his eyes. He choked back tears as the building's front door opened before him.

"Mr. Brigholtz? Oh my Lord, it *is* you!"

"Hello, Abel. Long time no see." As he stepped into the building's lobby, Jason hoped he wouldn't have to pick the dumbstruck doorman off the floor. He quickly glanced around and noted not much had changed. The only variation he could detect was the addition of some large black-and-white prints depicting various locales of the city from years past.

With a dry throat, the older man took several moments to find his voice again. Jason smiled at the familiar, kind-hearted soul, who was drained of all color and was looking at him like he was seeing a ghost. "Breathe, Abel." Jason smiled kindly at him.

"Mr. B, we all thought...we assumed...Mr. B, even your family believes you were in that tower when it was hit. They think you're dead, sir!" Realizing that he might be overstepping his station, might not be politically correct, he quickly stammered an apology. "I...I'm sorry, Mr. Brigholtz, to be so blunt, sir, but my goodness, I've never learned proper protocol for this kind of...um...event."

The man's face looked ashen. "It's okay, Abel." Jason thought his own genuinely cordial smile might be just as much a shock to the man as his apparent resurrection. "I'll just go on up and explain to my girls that I'm *not* dead." He didn't want to get into an explanation with Abel before he even talked to his family. He gave the doorman's shoulder a gentle squeeze and took a step toward the elevators.

"Mr. B, they aren't up there. Mrs. B and your daughter are on vacation, sir, in Hawaii."

Instantly, the wording registered with him. Abel still referred to Serene as *Mrs. B*. She hadn't remarried. A deep sigh of relief escaped his lips, and a shudder traveled the length of him. His legs suddenly felt like rubber.

"You all right, Mr. B? You look a little peaked."

"I'm fine, Abel. I think I'll just go on up and rest awhile."

"Yes, sir. Uhh." Abel was about to tell Jason that Mrs. Brigholtz had family staying in the apartment, that nice couple from Indiana, but just then, Mrs. Oppenheimer's poodle escaped her grasp again, as the elderly woman was stepping off the elevator. It was a frequent occurrence, and Abel was expected to capture the runaway canine before she could flee out the building's front door. "Oh, Abel! Stop her, Abel! Mitzi has absconded again!" The shrill demand completely redirected the man's attention.

While the wayward pooch dominated the attention of everyone in the lobby, Jason stepped onto the elevator and pushed the button for his floor, thankful that Abel's close consideration was no longer on him.

*****

Keith grabbed two cans of Vernors from the six-pack he and Callie had brought from home, since it was a favorite and that brand wasn't commonly available in New York. He nudged the door closed on the fridge and turned to leave the kitchen. His steps led him into the hallway just in time to hear the apartment door being unlocked. He stood shocked for a moment, staring at the door, unable to grasp who might be entering.

Jason pushed open the door to his home, entered, and dropped the worn duffel on the familiar catchall chair. When he lifted his gaze, it fell on a thoroughly stunned man standing in his hallway with a can of pop in each hand. They stared at each other for a moment, both dumbfounded by the unexpected presence of the other.

Jason found his voice first. "Hello, Keith." His face broke into a grin. "It's good to see you." He stepped forward quickly and wrapped his brother-in-law in a sincere bear hug.

"Jason…you *are* alive! Callie always said…" Keith's arms came around him and returned the embrace, Jason feeling the two cold spots on his back.

"Is one of those for me?" he asked, indicating the cans, when they separated to look each other over. "Or is my sister in this building somewhere?"

A spine-chilling shriek from his left answered the question for him. She seemed to be paralyzed, standing there barefoot in her sleeveless, pastel blouse, and short denim skirt.

Jason's grin widened. "Hey, baby sis…" Spreading his arms, he wiggled the fingers of both hands. "Come on, bring it on in."

She flew into his arms, crying like the baby he'd just called her. She was so overcome with emotion she couldn't speak yet. She just clung to him. In the back of her mind, she heard the words of Joan at the women's retreat: *I see a loving reunion hug.*

Thank You, Lord. Oh, thank You, Lord Jesus!

"Thank You, Lord Jesus!" Her tears were matched by those of the brother, who was squeezing the breath out of her.

CHAPTER 22

When she had finally found her voice, Callie began with, "Where have you been, you great big, wonderful jerk?"

"I'll tell you everything, Cal, every last detail, I promise." Smiling through teary eyes, he qualified his statement. "But before I get into what is a pretty long story, Sis, I need you to update me on my family...and yours too." He could see she was about to protest, so he quickly entreated, "Please, Callie. I need to know how Serene and Keisha are doing."

"They've endured a lot of pain, Jason. We all have. We had no reason to believe anything other than that you were buried in that giant pile of rubble." And bluntly she added, "In tiny little pieces."

Jason's heart ached for them, and a huge lump developed in his throat so that he couldn't speak for a moment. He'd processed every conceivable possibility in his mind, and it always came back to his family believing he was dead. Hadn't the doorman just confirmed it for him?

He realized that Callie was saying something now about the Holy Spirit giving her hope that he was still alive. She went on talking. "Keith and I kept in touch with them and tried to provide what comfort we could. Our communication has been mostly by phone and e-mail since we didn't want Serene to feel like she had to play hostess to us if we visited, and she declined our invitation for the two of them to come to Indiana for a visit. Serene has been completely focused on helping Keisha to cope, and Keisha hasn't wanted to travel until just recently, when Serene finally got her to agree to go to Hawaii."

He interrupted her. "I know this is a selfish question, Cal, but I have to ask if Serene has been…seeing anyone… dating?" He clarified, "It's hard for me to even say the word."

"She's not mentioned anything to me about having an interest in seeing anyone in a romantic sense, Jason. But being your sister, I might not be the first person she'd confide in if she were."

He knew she was right about that, but Callie was also not the *last* person Serene would tell. The two women had always been on friendly terms. The fact that Callie had not heard anything was encouraging, but only marginally.

Keith interjected, "I don't think her mind has been on anything other than helping Keisha through this, as Callie said."

"I'm gonna grab a drink." Jason gestured to the kitchen. "Can we all sit down and talk?" They both affirmed the suggestion.

He grabbed a bottle of water from the fridge, and the three of them sat down in the den to continue the discussion. After a couple of hours, stomachs growled, and the evening meal was finally considered. They ordered in from Jason's favorite Italian restaurant since Callie didn't think she could concentrate long enough to cook supper for the trio. The food, which would normally be considered heavy fare, seemed light after what had been heavy conversation. After they'd gratefully enjoyed the delicious ethnic meal, both men stayed in the kitchen to help Callie do the cleanup. Jason stayed because he was enjoying the company of his sister, who, just as he'd anticipated, had welcomed him with unconditional love and kindness. Keith wanted to be nearby so he wouldn't miss any of the conversation, which was like a mystery cake, two years in the baking, and was just now coming out of the oven. He was intrigued to partake in every layer of it.

They settled back in the den with coffee that Keith had made for them while the cleanup was being concluded. The conversation continued. Jason had related his difficulty in processing his grief and guilt over Michael's death, something Callie could fully understand, given their emotionally absent parents during their upbringing. He'd told his sister and brother-in-law how, with his pent-up pain, he'd decided to disappear from his stressful job, having also convinced himself that Serene and Keisha would be better off without him. Trying to keep the story short, he gave them the condensed account of Del Mayhew's role in the plan. Then he told how his strategy had inadvertently and quite amazingly coincided with the day of the terror attack. Keith and Callie exchanged glances and then returned their attention to Jason.

He guessed what they were thinking. "Yes, I know," he said. "The timing thing was God's doing. He took my stupid plot to abandon my job and family and turned it around to save my life, my physical life. Then He went to work on my soul. The short version is that He plunked me down on an obscure island southwest of Bermuda with a pair of the most radical Christian missionaries in His arsenal. Thurston and Rae Jean Judd are the most wonderful people you could ever hope to meet, and I'll be sure you do meet them someday." He had already shared about some of the ministry he'd received from this missionary couple.

"You've certainly changed, Jason. I can tell God has been working on you." Joy radiated on his sister's face, and tears glistened in her eyes as she softly and reverently gave voice to what she was seeing in her brother.

"The Holy Spirit has been working *in* me, Callie. But that's a story for later. I've about exhausted myself for one day. Only one more thing I want to be sure you know before we hit pause on this thing: I would *never* have stayed away this long if I'd known about the 9/11 attacks and the pain it caused my family, all of you. I found out about the attack four days ago. I was already on my way home when I heard about it."

"Oh, Jason…" Her hand went to her mouth. "So the pain of it is fresh for you…all your coworkers…"

He was nodding, pensive, and really looking exhausted. "Honey, I've got to shut it down for today. I'm too big for Keith to carry me to bed, and I'm just about to drop, so we'll have to pick this up tomorrow."

"I don't know what you have in that ratty-looking duffel bag, Jason, but if you'd like, I can loan you some pajamas."

"Thanks, Keith, but I'm too tired to do anything but strip to my shorts and fall into my bed, or maybe I should say Serene's bed." He got up and started for the hallway that led to the bedrooms. "Good night, you guys."

"Jason…are you going to call them?"

He paused. "I'll think on that tomorrow, Sis. I had hoped to be talking to Serene right now, right here, face-to-face, but now it's all up in the air again." He continued toward the hallway that led to the bedrooms. "I'm glad that I had this time with you guys, though. At the risk of sounding sappy, I love you both." Head and shoulders sagging with the weight of fatigue, he moved down the hall, and they soon heard the door of the master bedroom close.

Callie woke up the next morning at eight fifteen to the smell of freshly brewed coffee and found the other side of the bed empty. She wondered if only Keith was up or if Jason was as well. She quickly washed up and brushed her teeth and ran a hairbrush through her thick blond hair. Putting on a pair of shorts, her Indiana Hoosiers T-shirt, and a pair of sandals, she made her way to the kitchen, where she found her husband talking to Jason; his pen and ever-present legal pad was holding up its part in the discussion. From the gist of the conversation, Keith was deliberating the intricacies of reversing Jason's "presumed dead" status.

"Morning, babe. Can I pour you a cup?" He nodded to his coffee mug.

"I can get it." She kissed her husband's forehead as she walked by him to the coffeepot, planting another kiss on her brother's forehead en route. "Morning, Jason. I think I'd like one of those great-looking pastries too."

"Yeah, Danish from Della CaSees," Keith quipped. "Jason was up early and went for a walk. Try the cherry-almond cream cheese version. They're great."

"Thanks, Jason." Callie helped herself to a pastry, grinning at her brother, who smiled back and winked at her. She was still incredulous that he was actually here with them. Jason sat at the table, with his hands wrapped around a coffee mug, listening closely to Keith. He was wearing Bermuda shorts and a T-shirt, both faded and worn. She'd never seen him so dressed down in what was basically shabby chic, heavy on the shabby. Even as a kid, Jason had always liked to dress well. That it was no longer a priority to him was another evidence of the change in him.

Finding a pause in her husband's comments, she interjected, "Jason, would I be correct to speculate that you and I need to go clothes-shopping to recreate your wardrobe, the one Serene long since donated to charity?"

"Um, Keith and I have been talking about some legalities that need to be addressed, and it will require my meeting with someone from his former firm here in Manhattan, today, hopefully, since I plan to be on a plane to Hawaii tomorrow. We're waiting for the callback from his former colleague. I would love it, though, if you have some time and would be willing to pick up a few items for me. I don't need much, certainly no power suits or silk ties."

"On a plane, tomorrow?" She set her coffee mug and plate of pastry down on the table and pulled out a chair between the two men she loved. "Does this mean you are just going to show up there, or had you planned a phone call to warn them?"

"Every time I think or pray about it, sis, I can't seem to picture myself breaking this to them over the phone. I'm going to meet them, Serene first, face-to-face. I can't imagine the shock being any worse than getting a phone call from a dead man."

"Okay, I won't argue with you, but I will tell you this much"—her pointer finger came up with her remark—"if Serene calls me for any reason, I won't keep your secret. To not tell her would be a lie of omission, and I can't do that, Jason. I won't."

I should have known, he thought, keeping his grin to himself. "Fair enough, Cal. I can live with that. But please don't initiate the call yourself, okay? Can you do that much for me?"

"Okay." Turning to Keith, she gestured to his legal pad. "Now, give me a sheet of that paper, hon. I need to write down Jason's sizes and what he needs me to buy for him. Looks like I have some more shopping to do while you guys are handling your lawyer stuff."

*****

Jason sat with Keith, across the conference room table from Dylan Fielding, Keith's good friend and former colleague. Shortly after their conversation over breakfast, Dylan had returned Keith's call from the firm where Keith had worked years ago when he first met Callie. Dylan had agreed to see them on short notice. He didn't have much time; it would be just enough of a meeting to establish a file and go over what would need to be addressed in the days and weeks to come.

After they'd covered Keith and Dylan's concerns, the first question Jason had for Dylan was whether it would be better for him to book a plane ticket under the fake Jason Barnes ID or attempt to book it using his real ID.

"I think you could encounter some problems using your real ID since there's a possibility your name could trigger info on your *supposed* death, which, let's face it, is going to very likely put you into a suspected terrorist category with the airlines. For that reason, I advise against using it. I also do not advise you to travel under an assumed name. That would reflect poorly on me, professionally, you understand? So please don't let me know anything further about any travel plans you may be contemplating."

Jason and Keith shared a look. It was exactly the advice Keith had given him earlier. Neither of them mentioned to Dylan that Jason had already booked and flown two flights under his fake ID.

Keith and Callie had married within the first year after they met. They'd lived in New York for three years, but when Callie got pregnant, Keith wanted to take her home to Indiana, where his family was from and where they were all still living. He didn't want to raise his family in New York City; he wanted a more idyllic childhood for their children, like the one he'd experienced. However, he had maintained his law license in New York as well as in Indiana, and therefore, he actually could have handled this whole affair for Jason since he was knowledgeable and licensed in both states. However, it was not logistically feasible since he and Callie would be returning to Indiana soon. He had thought it through and explained it to Jason before calling Dylan that morning.

"Okay, to recap," Dylan was saying, "there's the land in Michigan that we believe Serene, as your legal beneficiary, has not disposed of yet. So that's not urgent. There is no pension, just the company-sponsored 401(k), which also will have reverted to Mrs. Brigholtz, also not urgent. The life insurance money will need to be repaid. I'll begin that process with a letter to the company explaining the circumstances. There could be a battle over interest and penalties on that one. We'll cross that bridge when we come to it. Of course, Keisha's dependent social security benefits will also need to be repaid. That will produce a lot of government red tape, but I can, at least, get the ball rolling on that for you. Keith, you're relatively sure that Serene did not apply to the 9/11 Victim Compensation Fund, correct?"

Keith confirmed it. "In previous conversations with Callie, Serene had mentioned that she had no intention of availing herself of that money. She felt that it should be there to take care of those survivors with more of a financial need. To my knowledge, she hasn't changed her opinion on that."

Dylan nodded. "Well, that certainly makes life easier for us." Then he went on, "There is no life tenancy on your apartment, so no issue there. Regarding your consent to investment transactions, you said you dealt with that before leaving by appointing an administrator. There should be a record of that since it was a computerized transaction, which would have been reproducible. If Mr. Barbour did not survive the attack, the company will have assigned a substitute."

Dylan looked satisfied that they had covered everything that needed immediate attention as he began to pull papers together into a fresh file folder. "I think we are good in the event that you decide to travel out of the city to reunite with your family." Looking Jason in the eye, he stressed, "Just be sure I have all your contact info, and don't go off the grid without keeping me in the loop. The thing we need to stress in putting your life back together is that you are not a criminal who faked your own death. Indeed, it's just the opposite: you are a victim of the 9/11 attack, as much as anyone else."

Jason couldn't leave that one alone. "No, Dylan, I'm not a victim. I have been a sinful man whose selfish, egotistical lifestyle took me terribly off course. And now you have the privilege of being one of the instruments the Lord is using to help me get recentered. I'll trust God to head up my defense team. You can be second chair."

Dylan looked at Keith, his expression pleading with his fellow attorney for support of his point.

Keith just grinned at him, poked his thumb toward Jason, and retorted, "What he said."

CHAPTER 23

It's been quite a while, Luke thought, *since I've had this sense of something about to happen, something that will require all my senses to be on high alert.* He'd had a dream, none of which he could remember, just that in the dream every cell of his body was ready to spring. When he awoke, however, that sensation had not left him even though the memory of the dream had. He might be unsure how to define it, but he was very familiar with it. It was that hyperawareness that he'd gotten on so many occasions while doing police work. Pressing into the Lord through the years had taught him to pay attention and let the Holy Spirit define it for him. Just having that instinct had proved very helpful in his job; having the Lord fine-tune it for him increased its value and, very likely, had saved his life on more than one occasion.

After spending time in the Word and in prayer, he was assured that he needed to be keenly aware of his surroundings today. He didn't sense danger; it was just a knowing that this was not going to be an ordinary day. Even without this instinctive sensation, he could have predicted an atypical day since he planned to meet Serene this morning and give her the feedback on Margo's *Frasier Crane* research. He was prepared for her shock and probable anger that he would presume to investigate her late husband without first discussing it with her. He was also prepared for her shock over the results of the investigation. But this Holy Spirit warning elevated his consternation over the meeting to a new level. And there was no indication in his gut that the warning applied to anything other than the meeting.

Serene took extra care in getting ready for her breakfast meeting with Luke. She had no illusions of his intentions in inviting her to breakfast. They had been on a friendly basis, but not more than that since the day he'd come so close to turning it into something romantic and then did a sudden, complete about-face. She admitted to herself that it, perhaps, was a little bit of vanity that made her want to look her best, to show him what he was missing. After being around dedicated Christian men the past couple of months, she had begun to think she might like to be married again, but with the Lord directing the selection process this time. She'd witnessed Wayne and Miranda's relationship and saw how the other men in the Bible study interacted with their wives. It stirred a desire in her to be valued like that by a marriage partner. She sighed. After their fateful date, she had to admit to herself that there was likely not going to be that kind of future with Luke.

As she applied light makeup, she thought of her conversation with Miranda after Luke's sudden rejection. Miranda had confessed to her that she already knew the details of what had happened because Luke had acknowledged the whole thing to Wayne, who then repeated it to Miranda so that she could be prepared to comfort her friend, if necessary. Serene had not been upset with Miranda for her secondhand knowledge of the incident—actually, Miranda had answered the one question that chafed inside Serene during the days following the *almost kiss*, as she'd begun to think of the incident. Being new at Christianity and at nurturing her relationship with the Holy Spirit, she wanted—no, needed—to know if Luke could have actually heard God's audible voice and had such a strong reaction to it. Miranda had assured her that, though it did not happen that way often, it could indeed have occurred just as Luke described it. As Miranda put it, a kiss is such an intimate show of affection that it would have caused Serene unnecessary pain when Luke eventually figured out that he was headed down a path that was unacceptable to the Lord. God's audible voice was like a passenger shouting to a driver, to bring his attention to a dangerous traffic situation. What Serene took away from their conversation was the knowledge that her Savior loved her enough to prevent the pain that a wrong relationship and breakup would have caused her. That left one unanswered question, one for which she might never have an answer: Why was she the wrong woman for Luke Vaughn?

She dressed in her favorite lime-green Hawaiian-print sundress, its flared skirt just skimming the tops of her knees, showing off her shapely legs without showing too much. She then slipped her feet into her favorite sandals. Pulling her hair back on just one side and catching it with a pretty dolphin-shaped mother-of-pearl barrette, she checked the mirror one last time and was satisfied that, if nothing else, Luke would be careful to check with the Lord before he ever entertained thoughts of planting his lips on another woman. It couldn't hurt for him to smart over this just a little bit. She had been very straightforward with him when he'd called to ask her to have breakfast with him. "If you are asking for a date, Luke, the answer is no."

His response was quick: "That's fair enough, Serene. So just to be clear, I'm not asking for a date. It's just two friends having a meal together because I've come across some information that I want to share with you, and it's not something to be discussed by phone." When she refused to meet him unless he gave her some idea what he wanted to discuss, he'd told her it had to do with a Hawaiian businessman who might have met her husband a few years back. She had reluctantly accepted his invitation but had insisted that Wayne and Miranda come along.

Luke had agreed to her terms, then had called Wayne and filled him in on the whole thing. Wayne agreed with Luke that she shouldn't have to deal with an audience when he sprang the news on her. That evening, she had asked Wayne, at dinner, if he knew anything about Luke's mysterious information, then asked if he and Miranda would be willing to come along if she met with him. Wayne had not yet had a chance to discuss the matter with Miranda when Serene's question was raised. He had affirmed that Luke had told him the essence of the matter. First catching his wife's eye, he told Serene that he was sure Luke's intentions were in her best interest and that, in his opinion, it would be better if she met with Luke alone.

Before Serene could respond, Miranda spoke up, addressing Serene, but also eyeing her husband. "Serene, I will leave the decision up to you, but Luke is already on thin ice as far as I'm concerned, and I am only willing to withhold my presence from this meeting because I trust my husband's perception of the matter, not Luke Vaughn's." Everyone at the table heard the warning in that. Keisha had not been present at that meal, or Miranda might not have been that forthcoming; none of them wanted Keisha exposed to any further drama.

The omelet was great, but Luke could hardly enjoy breakfast. His stomach was a little unsettled. Besides the fact that he was on high alert, this gorgeous woman across from him seemed to look extra attractive today, and he was only too aware that he was expected to look at her as he would a sister. Employing the attentiveness his training and his gut required of him, he had already picked up on the likelihood that they'd been followed to the restaurant.

The waitress brought the check to the table and asked if they'd like more coffee. They both declined. Luke pulled a credit card from his wallet and watched as the server departed with it. His eyes darted around the dining room again, doing another quick check of other patrons and what he could see of the parking lot through the windows.

He'd not said a word yet about why he wanted this meeting, and here he was, acting all distracted again. "Luke, what is going on with you? You've hardly said a word while we ate. You have been nervous as a cat since we got here—no, even before we got here. I'm beginning to wish I hadn't come today. Believe me, if not for Wayne vouching for you, I wouldn't have—"

"Let's just go, Serene," he interrupted. "If we go to the counter, the waitress will get the idea and check us out. Once we've settled on a bench in the park across the street, I can explain everything. I know I've been bad company and haven't even broached the subject I told you about when I called, but I need to be out of this restaurant first, where we won't be interrupted." His eyes pleaded. "Please?"

She nodded. "Okay."

After settling up at the checkout counter, they exited the restaurant, and with Luke's hand lightly on Serene's low back, he directed her across the narrow street into the shady circular park, the surrounding one-way street of which was graced with diagonal parking that fronted the small quaint shops on the park's outer edge. Five streets culminated here at the picturesque circle. Colorful flowers abounded on the circumference of the fountain that was the centerpiece of this small oasis and also bordered the walkways that wound through the popular park. This early in the morning, with the shops not yet open, it was virtually deserted, except for a few folks strolling or sitting.

There! Sunglasses, navy-blue T-shirt, khakis, loafers, and the newspaper—obviously a prop. Behind the sunglasses, and with slight head movement, the man's glance seemed to turn their way every few seconds as he leaned against the lamppost about thirty feet away from the bench they'd just settled on, the same man Luke had observed pulling into the restaurant's small parking lot right behind them in that taupe SUV with a rental car license plate, the same SUV he'd noticed following them for several blocks. The guy had quickly ducked his head when Luke tried to make eye contact as he and Serene had walked across the restaurant parking lot. Then, as they were being seated, the man had also entered the restaurant, still sporting the shades, and had ordered coffee to go. Luke had not seen him again during breakfast but had spotted him immediately as they left the restaurant, just leaning against his car, with a clear view of the restaurant's front door, seemingly engrossed in his newspaper. Now, here he was again and still seemed to have an inordinate interest in today's news in print, and to Luke's trained eye, he could tell, even with the shades, that the guy was still watching them.

In a way, Luke was relieved. He knew that he'd found the reason for the vigilance in his spirit, but it didn't decrease the adrenaline coursing through his veins, and there was no way he could have a conversation with Serene under these circumstances. It was time to deal with the situation. Luke had put all these puzzle pieces into place mentally in just the few moments it took them to cross the street and settle onto the bench.

Serene was looking at him expectantly, so he kicked it into gear. He put his arm around behind her on the bench, smiled warmly, and lowered his head closer to hers, as though to whisper, if you were a casual observer, and his mannerism was for the sake of their observer.

"Serene," he did whisper to her. "I need you to trust me. Just act casual. We are being watched—no, don't look around. I need to deal with this. I'm going to get up and walk away, and I need you to just sit here and not look around. Just pretend that all is well and you are just waiting for me. I promise I'll be back in just a few minutes. This is important. Can you do that for me?" He drew back to look her in the eye as he gauged her reaction. Her brows were drawn together in confusion, but he pleaded with his eyes for her cooperation, and finally, she gave him a slight nod.

Luke smiled at her once more and got up from the bench, giving her shoulder a quick squeeze as he moved away from her and also away from Sunglasses Guy, who was behind and off to the right of them. So he went left. He said a quick prayer that he wouldn't need it, as he casually lifted his shirt and unsnapped the holster of the Glock that was his constant companion. After a few yards, with plenty of small trees and shrubs between him and the stalker, he shifted direction, checking over his shoulder to see if their interested party had followed his movement or, instead, kept his eye on Serene. The man was openly watching Serene, and with her back turned to him, he seemed to be assured that he was safe to do so. With the man's attention so completely diverted, and with him practically drooling over Serene, Luke grabbed his opportunity and quickly approached, having circled around behind him. Whatever his motive, this guy surely wasn't a pro. He had no clue how to blend into the background and was oblivious to Luke's approach.

The temptation to turn and look around to see where Luke had gone and who was watching them had Serene nervous, bouncing her knee up and down and drumming her fingers on the bench. This must be what a cat felt like while waiting to pounce, she thought. In a couple of minutes, she was so anxious she could hardly sit still when she heard Luke's raised voice. "All right, jerk, let's have it! You've been following and watching us for the last two hours! If this is official, you'd better have some convincing ID! Otherwise, you'd better have some blasted good answers!" Serene jumped up and turned in the direction of Luke's voice. He had a man by the shirt front, backed up against a light pole, and Luke's face reflected the anger that had pervaded his voice. He looked like he might punch the guy, even though from this angle, the other man appeared to be in good shape and was a couple inches taller than Luke. She hadn't even noticed that she had been walking closer to the pair while taking in the scene.

Tricia had been carrying boxes into her little boutique, which she would be opening to the public in about half an hour, when she noticed the hot-looking guy by the lamppost across the street in the park. He seemed to be checking out the pretty redheaded gal on the bench. Being people-oriented and naturally curious by nature, she was wondering how it would play out when another guy suddenly approached from behind Hottie and, with one swift move, knocked his sunglasses off his face and slapped the newspaper out of his hand. Both objects hit the ground as hot Lamppost Guy got slammed up against the post, to the accompaniment of harsh words that she couldn't quite make out.

Serene's eyes were on the other man now, who was glaring right back at Luke. She wondered why he looked so familiar as she drew closer to them. Seeing her out of his peripheral vision, Luke cautioned, "Serene, stay back."

Serene couldn't tear her gaze off the other man. Just a few feet from the two of them now, recognition hit her—hit her *hard*. His face was a little thinner, his hair color sun-streaked, and he had a deep tan, but yes, it was him! She was sure. Her voice came out in a squeak. "Jason?"

Tortured deep-blue eyes fixed on her gaze. "Hello, Serene."

At that mutual greeting, Luke released his grip and stepped back, the whole scene coming together for him quickly. His mind whirled with thoughts as the implications of the stalker's ID sank in. The first and foremost thought that flitted through his mind was, *Oh great, now I'll never get to kiss her*. It frankly surprised him that he hadn't entirely given up on the possibility.

Staring at her suddenly resurrected husband, Serene forgot to breathe, causing the light around her to gradually fade to black. Her legs turned to jelly. Seeing what was happening, both men rushed to her, reached out to her. With just a slight lead, Luke swept her up in his arms just before she would have hit the ground. Jason wanted to deck the guy but refrained only to keep from possibly hurting Serene.

"Over here!" Tricia called out loudly and motioned to them. She had been watching the whole incident unfold from her position beside her car. "Bring her over here. You can lay her down in my shop, where it's cool." Even though they had heard her command and both men were coming her way, Tricia continued to bark orders. "Come on now. Don't dawdle." She held the door open. "Bring her in here. You can lay her right over there." Luke eased Serene through the doorway and into the little shop. He laid her down on the couch the shop owner was indicating.

Tricia's manner could not exactly be labeled as pleasant and helpful. She was a commanding presence with her five-foot, eight-inch height and ample hourglass figure, coupled with spiked heels in a bright purple shade that perfectly matched her stylish print dress. The word *commanding* also described her take-charge way of injecting herself into the current drama playing out on her turf.

"My good and gracious Lord!" she voiced as she picked up a menu for the restaurant next door from her checkout counter and began to fan Serene with it. She sized up the two men and said to Jason, "You! Go get her a cool bottle of water out of my little fridge in the back." Her instruction allowed that he might be simple, as she pointed the way. Then she turned with a scowl to scrutinize Luke.

Luke backed away from her and stood off to the side, finding a display counter to lean on. He was slightly shaky in the wake of his adrenaline rush, although it appeared to Tricia that she was doing a good job of intimidating him. When Jason returned with the water, Tricia turned her persisting scowl on him, took the water from him, and twisted the lid off. She laid the plastic bottle on her counter and continued to gently fan Serene. "Now, honey, you'll be all right." She crooned sweetly to the unconscious woman. She continued shooting little eye daggers at both men, obviously enjoying their discomfort. "You two banty roosters should be ashamed of yourselves, over there posturing and strutting, while this poor little lady had to endure your uncivilized behavior."

Serene moaned as she began to come around. Jason immediately knelt beside her. Tricia held out an arm, as though to physically restrain him. "I can handle this. She's my wife," he firmly protested to the self-appointed protector.

"Yeah! Like you've handled it for the last two years?" Luke was fuming but knew in his spirit that it was time for him to take a back seat to the action. The Holy Spirit was coming through loud and clear, even if the shop owner's reprimands were rolling off his back. He made no move to go to Serene, or to further challenge Jason.

Refusing to take the bait of Luke's rebuke, Jason didn't respond to the scathing remark.

"Now, honey, take a little sip of this water," Tricia gently coaxed as she held the water bottle out to Serene. "You're gonna be just fine. You just got a couple of hunky guys both wanting to be your knight in shining armor," she crooned softly, rubbing Serene's shoulder from behind the couch. "There's worse positions to be in, believe me." She winked at Serene. "My advice is, you make 'em work for it. You got the upper hand here."

Serene was still in a daze but was strangely grateful for the presence of another woman. Even though Tricia's simplistic conclusions weren't helpful, her sympathetic comradery was welcomed. She lifted herself up onto one elbow and took a sip of the proffered water. Then she turned her attention to Jason's tortured face.

Talk about mixed emotions. Every emotional fiber of her being wanted to grab him, wrap her arms around him— legs too—and hold on for dear life. Her husband was alive! Common sense wouldn't let her make the reach—too many unanswered questions. "You're alive." Was it a statement of fact or an accusation? Even though the whispered remark came from her own lips, she didn't know.

He inclined his head, a slight nod. His eyes held the look of extreme pain. Serene couldn't recall ever seeing pain like that in his expression, not even when Michael died. "There's so much I need to tell you, Serene. I was on my way to the Salengers' this morning to talk to you when I saw you leaving with *this* guy." His voice held attitude at the end of the statement as he hooked his thumb toward Luke.

He reached out his hand to her. She looked at the outstretched hand and tentatively presented her own. As he took it in his and covered it with his other hand, electricity surged through her body just as it had in that library in Michigan so long ago. An anguished moan escaped her lips, and she allowed great, weeping sobs to overtake her. Jason reached out and gathered her into his arms.

Turning, Luke walked out the door of the little shop and took a deep breath, then another. After the third deep breath, he settled his hip on the ledge of a large pot housing a plumeria tree, took his phone from his pocket, and hit a speed dial number. Miranda answered on the first ring. "Luke, what is it?"

"Miranda, would you be available to pick up Serene at a little shop in town called…" He turned and looked at the sign over the door. "Trending with Tricia?"

"I know the place, on the circle. Luke, what's going on? What have you done now?" Her voice conveyed her concern and slight disapproval.

"It's not me this time, Miranda." Trying but failing to keep sarcasm out of his voice, he continued, "Jason Brigholtz just dropped back into Serene's life, in person. She's pretty shook up. She could use a female friend right now, as well as a voice of reason."

A stunned pause, then, "Dear Lord in heaven! I'll be there in ten minutes."

CHAPTER

Luke pulled into the Salengers' driveway to drop Wayne off. His friend had called him earlier and asked if Luke could give him a ride home, since Wayne's pickup had been taken from the construction site to a garage for a brake job and Miranda, having gone to help her mother with her shopping, wasn't available to pick him up. As Luke had flipped his blinker and slowed to pull into the Salengers' driveway, Jason was just pulling out in his rented SUV with Keisha in the passenger seat. Keisha smiled and waved enthusiastically at them. Wayne responded with his own wave as the two drivers exchanged distrustful scowls.

To avoid the awkwardness of the moment, Jason continued talking to Keisha about Kalaupapa, the topic they'd been discussing when they'd gotten into the car to leave. "So as I was saying, some of the lepers were thrown overboard off ships after being told to swim to the peninsula. Their only alternative was to drown in their attempt to swim to shore. If they were fortunate enough to make it, they lived out their lives there between the cliffs and the sea, never being allowed to leave. The colony wasn't closed until 1967."

Keisha wasn't fooled by her dad picking up the subject of the Molokai leper colony again, rather than talking about that scathing look he'd just given Luke Vaughn. She decided she would choose another time to bring it up to him. "I think it's great that Father Damien devoted his life to those poor folks. He had to know there was little chance of avoiding the disease himself. I don't know if I could be as devoted as he was to helping people—it's a huge sacrifice."

"I know, Keish. Rae Jean Judd told me that if God calls you to do something outstanding like that, He also provides you with the gift and anointing to be able to handle it. She and Thud love the people they minister to as much as their own family."

She sighed. "I'll be glad when the Lord tells me what He has planned for my life." She saw the look her dad gave her. "I know, I know. Don't be too anxious. He'll reveal it to me soon enough, a little bit at a time."

He smiled at his daughter, who had taken his words to heart. "Delight yourself in the Lord and He will give you the desires of your heart. I think that's in Psalm 37. In other words, just keep having a good time getting to know Him, then watch what your heart begins to desire. It's probably a good idea to keep a journal of what comes out of your times of prayer and worship. Pretty soon you'll begin to see a pattern of things that appeal to you. Those are the bread crumbs He's leaving for you, leading you to your plan."

She smiled over at him. "I love you, Daddy." And with that remark, it felt like his heart was expanding in his chest to the point that it might burst.

Keisha dragged another french fry through the ketchup and bit off the half that was smothered in the condiment. She looked up to find her dad smirking at her across the booth. "What?" She grinned back at him. "Ketchup on my chin?" She swiped at her mouth and chin with her napkin.

"I just don't recall ever seeing you enjoy a burger and fries quite so much. It's kind of fun to watch." He took a long pull on his ice tea and pushed his fork through the veggies in his half-eaten salad. "I know I've already said it several times, but I'm so sorry to have missed being a part of your life for the last couple of years, and even before that, time I wasted by being self-absorbed."

"And I've already told *you*, Dad, you're totally forgiven, by God and by me." Her eyes teared up. "Don't you think it's time we stop focusing on the past and just enjoy today and look forward to our time together tomorrow?"

A little misty-eyed himself, he reached across the table and squeezed her hand. "How did you get to be so wise at the ripe old age of fifteen?"

"Well, I *am* going to be sixteen soon, and I'm sure part of it has to be good genes." Her mischievous smile touched his heart. "But hanging out with Alani and her church friends has also exposed me to God's wisdom, plus I've been reading my Bible a lot."

"It still fascinates me that the Lord was drawing you and your mom to Himself at the same time He was working in my life, halfway around the world."

With a teary-eyed nod, her smile lit up her whole face. "Clean up your plate, Big Kahuna. I'm ready for our hike into Waipio Valley...and a shave ice."

Renting a Jeep, Jason and Keisha made their way down the steep and narrow one-lane road into the Waipio Valley. They parked the Jeep and hiked back into the basin of lush vegetation, then along the mile-wide beach, enjoying the view of hills that rose on either side of the valley in steep, cliff-walled splendor and brilliant green color. As they sat on the beach, enjoying the gorgeous 360-degree scenery, the father-daughter duo breathed the clean air and discussed the history of the valley, which had been a favorite getaway of Hawaiian kings in the past.

In the weeks since he'd arrived, they had actually discussed a large variety of things. Jason had worried that he would not know how to talk to his daughter. But at the leading of the Holy Spirit, he just talked to her as he would any adult and found that the bright teen tracked with his conversation with more intelligence than he would have credited her. To his surprise, he had found over the past couple of weeks that she enjoyed discussing many of the same topics that interested him. Discussing the things of God and what they were each discovering in the Word was a favorite topic for both of them.

Keisha had told her dad about her experience when Pastor Dawson had, without knowing who she was, singled her out and basically told her that God was not responsible for the deaths of her brother and father. Jason was not ready to go into detail about his experience on the topic of Michael's death—it was so deeply personal. But he did tell her that God had assured him that Michael was okay now and that he knew they'd all see him again someday. Somehow it was healing to be able to talk about Michael, how they both missed him. Especially taking in the sights here in Hawaii. They knew Michael would have loved being here, enjoying it with them. Jason was surprised that Keisha, too, had been working through feelings of guilt over Michael's death because of her flyaway papers on the fateful day.

They had discussed their gratitude for how the Lord had, in spite of Jason's deceitful, selfish motivation, used his disappearing act to save him from the 9/11 attack. Keisha shared other stories she had heard of folks who'd been spared by various means. Her favorite was the man whose small son had been weepy and just didn't want to go to kindergarten that day, so his dad had agreed to take him to McDonald's for breakfast if he'd then go to school afterward. The time that it took them to have breakfast had caused the dad to be late enough that he was not in the building when the plane hit.

Jason's favorite had been the changed dental appointment that had saved John Barbour's life. It was one of the first things he'd learned from Serene when they began having their discussions. John was a devout Christian. Obviously, the God factor in John's life had manifested its importance on that day. Serene had related how she and John had both puzzled over Jason's decision to make John the administrator of the financial accounts, as well as the timing of it, the day just before he'd died or supposedly died. Serene had questioned in her mind if Jason had been suicidal and wondered if John had also speculated on that, though neither had ever broached the subject with the other. She now knew that Jason had written her a letter explaining why he'd entrusted their funds to John, a letter that had been destroyed in the attack, contributing to the confusion of the last couple of years.

Sitting on the beach next to her dad and taking in their surroundings, Keisha sighed deeply. "This is such a beautiful and peaceful place. It's hard to believe that the whole island is a result of the violence of a volcano. It's awesome how God puts things together." She ran the deep-gray-, almost-black-colored beach sand through her fingers.

He murmured a response and took a long drink from his water bottle, finishing it off. Considering his daughter's words drew his attention to his present circumstances, and he wondered if God could put Serene and him back together after the violence he had perpetrated on their marriage, their family. He couldn't help but speculate if Luke Vaughn would be a factor in the answer to that question. He scrunched his water bottle, flattening it. "What do you think of this Luke Vaughn character?"

To Keisha, the question seemed to come out of nowhere. She was well aware that her parents were trying to reconcile the rift between them and decide whether they could salvage their marriage. That was surely the context of her father's seemingly out-of-the-blue query. "Character?" Her raised eyebrows asked, "Did you really just say that?"

"I'm sorry, Punkin. I guess that isn't fair. It just seems he has an inordinate interest in your mom, and yeah, I guess I'm just a little jealous." He spiked the crushed water bottle into the sand.

"Inordinate. Huh, good word, Dad. I'll have to remember that one. But back to your question—we thought you were dead, Dad. Luke is a widower and was a part of the Bible study Wayne and Miranda were having at the house. I don't have to tell you, Mom's really pretty and"—she shrugged—"Luke noticed. It kind of took off from there with a few lunch dates." She wrapped her arms around her knees, pulling them into her chest. Looking thoughtful, she went on, "He's always been nice to me. But regarding Mom, he has totally backed off since you came back. I think he's a good Christian man who wants what's best for Mom, whether that includes him or not. I'm sure he won't try to influence her decision. You know what I mean? He won't try to force anything."

She turned and looked at her dad with a knowing smile. "By the way, I saw you glare at him today when we were pulling out of the driveway. Very territorial of you, Dad."

He blushed and grinned back at her. "I guess I've got some more growing up to do. The Lord has put me through the ringer in the last several months, but it seems there's always something more I need to work on. The Judds assured me that it will always be that way until heaven, that none of us can claim to have arrived at perfection."

Keisha took a long drink from her own water bottle. "I sure would like to meet the Judds sometime. I'd like to thank them for what they've done for you. They sound like really interesting people with a lot of godly wisdom."

"That they are! And I hope to introduce you to them sometime. I want them to see what a beautiful and wise daughter I've been given."

"If it helps, Dad, I'm pulling for you. You will always be my dad, and I will always love you. You can't do anything that will change that. But I happen to think it would be ideal if you, Mom, and I could be a family again—a better family this time. I think Mom would be on board, too, if she was convinced that things would be better. She just doesn't want to sign on for more of what we used to be like, like strangers who happened to be living in the same house. With God in the center of things now, it *can* be better. I believe that with all my heart."

Jason slipped off the rock where he'd been perched and sat closer to his daughter on the sand. Slipping an arm around her shoulder and squeezing, he asked, "Will you agree with me in prayer, right now, Keish? If any two agree on a thing, the Lord has promised that our heavenly Father will do it for us."

Nodding, she bowed her head. Jason began, "Father, You have told us that if Your people on earth agree on anything, it will be done for us in heaven. Keisha and I agree, Lord, that with You in the center of our lives, we can be a better family than we were before. Lord, I take responsibility for how pitiful our family life was before, and I promise You and Serene and Keisha that I will do everything in my power—no, everything in the power that You work in me—to be the best husband and father that I can be. I thank You that the Holy Spirit inside me is willing and able to empower me to be a better man for my family. We ask You now, Lord, to help Serene to trust, not in me, but in the work You are doing in me. I also ask You, Lord, to bring about healing for both Keisha and Serene, that they will need for us to be a family again, healing that only You can provide. Lord, even if Serene decides she cannot continue in our marriage, I still ask You to heal her and give her peace, Your supernatural peace that surpasses any natural ability to understand. We ask this all in Jesus' name. Amen."

"Lord, I agree with everything Daddy prayed, and I thank You, again, for bringing him back to me, whole and brand-new." She choked up on the last words, threw her arms around his neck, and sniffing back the emotion, hugged him with all her might.

"Amen and amen," he agreed and hugged her right back.

Letting go, she swiped at her tears and wiped a sleeve across her nose. "You owe me a shave ice, Big Kahuna, so pick up those water bottles and let's go!"

CHAPTER

"Well, that was a little awkward," Luke commented as he pulled the car up near the garage and shifted into park. "You did see that look he gave me, right?"

"I saw it. I also saw your answering glare." Wayne looked at him with raised eyebrows, his expression silently saying that the door swings both ways. Quickly changing the subject, he quipped, "But hey, the good news is that Keisha has adjusted well, and it's starting to get better for Serene too. She and Jason are having some really constructive discussions, from what Serene has told us. She doesn't go into a lot of detail, but she seems more settled than when they first started having their daily talks. He comes from his hotel every weekday while Reann is here. The rule is that he can't be alone in the house with Serene, so either Reann or Keisha has to be on the premises if Miranda isn't home. That was Serene's rule. She said she would feel too vulnerable being alone with him."

Luke just nodded. Wayne felt bad for his friend; he knew that Luke had been falling for Serene and this had to be very difficult for him, but it was not going to be helpful to anyone for Luke to hold out hope, which was likely false hope.

So Wayne plunged ahead. "Although, lately I think she might be more willing to suspend that requirement. Like I said, she's more settled, peaceful even, so she must be recognizing some positive changes in him, the kind of changes only the Holy Spirit could bring about." He looked at his friend to be sure Luke didn't miss the reference to God's influence in Jason. "She is still having to deal with the pain of essentially being abandoned, but I think the Lord is starting to bring healing to her heart in that regard."

"I'm glad for Serene, then." Luke's facial expression looked anything but glad. It brought a squeezing pain to his chest to force his mouth to speak the words, but he did want her to be happy. "And for Keisha. She looked like she's pretty happy to have her dad back."

"Wow...Keisha," Wayne responded with a grin and shook his head. "When Jason followed Miranda and Serene back here that day and that little gal saw him get out of his car, she screamed like a crazed groupie spotting a rock star. With tears streaming down her face, she virtually flew into his arms. She just kept repeating, 'Daddy, Daddy,' and cried uncontrollably. She had all of us in tears—quite an emotional day."

Tell me about it! Luke thought but kept the remark to himself. He had wanted to cry uncontrollably too, but for pretty much the opposite reason.

"Speaking of Serene, she just stepped out onto the lanai." Wayne lifted a hand in greeting to her.

Luke looked over at the pergola-covered porch, partially shaded with its vining foliage and hanging planters of brightly colored flowers. He spotted the brightest one of all; in her tangerine-colored top and white shorts against her golden tanned skin, she rivaled any beauty that the flowers portrayed. She gave him a slight smile and wave. He nodded in response.

"Why don't you take a few minutes to say hello? You know, she could have ignored you and just stayed in the house, so she probably came out, hoping to talk to you. You haven't seen her since that day, have you? What's it been, three weeks?"

"Yeah, about that. I figured it was time for me to take a step back and let her sort things out. Lord knows she has enough going on without any further complications."

Wayne looked at his friend with compassion. Slugging him lightly on the shoulder, he commented, "Then don't be a complication, be a friend and go say hello."

With a lump in his throat, Luke shot his friend a "You don't know what you're asking" look, but he cut the engine, released his seat belt, and got out.

As he walked by her, Wayne squeezed Serene's arm affectionately, winked, and walked on into the house.

Right behind him, Luke approached. "Hello, Serene. You're looking well. Your color is much better than the last time I saw you." She smiled at his ability to keep things light.

"Hi, Luke. Yes, I'm feeling better than I was the last time you saw me." She gave a little chuckle. "I was more concerned for you and Jason that day. Tricia was breathing fire, and I'm pretty sure I saw her sharpening her claws."

He grinned. "She's quite a character, for sure. Although I believe she brought perspective to the whole scenario, which was likely the Lord's doing. Otherwise, there could easily have been a fistfight." They smiled at each other, but their eyes belied a mutual sadness.

"And I want to thank you for calling Miranda to pick me up too. I was so confused. It was a huge relief to see her coming through that door."

He nodded and watched the breeze pick up a few strands of her fiery red hair, sweeping it across her face. Pulling his thoughts from the desire to reach out and tuck the wisps behind her ear, he put his hands in his pockets and cleared his throat. "Um, I just gave Wayne a lift home and thought it would be impolite not to say hello." He glanced back at the driveway. "I noticed Jason was just leaving. I hope the two of you have been able to work through some things."

She sat on a patio chair, crossed her legs at the ankle, and patted the matching chair, an invitation for him to take the seat that was angled toward hers. She began, "We've had some pretty productive conversations, yes." As Luke took the other chair, she looked down at her hands, and he didn't miss the heaviness in her expression. "There's still plenty of *working through* to be done." She was thinking of today's discussion, which had brought out his affair with Jennifer, a particularly hard confession for Jason to make and for her to hear and process, although if she was honest with herself, she'd had her suspicions at that time.

Luke recognized a detour was needed, "And how is Keisha adjusting to this major change in her life?"

A smile came over her countenance that depicted a measure of relief at the shift in the conversation. "With the unfailing resilience of the young. And she has grown so much spiritually in the last couple of months. She seems to have the wisdom of an ancient scholar. The way she put it was, 'Mom, I had lost two of the three people I loved most in the world, two-thirds of my family. And now God has given my father back to me. I'm just so grateful to the Lord for that I find it hard to be upset with Daddy, even if he *has* done some things wrong.' Then, in that same wise vein, she hugged me and added, 'I know that, as his wife, it may not be that easy for you. So I will just pray for you and Daddy. It's all I can do.'"

She sighed, and then with a deep, bracing breath, she looked up at him. "And how are you doing, Luke?"

"Doing well enough…keeping busy. God is good. There's plenty of healing to go around." He shot her that beguiling half-grin, one of the things she loved about him, and it momentarily broke her train of thought.

"Now, what was it I wanted to ask you? Oh yes, I just happened to think, on the day Jason showed up, you had been about to tell me something and never got the chance. Was it something I should know about now?"

Okay, he thought, *the shock factor has been neutralized. Just tell her.* He was nodding slowly. "One of the investigators in my office had done some digging for me." He leaned forward and put his elbows on his knees, looking her in the eye. "What I had planned to tell you that day is that the information she turned up determined that Jason hadn't died in the 9/11 attacks." He paused. "Jason's appearance obviously canceled out the necessity of telling you about it."

"Oh." She paused, thinking about what he'd said. "Wow. I'm impressed with your profession, that you and your team can unearth that kind of information. How long had you known about that, Luke, before you decided to tell me?" In the question, not very well disguised, was the desire to know if his timing had been self-serving.

He didn't miss her implication. "The day I found out, I called you about getting together. I'm sorry, Serene. I hope I haven't offended you by taking it upon myself to look into your personal life, but I had a feeling that *that* might be the reason the Lord was holding me back from pursuing a relationship with you, and if that *was* the reason, no matter the circumstances surrounding his disappearance, I figured you had every right to know about it. I'm guessing Jason's disappearance on 9/11 has been a part of your discussions, so I won't go into the details, but if you ever want to read Margo's report, just say the word."

Ignoring the part about reading a report, she just sighed deeply. He noticed that she looked tired around the eyes. "I can't be offended at you, Luke. You did what you did out of concern for me. I know that." She paused, looked up at him, and her eyes misted over. "You are a very good man, Luke Vaughn, and I count it a privilege to have known you these past months." She blinked back tears and rose, signaling the end of their conversation.

He also rose and stepped closer. "I just want to say one more thing, Serene, and I say it from experience. If you decide to stay married, Jason is going to need three things from you. Besides your love, of course, which I'm thinking he never lost, he'll need your loyalty, your patience, and your trust." He reached out and took her hand; tenderness filled those caring blue/green eyes, and his voice softened. "If you, for any reason, are not willing or not able to give him those things, please let me know and I'll ask Father if I can have another go at winning your heart."

Just before her eyes misted over at his implied sentiment, blurring her vision, she caught a glimpse of the deepened color of his aqua gaze and that flirty, lopsided smile that had become so familiar to her.

He couldn't believe he was adding this last comment; it was as though the Holy Spirit had initiated it. "I was once a pretty crusty heathen." Like Jason, though he didn't add that. "And knowing full well what kind of a past I had, my Caroline was willing to take me on, and along with her love, she also pledged to me her loyalty, her patience, and her trust. I surely didn't deserve it, but just as surely, I have praised God every day for her commitment to me. It helped me become a better man." With a lump in his throat, knowing that he had just turned her over to his rival, he squeezed her hand and let it go. "Goodbye, Serene." It came out in just a whisper. Turning, he walked resolutely back to his car and out of her life.

C H A P T E R

She rolled over and looked at the digital clock: 4:47 a.m. Serene had awakened early and was now thinking about her conversation with Luke the day before. With hearing Luke's endearments, coming on the heels of Jason's confession about his affair with Jennifer, it made her feel empowered; it was a feeling that was strange to her. It was like she was just discovering that she had options. She had never in her married life thought of being disloyal to her marriage vows, but since Jason had broken the vows of that union, she believed that, scripturally, she could be released from the marriage if that was what she chose to do. So now, patching things up with Jason was just one option. Luke had as much as told her that a relationship with him was still a possibility. She was beginning to feel strong and whole as an individual and not *just* because two men showed interest in her but also because of her growth in the Lord. She had begun to realize that she was not valuable *just* because of being someone's wife or mother or potential wife material. She was valuable because Jesus loved her unconditionally and had sealed her identity in Himself as a member of the family of God.

Holy Spirit, please help me to get ahold of what You are showing me here.

As she continued to meditate, it came to her that she'd never really talked to Jason about her feelings; it had always been about what was going on with him or the children. As she considered talking to Jason now about her feelings, she began to realize that in her attempts to help Keisha and Jason work through their grief over Michael's death, she'd never really worked through her own emotions. Then, after Jason's disappearance, her whole existence had become about saving Keisha from the demon of deep grief, a sorrow that wouldn't let go. Her discussions with Miranda subsequent to 9/11 had begun to point her in the direction of the only one equipped to carry that Savior mantle that she'd been trying to carry for Keisha. So when Miranda and Wayne had invited Keisha and her to have an extended vacation with them in Hawaii, she had readily agreed. Once here, Miranda had begun to point her in the direction of her own healing, through the Word and through Christian counseling and praying with other believers. But the Holy Spirit seemed to be prompting her now to discuss her feelings with Jason.

He's always made me feel intimidated whenever I've tried to talk to him about how I feel about something...or maybe there has been a fear of being open with him that came from me. What if I did all the talking? It would be like reading a letter without his response until the end. I wouldn't even have to look at him, if that's what's necessary to stay focused on my thoughts.

"Okay, Jason, today I want to take a different approach to our discussion. I've listened while you've explained yourself, your misguided attempt to remove your misery from our lives by removing yourself. You've related how messed up you were in the months, years even, leading up to that decision. I've heard all about the way in which you facilitated your disappearance, about your subsistence period as a societal dropout, then your revival when the Judds befriended you.

I've heard how you came to be in that circular park the day you re-entered my life."

That sounds almost confrontational, Jason thought. *Serene's never displayed attitude with me before.* This was strange for him, and he wondered where it had come from and where she was going with it.

They were sitting at a right angle to each other in the Salengers' family room, Serene on the couch and Jason in an easy chair. The refreshments on the nearby coffee table that Reann had prepared went untouched and ignored. She continued, "Now I want to talk to you about how things were *for me* while you were struggling through this reinvention of yourself that you started and God finished for you."

"I'm anxious to hear what you were experiencing, Serene. Your feelings—"

"No, Jason." Her pointer finger came up, halting him. "Don't talk. Just listen. I've begun to realize that, in all our years together, you've always been about your own purpose and goals and you've never cared to hear about my feelings, unless I was discussing my support for you. I'm not entirely blaming you. I enabled you. I valued myself only as how good a wife I could be or how good a mother I could be. I now know that my value is based on who I am in Christ. And on that basis, I have a valued and secure identity…complete, because it's based on Him and His righteousness, not on any qualifications of my own." *Wow! That felt good!*

He took a deep breath and opened his mouth to speak.

"Nope." The finger had come up again. "This is not a conversation. It's a monologue. I don't want to monopolize the discussion out of any sense of deserving, but I *do* want to monopolize. I need to be able to express myself—my feelings—and if you speak, I might lose my train of thought. So please just hear me out."

He nodded at her, suppressing a smile; he didn't want her to feel patronized. Inside, he was sincerely glad that she was going to express her feelings. It was long overdue. He knew that she *did* deserve to be heard; he just hoped it wouldn't end by her deciding that she didn't need or want him in her life.

She was looking down at her hands, folded in her lap. "When Michael died, do you know what I did, Jason? Emily Markus interrupted the board meeting. She looked at me with abject pity in her eyes and said, 'Serene, it's urgent that I see you in the hallway right away. There's been an accident.' I guess that, right then, I went into the first stage of grief, denial. I said to myself, it can't be as bad as she's making it look. I'll just go out into the hallway and straighten this out. I'll be an example of how to compose yourself in these situations. Of course, when I got out into the hallway, there were two uniformed police officers there to tell me that my son was dead." She choked up a little bit as she finished that sentence. "It took just a moment for me to process what they'd said. Then I asked them if they were sure of their facts. After all, I told them, it was very upsetting to make such a statement if it, indeed, was not the case. They gave me enough details to convince me they'd *not* made a terrible mistake. So I allowed Emily to help me, and I sat down on the bench that was close behind me. It's strange what you think about in that kind of a situation. I can remember thinking, 'Why would anyone put a bench in the hallway?' I asked myself if some designer had anticipated such a need as I now had—wobbly legs that would not hold me in an upright position."

She continued in an emotionless monotone. "The female officer appeared at my side with my purse and my sweater and said they'd drive me to the hospital where he'd been taken. Apparently, he needed to be pronounced dead, then on to the morgue in the hospital's basement. The next thing I realized was that I was in the back of the police car and it was pulling out into traffic. Being the pragmatic person that I am, I realized this was the perfect time for me to lose control—the audience was limited, the car ride would be about the right time frame. I would soon be called upon to be strong for you and Keisha, so other opportunities would likely not arise. I'd better have my cry now. So I gave my mind permission to remember my beautiful little boy and the reality that I would never see him grow to be a man. I wouldn't help him pick out clothes for his first date. I wouldn't see him graduate, or get married, or become a proud father of his own children. With the sweet little-boy pictures of him that came to me, a tear slipped down my cheek. Before I knew it, I was sobbing and keening and trying not to be physically sick."

Jason sat mutely, as he'd been instructed, though the sun had the audacity to shine in through the gauzy curtains as though everything was all right. He was ashamed that he'd never before listened to Serene's details of her grief. Silent tears slid down his face.

"The next awareness I had was of the female officer holding open the car door and handing me tissues, telling me softly that we'd arrived. I was angry then, angry that I now had to be strong. My remaining family needed my strength, and all I wanted to do was collapse. I know police officers must see a wide gamut of emotions in their work, but I bet I pushed the envelope of their previous experiences. I took a deep breath, wiped my eyes, blew my nose, and forced myself to become the paragon of strength."

Her chin quivered, her vision blurred with tears that refused to be suppressed then spilled over onto her cheeks. "You never helped me through my grieving, Jason. Instead, you consumed me. I knew you were struggling with guilt along with your own grief and that the guilt just compounded the weight of your grief. But you refused to face it, refused the counseling. You rejected my attempts to talk with you about it. You put us both in a position where neither of us could heal." She sensed his movement and put her hand out like a traffic cop. "So I concentrated on helping Keisha to heal. And while I did that and you stuffed down every emotion you had, first trying booze, then the affair, our marriage spiraled into disintegration. You abandoned Keisha and me long before you walked out that door on the morning of 9/11."

Wiping her eyes and blowing her nose on the tissues she'd grabbed from the nearby table, she took a deep, ragged breath. "Our Hawaii trip, meeting Miranda, was the first ray of sunlight in my life since Michael's death. I needed the Lord's healing so badly, and I began to see, in Miranda, that she had more of God than I did, though I thought I knew Him. After we returned home, my regular phone calls with her were a lifeline to me."

"And then after 9/11…" Her voice cracked, and Jason couldn't sit quietly anymore. He rose, took two steps, and dropped down by her side on the couch, pulling her into his embrace, then onto his lap. He rocked her gently. "Shhhhh. Shhhhh. It's okay. It's okay now." He spoke softly into her ear as great racking sobs took over her body. "You were married to a hurting, angry, self-centered little boy in a man's body. You did all the giving and I did all the taking. I'm so sorry, Serene. So sorry. I was such a selfish jerk. I know I failed you, miserably." He rubbed her back and continued gently rocking her. She was openly moaning now. "It's okay, just let it out. Let it all out. I want to be strong for you now."

Reann had started into the room to ask if they wanted anything more before she left for the day. Seeing the scene before her, she quietly backtracked into the hallway, turned, and retreated to the kitchen. She grabbed her purse and quietly left through the kitchen door.

Jason just continued to hold Serene, murmuring encouragement to her occasionally and allowing her to cry. Her sobs subsided after about twenty minutes of deep anguish being cleansed from her system. He kissed her forehead and set her down on the couch next to him. He arose, handed her a few more tissues, and then poured her a glass of ice tea. Coming back, he knelt before her and wrapped her hand around the drink.

As Serene drank deeply of the refreshing liquid, Jason began, "I want to share with you an experience I had on that island, Serene. It might have been a dream, but I don't think so. I believe I was actually in heaven." She handed him the glass, which she had drained. He set it on the coffee table. Then he took both of her hands in his, leaned in close, and said, "Serene, I saw Michael."

She sat mutely, continuing her self-comforting, gentle-rocking motion as Jason shared in detail the experience he'd had, stressing that Michael was at peace and that he wanted them to be happy. "Serene, more than anything, I want you, Keisha, and me to be a family again, but I *don't* want that at the expense of your happiness." She sat very still now, just watching him. He hoped she was hearing him. "We'll all see Michael again someday, and I want to be able to tell him that we were happy, that we lived out the rest of our lives here in contentment. If that, for you, means that you can't be married to me anymore, I'll understand…and I'll not fight you in a…divorce." His mouth had gone so dry he had to choke out that last hated word. "But if you can find it within yourself to try with me to salvage our marriage, I promise I'll do everything I can, with God's help, to make it better than it's ever been."

She said nothing in response. Recognizing that she had exhausted herself, he helped her up and led her down the hallway to the bedrooms. She seemed to be in a daze, so he asked her which bedroom she was using. Her eyebrows came together as she turned and looked at him. And he realized then that she was questioning his motives. And why shouldn't she?

"Honey, you need to lie down. Here's what I'm going to do: I'm going to call Miranda and tell her our discussion was somewhat intense and that you are resting. That way, you won't be disturbed until you want to be. Then I'll pick up our dishes, take the tray to the kitchen, and leave." He could see her relax again.

"It's this one." Barely audible, she pointed out her room.

He opened the door, led her in, and sat her down on the side of the bed. He knelt before her. "Can I get you anything, maybe some ibuprofen?"

She slowly shook her head.

He slipped her sandals off, took her by the shoulders, and gently pushed her down onto the pillow, lifting her legs onto the bed. He reached for the quilt folded on the foot of the bed, unfolded it, and covered her. Kneeling next to her, he caressed her cheek, pushing hair, still damp from her tears, back off her face. "Should I come back tomorrow or give you some time?"

"Tomorrow," she whispered and closed her eyes.

"Rest now." With every fiber of his being, he resisted the strong urge to kiss her. He quietly crossed the room, looked back at her already-sleeping form, and left, softly clicking the door closed behind him.

As promised, Jason cleaned up their dishes and made the call to Miranda, who, mercifully, didn't ask for details. As he left the house, he expressed his gratitude to the Lord that he'd been given his wife's permission to return the next day.

CHAPTER

It was Thursday, and Serene had the house to herself. Miranda was working at New to Me today, and Keisha was on a day trip to Oahu with Alani and her parents. Wayne, of course, was at work. Reann had just left, after doing a preliminary prep of supper and cleaning up the kitchen. She had readied a casserole that just needed to be popped into the oven later.

Serene expected Jason anytime now, chiding herself for feeling slightly nervous about being alone with him. It wasn't the first time they'd had the house to themselves, and he had not been pushy or manipulative with her yet, so why be nervous about this visit? *Because you've begun to want a romantic relationship with him again—admit it.* She did admit it to herself. She was beginning to become attracted to this new Jason. He seemed genuinely remorseful for abandoning her and Keisha, and that remorse was intensified because it had inadvertently resulted in their believing he had died.

Since the day that Serene had broken down in front of him, she and Jason had further discussed Michael and how each had coped with his death or, in Jason's case, had neglected to deal with it at all. Serene was able to draw comfort from Jason's experience of seeing Michael in heaven. In the last couple of weeks, Jason had opened up to her about his feelings of guilt and failure, his pride that wouldn't allow him to be vulnerable with her, his fear that he'd never be a good-enough father to Keisha.

He'd also told her repeatedly that he loved her and the children, that he always had and always would, but that he would not pressure her if she chose to walk away from the marriage. He reiterated what he'd written in the note to her, the one that she'd never gotten because of the attacks. The two things that stood out to her were his admission that he didn't know how to show his love because of the poor role model his parents had been and the misery that he'd heaped on himself, not understanding about God's forgiveness of him and his need to forgive himself.

She recalled the afternoon she had lain on the bed in the guest room right here at the Salengers' house and mourned the Jason of the early years of their marriage, wanting so badly to have *that* Jason back. And the Jason who'd been meeting with her these past few weeks was even better than the early-years version. He talked about God and the things he was learning in Scripture. He had a genuine interest in Serene and her pursuits and wanted to hear Keisha's thoughts and opinions on things that were important to her. He seemed very determined to be a godly man, desiring to put his family's best interests above his career. In fact, he'd indicated he did not want to go back to investment banking, a career that had been devouring him in the years leading up to his disappearance. He had been seeking the Lord about a new direction and seemed to be patiently waiting on the plan, patience being something the old Jason could never have pulled off. And that was what was convincing her that Jason's dramatic changes weren't just the proverbial *jailhouse religion*.

The doorbell roused her from her musings. Her stomach did a little flip, reminiscent of her college years, when he was picking her up for a date. She put down the magazine that she'd been voraciously ignoring, while more evocative thoughts had fully engaged her attention.

He stood on the stoop, holding his Bible and the bright-pink flower he'd broken off a bush on the hotel grounds. He took a deep breath and tried to calm himself. In his prayer time this morning, he had whined about how much he loved her but didn't want to scare her by causing her to feel manipulated. The Lord had simply said, "Let her make the first move." He was repeating that to himself as he rang the bell.

As she opened the door, a big smile involuntarily overtook her face. He quickly returned the sentiment, his deep-blue eyes beaming at her. She breathed in the manly scent of him, mixed with the aroma of the bloom he held. "Come in, Jason." As she stood back, she asked, "Is the flower for me?"

"Oh yeah." He seemed to just now realize he was holding it. He handed it to her. "I have to admit, I pilfered it from the hotel landscaping. Its beauty reminded me of you. I couldn't resist." Wow, he thought, that sounded lame. Though she didn't reply to his remark, the roll of her eyes said that she agreed with the lame observation.

"You look great, Serene, as always." His remark followed a politely quick perusal of the outfit she'd chosen for today, a print sundress in shades of navy and teal. The hues complemented her coloring, and the fitted cut of the dress accentuated her feminine physique, still youthful and firm.

Thanking him, she turned and led the way into the family room, where a pitcher of ice tea, two glasses, and a bowl of hummus, surrounded by veggies and pita chips, awaited them on the tray resting on the coffee table.

Jason swallowed hard and tried valiantly not to leer at her, but as she walked ahead of him into the room, he couldn't help but allow himself a prolonged appreciation of her retreating curvaceous form. *Lord, help me behave myself!*

Sitting a safe distance apart on the sofa, they engaged in a few minutes of small talk. When there was a lull in the conversation, Serene quietly commented, "You've changed so much, Jason."

"This is what's changing me, Serene," he remarked, holding up his Bible. "I want to show you something." He opened the Bible and turned to the latest portion of Scripture that had been feeding his spirit.

"It's just fascinating to me that you can actually live your day-to-day life on what's in here. For instance, this second chapter of First Corinthians talks about the Holy Spirit searching out the things of God, then freely giving us those things, things that God has prepared for us beforehand. He's so good, Serene! It's wisdom the world doesn't have to give and can't produce. We have the mind of Christ! This is why I have newfound patience about the plans God has for my life. That wisdom is always going to be available to me. He's already shown me it will have something to do with finances. I can see myself helping people get out of poverty, for instance, young people coming out of foster care situations with no prospects, those being released from prison who need to transition back into honest jobs, helping Christian ministries to make the most of their funding. I don't have all the details yet, but I know my general direction, and I have total peace about it."

He held the Bible up. "This is the real treasure, Serene. I've spent my whole adult life trying to accumulate money, and no quantity of the stuff has ever satisfied me. I've found the real treasure, or I should say, He's found me."

His excitement was contagious. She didn't question where she and Keisha fit into his vision. He'd already made it abundantly clear that he wanted his family back. His face glowed when he spoke like this, and she wondered if she'd ever seen that visage on him before. She realized she'd been staring at him like a hungry pup watching his master open a can of gourmet dog food, and he'd noticed it too; recognition of her longing was reflected in his eyes. He was leaning in very slowly. His eyes, now in their stormy ocean-blue shade, moved to her lips.

Jason felt himself losing the battle to keep the visit platonic. *Direct some of that patience into this relationship, man. Let her make the first move!* The coaching came from his spirit; his flesh wanted to go full throttle.

Uncertain and intending to break the tension of the moment, Serene fumbled for her glass of tea. Slightly shaky, she tipped it over instead. "Oh!" she gasped, grabbing for napkins. "How clumsy of me!" They both mopped at the liquid that flowed across the tabletop, but when their hands inadvertently touched, she felt the sparks. Jumping up, she quipped, "Um, I'll go get a towel from the kitchen."

But as she moved around the table, the toe of her shoe caught the table leg, rattling the tray and jostling her balance. With record reaction time, strong arms caught her around the waist in a loose embrace. Instinctively, she laid her hands flat against his chest. Wow, that was a rapid heartbeat beneath her palms! She slowly ran her hands up the soft knit shirt that covered that firm, muscular torso, oblivious that she was blazing a trail of heat as she went.

Her balance was restored, but he couldn't seem to let go. His eyes were locked on hers.

She dared to raise her gaze up to meet those cobalt eyes; it was her undoing.

"Oh, Jason…" Just a whisper. Wrapping both hands around his neck, fingertips tingling in the neatly trimmed scruff at the back of his neck, she slowly pulled him in. His arms tightened around her waist. Their lips met. Fire shot through her as she was instantly transported back to their first date. She relived that first kiss. He was transported back to the last time he'd shared her bed. The kiss mutually deepened.

Coming up for air, he continued to deposit small kisses on her eyelids, her jawline, her ear. When the heat of his mouth touched the pulse in her neck, a small moan escaped from deep in her throat. It had the effect of a magnet, pulling his lips back to hers. He thoroughly lost himself in the pleasure of the moment, until it abruptly ended as she pushed him away.

He stood stunned, drawing in a ragged breath as Serene backed away, putting several paces between them. "I'm sorry, Jason," she protested from behind her outstretched palm, tears springing into her eyes. "I had a sudden image of you kissing *her* like that." She hesitated, then shook her head. "I don't think I know how to live with the possibility of that kind of betrayal happening again."

She was remembering what Luke had told her, that for a reunion to work, Jason would need her love, loyalty, patience, and trust. Love him, she could and did. Loyalty and patience, she could give him, but she wasn't sure she could trust him not to betray her again with another woman. Her stomach clenched. It hurt just to look at him. So she turned her back to him.

"Serene, I…"

"No!" Then softer. "Just leave, Jason…please."

Silently he picked up his Bible and walked slowly to the door.

That night, after Keisha had happily regaled her mom and the Salengers with a synopsis of her day trip to Oahu, she kissed her mother good night and went to bed. Before Miranda went to bed, she had offered Serene a friendly ear if she wanted to talk about her obviously pensive mood. Serene had turned her down, opting instead for an encouraging hug from her good friend and a promise to talk later. She went to her room. Sitting on the edge of the bed, she bit back the tears that she'd been holding on to since Jason had left. *Okay, I'll give myself fifteen minutes to cry over this, then...no! No more of that kind of quick fix, which never really resolved anything anyway. What really works is to pray it through, talk to the Holy Spirit about it, and then allow His wisdom and love to surround you.*

She decided to get ready for bed first. In the adjoining bathroom, she completed her bedtime ritual, then settled into bed with her Bible to read a chapter or two before she prayed. Her silky ribbon bookmark directed her back to where she'd been reading in Second Corinthians. When she came to the second verse of chapter 7, the apostle Paul coaxed, "Open your hearts to us. We have wronged no one, we have corrupted no one, we have cheated no one." Wait a minute! What was he saying? She reached for the heavy concordance on the lower shelf of the nightstand and pulled it up onto the bed. She was sure this was the same zealot who'd harassed Christians, arrested them, and even oversaw their executions, for no more wrongdoing than just believing in Jesus. How could he say he'd wronged no one?

She searched the big reference book for her answer. She found the passages in the book of Acts, chapter 8, how Paul ruthlessly persecuted the early Christians. With her finger on the page in Acts, she looked up and asked, "So what about that, Lord? How can he claim that he's wronged no one?"

Read on. The man you're talking about died on the road to Damascus. There, he received his forgiveness and had no more consciousness of sin. Old things passed away and all things became new.

She did read on to confirm what she'd heard. She basked for a few minutes in the fact that she'd clearly heard the voice of the Holy Spirit in her heart. She meditated on what the apostle Paul's transformation meant for him and to the people he influenced. It didn't take her long to make the connection, to see what the Lord was saying to her personally. The same thing Paul had experienced applied to Jason. The old Jason died on that remote, nameless island in the Atlantic. Why should she have any more consciousness of his past sin or, God forbid, expect *him* to be reminded of it? She looked over at her clock: 11:17 p.m. She didn't care. She needed to get this thing settled. She picked up her cell phone and dialed his number.

Jason answered on the first ring, having seen her ID come up on his phone. "I've been in discussion with the Lord, Jason." She dived right in. "I need to talk to you as soon as possible. Can I meet you for breakfast at the restaurant in your hotel, say, 9:00 a.m.?"

"Absolutely. I can be there earlier if you want, or I can come to you." He focused on her "discussion with the Lord" comment. It alleviated some of his trepidation of what she wanted to talk about. Earlier that day, after leaving the Salengers' house, he'd spent a short time fretting over how the encounter with Serene had ended. Then he'd turned the situation over to God. After praying in tongues for several minutes, he allowed the Lord to wrestle the matter out of his hands. "I'm letting go of it, Lord. You know what *I* want, but You've already made me see that You won't violate Serene's free will, nor should I." If she couldn't forget his infidelity, he had to accept that. It hadn't been easy to resign himself to that, but he'd gotten peace about it when he finally did release it to the Lord. Whatever she'd concluded, he accepted that things would be all right, even if he had to go on with his life without her in it.

"Nine," she repeated into the phone, "at your hotel. See you then."

She disconnected the call. This was not something to discuss on the phone.

C H A P T E R

Jason was thoroughly enjoying his morning showers these days. *I never thought I'd have such an appreciation for hot water and plentiful soap,* he thought. What a luxury! One he'd never again take for granted after bathing in the cool water of the small creek with the other men of the village all around him. After much prodding, the Judds had finally gotten the villagers to agree to the women and children bathing first in the small section of the stream graced with a moderately-sized waterfall, where the water was knee-deep, and then when they'd all returned to the village, it was the men's turn to have their bath. And they still had to be watching for water snakes and leaches the whole time and share the few slivers of soap that were available. Then there was the matter of dental hygiene. Although the bark from the neem tree with its natural healing properties had done a satisfactory job of cleaning teeth, having a toothbrush and toothpaste was another luxury he often thanked the Lord for these days.

Dressed, shaved, and slightly on edge, he arrived in the lobby and claimed a chair where he could watch the door at 8:45 a.m. She walked into the hotel at 8:55. He immediately got up and approached her, giving her a tentative smile, but was unable to read her face. "Good morning, Serene."

She nodded, gave him a brief smile, and gestured toward the large entryway to the hotel's restaurant. "Let's have some breakfast. I'm starving."

When they'd been seated at a small table for two in the middle of the busy dining room, she wondered about the location she'd chosen. Perhaps something more private would better serve her purpose, but she really was hungry, having eaten next to nothing last night at supper. *Oh well,* she thought. The Lord could handle this, no matter the setting.

"You wanted to talk?" he asked as soon as the waitress had taken their orders, filled their coffee cups, and moved on.

"I don't want to be interrupted by the waitress, Jason. Let's have our breakfast, then we can talk."

He nodded, but inside he wondered if she was going to break his heart and if that experience might be better processed on an empty stomach.

"Keisha had a great time on Oahu yesterday." A safe topic for light conversation. "They did the circle-the-island day tour, a lot of sightseeing and historical information. She loved it. She's always been interested in history."

"I know," he replied. "She called me last evening and talked about it for almost an hour. Maybe we could all go over there sometime and spend enough time to really appreciate it." He realized that what he'd just said presumed that they would be doing things together as a family in the future. He watched for a reaction from her, but she gave no hint.

While they ate their breakfast, they continued to talk about Keisha, about how good the food was, about the Salengers and island points of interest; everything was kept on a superficial, nonconfrontational level. After the dishes had been cleared and cups refilled one last time, she opened with…

"So the apostle Paul told these folks in the seventh chapter of Second Corinthians, 'I have wronged no one.'"

Say what? That was strange, but over the years, she had occasionally done this, just began to speak her mind, even if it did sound like it was coming out of the wild blue yonder. He'd always thought it was kind of cute. "Okaaay." He dragged out the word to relate his confusion about where she was coming from and where this conversation might be headed.

Rather than explain herself, she just continued her thought. "Now, the comment kind of struck me as being less than honest since the man Saul, who persecuted the Christians in the book of Acts, is the same man that we know as the apostle Paul."

He nodded slowly, trying to follow her logic. "Yup, same man."

"So first, I got my concordance and found where it was written that he'd done those heinous things—arresting people, stoning them, executing them. It's chapter 8 in Acts, by the way."

He nodded again and let her keep talking, hoping that eventually he'd find the point in her discourse.

"So I asked the Lord, politely, since I know the apostle Paul is one of His big guns. You realize he wrote about two-thirds of the New Testament, right?"

Jason nodded again, a slight grin at the "big guns" observation. "I am aware of that."

"So I asked Him what's up with that 'wronged no one' comment. How can he say that?" She leaned forward a little and lowered her voice just slightly as though this part was confidential. "And I heard the Holy Spirit say, 'That man died on the road to Damascus. He was forgiven, and he had no more consciousness of sin. All things had become new for him.'"

Jason was mesmerized now; it thrilled him that she'd received revelation of the Word directly from the Holy Spirit, and he was fascinated to hear where she was going with this.

To his surprise, she reached out and covered his hand where it lay on the tablecloth. "And then, Jason, I realized what he was saying to me." Her fingers briefly caressed the back of his hand. "He was telling me that *you* had died on the road to Damascus, and who was I to remind *the new you* of your past sin when He has made all things new for you? And if the Lord can trust the apostle Paul after what he'd done, who am I to withhold my trust from you, the *new* Jason?"

He blinked a couple of times. *Would she make a grown man cry, right here in public?* The lump in his throat, moisture in his eyes, and burning in his nostrils were his answer—yup, she would.

She clenched it with her next comment, a question, actually. "So, Jason, the *new* Jason," she clarified, "will you marry me?" A slow grin mischievously played across her face. "I don't have a diamond ring for you, but I have love and loyalty. I'll have patience and…trust. I've made a decision to trust you, Jason."

Both of them were teary-eyed now. Jason sniffed, rose from his chair, and took the two steps his long legs required to reach her side of the small table. He took her hand and raised her from her chair, the napkin drifting from her lap to the floor. He pulled her close and whispered in her ear, "Yes, my beautiful Serene, I'll marry you—again."

He lifted her in a bear hug and twirled her around as she giggled like a schoolgirl. By now, everyone in the dining room had stopped what they were doing and watched them. When Jason realized they had an audience, he smiled and announced to the crowd, "She just proposed to me…and I said yes!" Applause, whistles, and cries of "Congratulations!" broke out in the place.

Somewhere in the back of the dining room, a chant began: "Kiss, kiss, kiss, kiss, kiss!" It picked up in volume, accompanied by fists hitting tabletops. Utensils, jumping with the impact, added a jingle to the chorus. Serene blushed openly, but Jason knew he had to accommodate their spectators, since he'd made the happy announcement to the roomful of strangers. He grinned at her and lowered his lips to meet hers. He kept it long enough to satisfy his audience, but chaste enough so as not to embarrass Serene any further. Her smile told him it had been just right. The warmth of pure joy began in his belly and spread throughout his being.

*****

Luke pulled his damp T-shirt back over his head. Having gone straight to his bedroom upon returning from his run, he'd just shed the shirt and his running shoes and socks when he was rudely interrupted by his doorbell. His running shorts would have been next, as he was headed for the shower. Who would be ringing the doorbell at seven fifteen on a Sunday morning? The bell repeated its demand for response. If it was old Mrs. Claxton, his nosy neighbor, maybe he should leave the shirt off. He was in no mood for the gossipy woman this morning. He might be able to shock her into keeping her distance by appearing at the door in nothing but his speedos. But as he checked the peephole, there was no nosy neighbor; it was his brother who stood there, waiting to be admitted.

They were both early risers, both having developed the habit in the military, so the early hour for a fraternal visit was not surprising. He jerked the door open. "This better be good. I was just about to get in the shower."

"No problem. I was just about to locate your spare key and let myself in. In fact, you should shower, because I am about to invite you to blow off church and go fishing with me, and I don't want you to stink—it would scare the fish."

What Caleb was not saying was that he'd made the last-minute plan because he'd noticed that Luke had been uncharacteristically quiet around the office lately, and being focused on the Steele case was not a credible excuse for the social withdrawal, even though that had been what Luke alleged. Then it had finally occurred to Caleb that Luke might be struggling because it was coming up on the anniversary of the date of Caroline's death. It had been four years ago today, and all too fresh in Caleb's mind now was the night he had gotten the call from his distraught brother from an emergency room. He'd immediately left the poker game he'd been play-ing with his buddies and spent the next full week at Luke's home, sharing in his grief, because being there to share it was all he could do. He had no clue how to alleviate the pain; he could only pray that his brother wouldn't self-destruct. After a week, Luke had kicked him out, assuring Caleb that he would *not* commit suicide and that he *would* stay in touch.

"Oh yeah…where're you going fishing?"

Realizing that his brother had responded to him, and detecting no despondency in his voice, he came back with his reply, "Milolii Village. My buddy Zeke can get us hooked up with a boat and fishing guide, no prior notice needed. He's got an in with the locals. My mouth is watering for some parrotfish, not to mention a day of fishing without the whole touristy atmosphere."

"Sounds great, Caleb." A genuine response. "And I'd love to join you, but I'm on the schedule for security this morning. I'm not going to blow that off."

"Come on, Luke! You know they've got plenty of guys to cover for you. It's not like the other five or six guys can't handle whatever may come up. Surely, one of them can quick-draw his weapon if a kid sticks gum to the bottom of his seat." He chuckled at his own joke. With a more serious look, he added, "Besides, this might be a good day for you to have a pleasant distraction."

What was that supposed to mean? Caleb couldn't know about Serene and Jason's renewal of their marriage vows, could he? No. He knew nothing about them, and Luke was confident that Margo would not have said anything. And even she didn't know his motive behind wanting the information on Jason. Caleb's meaning suddenly dawned on him.

Sinking down onto the arm of an easy chair, he addressed his brother. "Caleb, I appreciate your sentiment, really. You are one of the most emotionally challenged people I know, so for you to show concern for me on *this* particular date is commendable. But I'm not a person to be hung up on anniversaries. Just because Caroline died on August 22nd doesn't mean that I hurt anymore on this date each year than on any other day. *Whenever* I think about her, there's pain, no matter the date. I work through it. The Lord helps." He paused for a deep sigh. "So go, enjoy your fishing trip, and tell Zeke I said hi. It sounds great, and I hope you invite me again sometime. And if you snag one of those parrotfish—what do the locals call them, uhu?—save me a hunk of it. I've never tried it, but I've heard it's really good."

After some further coaxing, Caleb agreed to go ahead without him, and as he prepared to leave, the brothers shared a brief hug. "I love you, bro, but ugh, go take your shower, man."

An affectionate slap alongside the head escorted Caleb out the door. "And by the way, bro, remind me to talk to you soon about Margo's Frasier Crane file. It's still not something to be discussed around the office, but you and I need to talk about promoting Margo. She did a fantastic job of research on that one. We've obviously not realized her full potential." Caleb was nodding even as he backed away toward his pickup. "See ya later! And seriously, man, thanks for stopping."

C H A P T E R

It was a beautiful, breezy Sunday morning following on the heels of Jason and Serene's pivotal breakfast on Friday. Having stayed on after the second morning service, they were in church to renew their marriage vows before Pastor Dawson, with Keisha as maid of honor, Miranda as a bridesmaid, and Wayne Salenger filling the best man slot. Along with the pastor's wife, that was the extent of the guest list. Specifying no gifts, Miranda had planned a small reception for them at the Salengers' home on the upcoming Wednesday evening. The guests for that evening were to consist of the few people the Brigholtzs knew on the island. When Wayne had told Luke Vaughn about the vow renewal and the Wednesday-evening reception, to which he was being invited, Luke politely declined, citing a prior commitment. When Wayne had asked, the way he had explained it was, "I'm committed to being anywhere but there." Wayne understood and excused him.

The second service had concluded about an hour ago, and the church had emptied of congregants except for a few stragglers, those involved in various help ministries who sacrificed their time to serve on Sunday mornings and thus were the last ones out the door. This particular Sunday, Luke Vaughn walked out the back entrance while exchanging friendly banter with another security team member and a man from the counting team. The two security guys had waited while the offering had been counted. The other security person would now accompany the counting team member to the bank to make the deposit drop. They said their goodbyes, and Luke went his separate way across the parking lot to his vehicle.

Jason alighted from his SUV, where he'd gone to retrieve the box with his boutonniere and Serene's bouquet. There was only one other vehicle, a dark-gray pickup, in this part of the parking lot, now that most everyone had left. It was just two spaces over from his own vehicle, and when he'd come out a few minutes ago, he had thought the truck looked familiar, but couldn't quite place it. Now, as the truck's owner approached it and held the car keys out, prompting the *chirp chirp* sound of the unlocking door, he knew why it was familiar—Luke Vaughn's truck.

"Brigholtz." The begrudging greeting came.

"Vaughn." The response held matching attitude.

They sized each other up for a moment. Luke noticed the florist's logo on the box the other man held. He thought about how pretty a plumeria bloom would look in her gorgeous red hair, perhaps pulling it back behind just one delicate ear. *Don't go there,* he silently prompted himself.

Luke slowed his steps. "Look, Jason, I'm actually glad I ran into you. I feel like I owe you an apology for the slamming-against-the-light-post thing, as well as…" He paused, searching for the right wording. "Remarks that I made." *That'll have to do it, Lord. I don't know what else I can honestly say to the guy.*

"Hey, I understand that with your police background, I probably did look like a stalker, so no offense taken. I also apologize that my actions put Serene in the awkward position she was in—the whole dating one guy while unknowingly still married to another. I appreciate that you didn't push the issue. We've needed the time to work through things."

Luke slowly nodded, but his expression remained serious. As he opened his pickup door and put one foot up to get in, he stopped and looked at the other man over the roof of his truck's cab. He couldn't resist one last prod. "Be good to her. I tracked you down once. I can do it again." His defining half-grin didn't quite reach his eyes. He finished climbing into the vehicle and closed the door, started the truck, and glanced over his shoulder as he pulled out. The *groom* was just standing there, watching him. *One more reason to hate this date,* Luke thought.

Jason fought his emotions. *That was uncalled for. She's my wife—has been all along. What makes him think he gets to monitor my conduct with my own wife?*

Leave it be, son. He's speaking from more hurt than you know of.

As he drove away from the church, Luke thought, *Too bad it's too late to catch up with Caleb and Zeke.* He realized he was craving a drink; more than that, he was actually contemplating where he might go to get one. *Call Al.* He knew where that thought originated. He ignored it. *There's a little dive a couple of miles from here where I can get a greasy burger, and they have no qualms about serving liquor on Sunday.* He knew that giving place to that thought was just being argumentative with his friend the Holy Spirit. The admonition came again. *Call Al.* His employee and good friend was a sponsor in AA. Early in their friendship, Luke had discussed with Al his days of rampant drinking after getting out of the service. The older man had congratulated him for kicking the habit with the Lord's help and without joining any support group, but also had told him to call anytime if he ever felt the need to talk to someone.

Remember the day you told Me to let you know if you were veering off course? Back there in that parking lot, you let your flesh lead you, and it opened a door to the enemy. Now, if you really want to live before Me in an honorable way, call Al! Luke pulled his truck over into the parking lot of a gas station and pulled his phone from his pocket. He hit speed dial and called Al.

*****

Jason stood in front of the mirror in the men's room of the church and tied the bold-colored, Hawaiian-print tie that he'd borrowed from Wayne, who stood a few feet away, the only other occupant of the facility. This was the last-minute inspection before the ceremony. "I don't deserve this. I'm so grateful to the Lord for all that He's done for me, including helping Serene to get beyond my betrayal of her, but I keep thinking I don't deserve this."

Wayne, leaning against the doorframe with his arms folded over his chest and one leg crossed over the other, smiled at the image of Jason in the mirror. "Of course you don't. But that's what grace is all about. We've all done things that preclude God's goodness toward us, but He forgives and blesses us anyway. He can't do otherwise. It's a part of who He is. The problem comes when we are stupid enough to think that we *do* deserve His grace."

Jason turned and looked at him with appreciation. "Wayne, I know I've mentioned it before, but I want to be sure you know how grateful I am to you and Miranda for being such good friends to my girls. Serene's friendship with Miranda has been a real lifeline to her. I'm eternally grateful to the two of you for your generosity and Christian kindness to them."

"It was no problem. Just doing what's right because it's right. And we've greatly enjoyed having them with us."

Since they were alone and had a few minutes, Jason dared to address the question to Wayne that he'd wondered about for a while now. "Is today a little bit hard for you, Wayne? I mean, it's obvious that you and Luke Vaughn are pretty good friends. It's just as obvious that Luke has developed feelings for my wife." This morning's encounter in the parking lot was still fresh in his mind. "You must have supported him in his desire to see this thing take another direction." Jason ran a small comb through his already perfectly styled hair as he eyed the other man in the mirror.

Okay, then, Wayne thought. *Cards all on the table.* Looking Jason right in the eye, he didn't hesitate to respond, "Yes, Luke is a very good friend. I've known him for years, and there's no better person I could hope to have for a friend. I am completely supportive of him, as he would be of me. You're also right about Luke's feeling for Serene. To be perfectly candid, he was falling in love with her. These last few weeks have been painful for him, and it's hard for me to watch him hurting."

Jason hung his head; he felt small, humbled, just one more person—make that two—who'd been hurt by his selfish, sinful decisions.

"However, Jason, as to your question about today being hard for me, no, it isn't. This is the outcome God intended. I know that. And by the way, Luke knows it too. He had begun to back off *before* you showed up on the scene, because he's a man who's sensitive to the voice of the Holy Spirit and has the integrity of instant obedience to that voice. Under other circumstances, I'm convinced that *you* and Luke could have been good friends. Like I said, there's no better friend a person could hope to have."

Jason nodded thoughtfully, remembering the day in the park with remorse; his jealousy and animosity toward Luke had nearly resulted in physical blows. Yet today Luke had put forth an effort to be gracious about the whole thing.

A few minutes later, the wedding march rang out in the sanctuary, played skillfully by Mrs. Dawson, as the wedding party all came forward down the center aisle—first Wayne and Miranda, followed by Keisha, then Jason and Serene. No hard-and-fast rules of ceremony were being employed since the situation was far from the norm. Serene, dressed in a new cream-and-soft-yellow-colored Hawaiian-print sundress and carrying her bouquet of tropical blooms, beamed up at her husband/husband-to-be. In his dark-gray dress pants, white shirt, and borrowed tie, he'd never looked better, Serene thought to herself. She was just as thrilled today as she had been as a college girl, the first time she'd pledged herself to him. The look he returned to her was filled with love, humility, and gratitude. She drank it all in. The love had been in his eyes the first time they did this, although she didn't recall noticing humility and gratitude that other time. Yup, she liked this new Jason—a lot.

That Sunday evening, with a new sense of their being a married couple, Serene joined Jason in his hotel room. They hadn't had any alone time since they'd made their announcement the previous Friday. By the end of the upcoming week, the three Brigholtzs planned to fly out together to return home to New York. The arrangement was that Serene would stay with Jason at his hotel room while Keisha would continue as a guest with the Salengers for those last few days on the island.

When Jason came out of the bathroom dressed for bed, in plaid flannel pajama bottoms and a T-shirt, Serene stood next to the bed, looking slightly nervous in her silky, new champagne-beige nightgown and robe—Miranda hadn't been able to resist just that one gift. The lingerie fell a few inches above her knees, showing off her shapely legs. He drank in the sight of her. Her fiery hair was unconfined by any accessories, skimming her shoulders in soft curls. Those sparkling, jewel-toned golden-brown eyes held his own in a tentative smile. He held her gaze as he crossed the room.

Serene tensed slightly as Jason reached out to embrace her. Beneath his hands, he felt her marginal resistance and saw uncertainty in her eyes. He buried his hand in her soft hair and gently tugged her closer. "It's all right, Serene," he whispered in her ear. "I can sleep on the sofa tonight. There's no need to hurry anything." He hesitated a moment. "If I can help you work through your doubts, I will. We'll talk about it in the morning." Letting her go, he reached behind her to take a pillow from the bed, kissed her forehead, and headed for the sofa in the sitting area of the room.

Her heart pounded. She had thought she was rid of her concerns about another woman. Why was she having these doubts now?

You've pledged him your trust, daughter. Take your thoughts captive to the obedience of Christ.

He plopped the pillow onto the sofa, which was perfectly comfortable for sitting, though he wasn't so sure about sleeping on it. *Come on, Jason, you slept on a straw pallet in a bamboo hut for almost two years.* He grabbed an afghan from the back of the sofa, and just as he was about to lie down, he heard her soft voice. "Jason…"

He turned back to her and watched as she switched off the bedside lamp, slipped out of the sheer robe, and dropped it on the foot of the bed. Moonlight from the window backlit the room, accentuating the curves of her silky silhouette. Her soft invitation reached out to him. "Come to bed, Jason. I just want to cuddle."

CHAPTER 30

Jason sat in front of his computer screen in the room they had designated as his office. The new house was perfect for them; it was spacious and had been recently renovated. It was in a great neighborhood in Spring Lake, a suburb of Grand Rapids, and just a few blocks from Keisha's new school. He was surrounded by paperwork relating to his newly established 501(c)(3) foundation that would be aiding various individuals and organizations with finances, financial planning services, and financial management training. He already had several donors on board to help fund and operate the endeavor. When John Barbour, for one, had heard about it, he did not have to be solicited; he was anxious to assist Jason, whose testimony of transformation had so greatly impressed him. In fact, John had become a good friend to Jason, who was impressed with the wisdom with which John had managed the funds Jason had turned over to Serene before his disappearance. The sharp downturn of the market after 9/11 had had minimal effect on Jason and Serene's investments and on John's own, thanks to the man's astute handling.

As Jason studied the document on the screen from the Judds' missionary group, Serene walked into the little office dressed in a soft-yellow sweater and tan dress slacks, a complementing, multicolored scarf artfully tied at her neck. "How's it going?" she asked, coming up behind him. She began to gently massage his neck and shoulders.

Moaning with pleasure, he turned in his swivel chair and pulled her onto his lap. "Serene." He spoke it reverently, gently pulling the colorful scarf away from her neck and planting a kiss on the soft flesh beneath, breathing in the scent of her and enjoying the feel of goose bumps his lips had prompted. "Have I ever told you that you are perfectly suited to your name?"

"I believe you've mentioned it a few times before." A few dozen was more like it.

"You have the calming appearance of a smooth-as-glass lake bathed in warm sunshine. Your scent is like a breath of fresh mountain air kissed by spring flowers. Your voice reminds me of a tinkling brook and sweetly singing birds. You are a delight to all my senses."

Latching onto each of his earlobes, she playfully squeezed until she got the grimace of pain she was looking for. "Okay, buster, you want something. What is it?"

He grinned impishly. "Nope, nothing. Just trying to accumulate points to store up for future access." She released his ears. "But you came in here for something. Was it just to bless me with your serenity, or did you have another purpose?"

Her expression turned serious. "Well, you know how I've been feeling a bit icky lately? I've made a doctor's appointment, with that general practitioner the neighbor Mrs. Henley recommended. It's for this afternoon at two. I just wanted to let you know."

"I'm coming with you." He said it quickly and sternly, before she could proclaim that she didn't need to be con- cerned. He *was* concerned. He knew his wife well enough to know that she always made light of her own needs, so if she felt that she needed to see a doctor, he wanted to be there to be sure she didn't downplay it.

He breathed deeply of the somewhat-stale air in the third-floor doctor's office waiting room. Jason was indeed waiting, nervously waiting for Serene to come out from her examination. She had adamantly refused to let him go in the examining room with her, due to the discussion of female things, she'd said, which might be sensitive and therefore embarrassing for him. She'd been nauseous lately, had little appetite, and tired easily. There had certainly been a lot of stressors in her life recently. For one, the lawyers getting everything settled up with Jason's return to the ranks of the living, including the legal battle to clear his name of any criminal acts regarding his disappearance. That had been stressful for them all, but thank God, it was all settled now, with no charges leveled against him. Then the move from New York back to Michigan, getting Keisha settled into a new school. But even so, it was so unlike Serene to lack physical energy.

He wavered between trusting God for her healing and worrying that some serious malady had overtaken her body from all the tension in her life over the past few years, all of which was traceable back to him. He knew better than to revisit the bad decisions and selfish behavior that marked his past. Sin consciousness was a slap in the face to the Savior, who'd removed his sin from him, as far as the east is from the west.

He sat with his elbows on his knees, his head bowed in silent prayer, trying to ignore the conversations of others in the waiting area, and so he didn't notice when she came out into the reception area until he heard her voice settling up with the doctor's clerical staff. He looked up. When she turned toward him, he stood abruptly and began to approach her. She met him halfway across the room. "It's okay, I'm ready to go now." The smile she gave him was weak. She kept her head lowered.

"Serene?" he pressed her. "What is it? What did the doctor say?"

"Let's go, Jason," she said quietly, settling her purse strap onto her shoulder and glancing around the reception room. "I don't want to discuss it here. Let's just head to the elevators, then we can talk."

Leaving the office, they walked several yards down the hall, and when they'd almost reached the elevators, Jason stopped her, looked at her expectantly. "There's no one around us, Serene." When she acted like she'd walk on, he stressed, "Stop! I want to know what you found out in there. Are you all right, sweetheart?"

Past the elevators at the end of the hall was a bench, tastefully padded with nubby fabric that coordinated with the muted-blue wall color. It was located under a tall narrow window. She pointed it out. "Let's sit down over there for a minute, Jason."

He took her arm and gently urged her toward it. The lump in his throat was growing. He had trouble drawing a deep breath. Just as they sat down, the sun appeared from behind a cloud and poured through the window behind them, bathing them in warmth and light. Jason felt like God was telling him, "I've got this, don't worry."

She sighed deeply, looked him in the eye. "Jason, there's been a lot going on in our lives lately. Dr. Montrose pointed out what I already knew, that stress can be a causative factor in the abnormality or interruption of the monthly cycle. So I didn't question it when mine became irregular, then stopped altogether a couple months ago."

He could barely breathe now. He certainly wouldn't let the word *cancer* come out of his mouth and tried not to let it permeate his thoughts. "Did the doctor find something else that would have caused...uh, *that* problem?"

"Yes." A slight pause. "Jason, when I thought you were gone—had died—I went off the birth control pills." I had discussed it with my gynecologist back in New York, and she agreed that it might be a good time to give my body a rest from the pills. It's still controversial whether or not the pill has negative side effects, so it just seemed the prudent thing to do."

He looked at her intently. "What is it, Serene? What are you telling me?"

"We've been busy, Jason. I would think of it, but then it would slip my mind again." She was looking at him, intently now. "I never got a refill of the prescription." She shrugged her shoulders. "I'm pregnant."

His face drained of all color. "Wha...wha...*that's* why you've been so tired, queasy, no appetite?"

"Those are pretty common symptoms with early pregnancy, Jason. You should remember that."

"It's been a long time, Serene." His head was turned. His voice was small. He was thinking of Michael. Was it disloyal to Michael to have another child, to love another child, to replace Michael with another child? It didn't occur to him that the sad demeanor on his face was sending a wrong signal.

She bit her lip. "You're not happy about this. I was concerned that would be your reaction."

"Oh, babe, I'm sorry." He reached for her hand, kissed it, and held it tightly between his own. "I was remembering you pregnant with Keisha, then pregnant with Michael, then Michael...gone." He swallowed against the lump in his throat. "My head knows it's all right for us to be pregnant again, to be happy again, to love and enjoy a new baby..." He held her eyes now, moisture in his. "But my heart almost wants to apologize to Michael. Does that make any sense?" He waited for her answer, then shook his head and answered his own question. "Of course it doesn't."

They were both quiet a minute, considering what he'd said about Michael. Then Serene voiced what the Holy Spirit had just spoken into her spirit. "Should we apologize to Michael for continuing to love Keisha? Or maybe we should be sorry for finding a love for each other like we've never had before, a love that allows the Holy Spirit to lead us, one that has resulted in a conception that has nothing to do with replacing our beloved Michael?"

He looked thoughtful at his wife's sage comment, then scooted closer to her on the padded bench, took her in his arms, and hugged her for all he was worth. "Oh, Serene, I love you so much. I'm so relieved that you aren't sick. And I'm absolutely delighted that the Lord has chosen to bless us old folks with another child."

To seal his declaration, he smothered her face with little kisses. She chuckled, then began to laugh full out. Then the laughter turned to crying, softly at first, then uncontrolled, gulping sobs. She pushed him away and groped for her purse. "I need a tissue!" She sobbed, pitifully, thrusting her purse at him in a further demand for help.

"Honey?" He unzipped the bag and fumbled inside until his hand happened on the vital, lifesaving softness of the small packet. He brusquely ripped open the plastic and yanked several tissues from their confinement, mangling most of them as they emerged.

She managed to blow her nose on the mangled mess of tissues he handed to her. She then deposited the used, along with the unused, back into the purse, the good, the bad, and the ugly, converging together within its depths. *Yuck* would define the expression on his face as Jason pulled the zipper closed on the disorder. With little gasps of breath, she regained enough control to whine, "I love you too, Jason, and I'm not old!" The sobbing began again as she melted into the embrace he offered.

Epilogue

The agreed-upon time for the visit was 6:30 p.m. It was right at 6:20 when Jason pulled the SUV into the circular drive at Perennial Gardens Assisted Living in Port Huron and slowed to a stop under the front portico of the facility. From the drive, the beautiful gardens overlooking Lake Huron gave off a golden glow in the early-evening sun, sun that had not arrived by traversing the huge expanse of the lake, since this was known as the sunrise side of Michigan's lower peninsula. Nevertheless, the receding sunlight was beautiful, the scene was peaceful, the cool early June breeze held the watery scent of the lake, and Jason exuded an excited hopefulness; it would be so satisfying if Ellen Devereau would be tranquil enough to receive her visitors. He and Callie had been warned by her daughter, Sharon, that sometimes the Alzheimer's patient would become agitated and even combative with unfamiliar visitors, feeling threatened by them.

Keith alighted from the front seat of the SUV and opened the back passenger door for Callie and Serene. He offered a helping hand to his wife as she alighted from the vehicle, then did the same for Serene. The delightful, newest member of the Brigholtz family, eight-month-old Judd Michael, was at home in Spring Lake, holding court for his adoring sister, three cousins, and Mrs. Henley, the middle-aged neighbor lady who loved kids and was delighted to stay with them for a few hours.

"We'll wait for you in the lobby," Serene assured Jason. "You and Callie will want to go in together, if you're able to see her."

Jason nodded, admiring his wife and thinking how quickly she'd regained her figure after Judd was born. When all the doors had been closed, he proceeded to the section of the lot where he could park the vehicle. Locking the doors and pocketing the key, he breathed deeply of the brisk lakeside air as he walked back to the entrance. It felt good to be back in Michigan. He was glad he and Serene had decided to bring Keisha back here to make their home after leaving New York. You could pick your pace here, like spending weekends *up north*, as the Michiganders referred to the northern part of the state, which was more geared to hunting, fishing, boating, camping, and just plain relaxing. He was getting to know his family again—or perhaps for the first time. The Revelle family had come from Indiana to spend a couple of weeks of the summer vacation with them, and the plan was to take in a lot of *up north* experiences while they were here.

There was a clean, modern sitting area for guests just inside the entrance of the assisted-living facility, and Jason's wife, sister, and brother-in-law had made themselves comfortable there. As he entered, they all stood. "Well, are you ready for this, Callie?" Jason addressed his sister.

"More than ready. I just hope we'll be able to talk with her, even if she isn't able to recognize us and understand the context of our visit. Just to be able to share it with her will be enough. I believe, in her spirit, she'll be able to hear us."

"Amen to that." Jason's slight smile and nod also expressed his agreement.

Serene touched her husband's arm. "Keith and I have agreed that we'll wait out here. We don't want to overwhelm her since receiving visitors can be taxing for her."

Callie and Jason entered the pretty room to which they'd been directed, painted in a soft shade of robin's-egg blue, with homey touches of knickknacks and family pictures gracing it. Sharon was just getting her mom settled in an easy chair. A cordial attendant, who introduced herself as Genevieve, was on her way out with a tray of the elderly woman's supper dishes. After exchanging pleasantries with Genevieve, they greeted Sharon, Callie giving her a big hug. "It's been so long. I think it must have been in high school the last time we saw each other. I wish Shellie could have been here too, but I understand about the baseball tournament. Kids need the support of parents for those things."

While that exchange took place, Jason looked over at the older woman, marveling that only a slight resemblance remained of the woman who'd introduced his sister and him to Jesus so many years ago. Surrounded now by wrinkles, it was the kind eyes that placed her in his memory. Either she'd changed that much with age or he'd been too young to retain a good memory of her face. Nodding toward Mrs. D, Jason asked, "How's she doing today?" The Alzheimer's patient sat looking out the window, expressionless.

Sharon gazed over at her mom. "She's having a relatively good day. She's calm, but not responsive. She doesn't recognize me, except as the lady who sometimes brings her saltwater taffy. But that's not unusual. It's been about four months now since she knew who I was, about six months since the last time she mistook me for Shellie. Even then, it only lasted a moment." The sadness of one who daily lived with this kind of relationship loss embodied her words.

Recovering her composure, Sharon addressed the older woman. "Mom, you have some visitors. This is Jason and Callie Brigholtz. You remember, they went to school with

Shellie and me. And they were part of your afternoon Bible study when we were just little." There was no response.

"Sorry. It looks like you won't get any interaction, but go ahead if you want. I usually just talk to her as though she were well. It's what the doctors recommend."

Jason had brought two chairs from a small table that was in a corner of the room and set them down near the two easy chairs. He indicated Sharon should take the unoccupied easy chair while he and Callie took the hardback chairs.

Callie led off the exchange. She began by thanking Mrs. D for taking the time with the neighborhood kids to share Jesus through the Bible stories, going on to explain how it had been her lifeline throughout her growing-up years. She concluded with telling her about her husband and family and their involvement in their church in Indiana. When she was done, there being no response—not even a glance from Mrs. D—she sat back and looked over at Jason. Her slight smile didn't disguise the disappointment in her eyes.

Leaning forward, Jason addressed the unresponsive woman, encouraging himself that, in her spirit, she would be able to hear him. "Mrs. Devereau, I'm Jason, Callie's brother. I want to begin by saying thank you for the frosted graham crackers and milk. They were great snacks, and I'm not sure I ever properly thanked you for them." Smiles broke out on the faces of the two younger women in the room as they exchanged a glance. "I can't say that the seed you planted in me enjoyed the same growth as Callie experienced, at least not until much later in my life. But the Lord has been at work in me, in spite of my years of neglecting Him. I was a sinful man throughout my adult life, until recently, when He snatched me up, saving me from a terrorist attack, and sent me halfway around the world to receive love and godly coun- sel from a missionary couple. He has drawn me to Himself through the Word and restored my family to me. They have graciously forgiven me." His words were slow and deliberate. "He continues to provide me with Holy Spirit guidance and council on a daily basis. That is all thanks to you and the ministry you provided to my sister and me as children. I want you to know that I will be eternally grateful to you for that."

Jason sighed and leaned back in his chair, happy that he and Callie had gotten to express their gratitude to this selfless servant of God, even if her mind was not able to comprehend it. He looked over at Sharon, preparing to express gratitude for allowing them to visit and politely make their departure.

But then it happened. Ellen Devereau slowly turned her head and looked him right in the eye. A voice, creaking with age and disuse, arose from the timeworn face. "Jason, I have prayed for *all* the little ones He allowed me to touch back then. Our Lord has kept you especially in my heart all these years." A shiver started at Jason's toes and spread rapidly to the top of his head. Silence from the three younger people indicated they didn't want to miss a word of this, or perhaps they were just too stunned to make a sound. "For years, I prayed for you faithfully every day, as He led me to do. You've been a tough nut to crack, young man, but He never gave up on you and wouldn't allow me to either." With a tear in her eye and a crack in her voice now, she concluded, "I can't tell you how it blesses my heart to hear your testimony." Heartfelt emotion embodied the words, and a slight smile reshaped the creased features of the aged face that seemed now to emit a radiant glow.

A collective shudder had traveled up and down the spines of the three younger people in the room as soon as Mrs. D had spoken her first word. Now they all sat with round eyes and open mouths.

Sharon recovered first. "Mother, it certainly is delightful that we could enjoy this visit with Jason and Callie today. Don't you agree?"

But the haze of incomprehension had once again descended over Ellen's countenance, and her head gradually turned again to the window. "No, I don't want to receive visitors today. I'm tired." The words came out slowly, indeed sounding tired. "Please tell Genevieve I'd like to lie down now."

About the Author

Karen Spickerman resides just outside a small town in Michigan but also enjoys spending several months in Florida during the winter. She always has a good book within reach.

Karen has three married sons, nine grandchildren, and two great-grandchildren.

The God Factor is her first novel, and she fully credits the Holy Spirit with inspiring the story.

CPSIA information can be obtained
at www.ICGtesting.com
Printed in the USA
LVHW091450130321
681461LV00035B/335